# OMENS OF FURY

## THE DAYS OF ASH AND FURY VOLUME ONE

### AN EPIC FANTASY BY
### SEAN HINN

BOBDOG
BOOKS

Published in the United States of America by Bobdog Books.

Second Edition, First Printing

Originally titled *Tahr*, published July 2016.

July 2017

10 9 8 7 6 5 4 3 2 1

ISBN 978-0-9980960-2-5

seanhinn.com

facebook.com/TahrSeanHinn

twitter.com/SeanHinn

# TABLE OF CONTENTS

For Lady Emily, my heroine and queen.

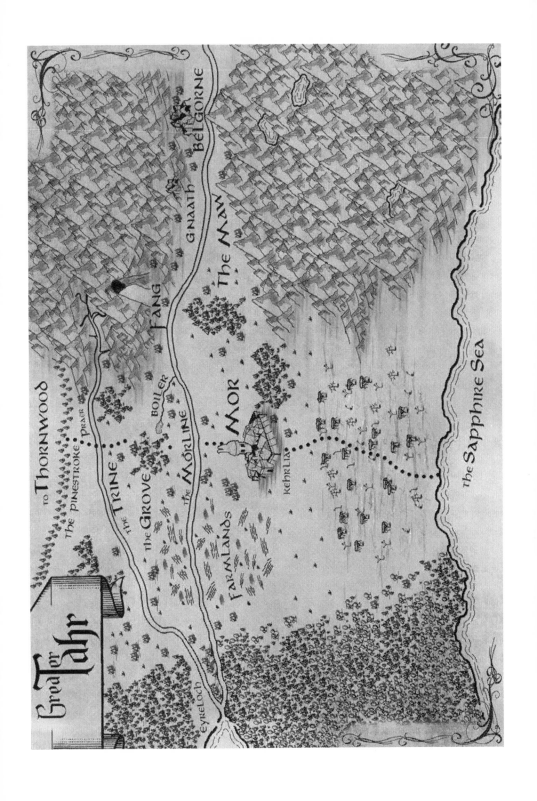

# PROLOGUE

he scene before Lucan reminded him of stories he had heard as a boy, of horrors millennia past. He recalled nightmarish tales of when Fang had first emerged, the great volcano that towered at the muzzle of the Maw. In that all but forgotten age, the mountain had not sprung from the world in a violent birth, but had gradually risen, lava spilling from its mouth, cooling, then spilling again over the course of many cycles, finally resulting in a soaring black thorn that protruded from the center of Greater Tahr. The land then had been covered in ash, it was said, as it was now in the scene before him. Horrific, indescribable creatures from the deep fiery pits of Fury had clawed their way from their eternal prison to make war upon the living and claim the world as their own. Lucan had once believed that the stories were little more than a way to ensure the behavior of children; if the boys and girls of Tahr were not good, adults warned, their mischiefs would call the evil up to the world of the living again. The worst boys and girls would serve as the first meals of the devils.

Lucan stood beside the elf, watching, on the ridge overlooking The Praër of Thornwood, the vast expanse of grassy slopes that stretched for a radius of miles around the Trine Crossing. Below their position and to the right, the Pinestroke ran from the eastern foothills to the western forest, parallel to the Trine, which lay to Lucan's south. The once endless procession of ancient emerald trees marked the entrance to the homeland of the elven people. It now stood lifeless, branches barren of needles, blanketed in ash. A few days' ride beyond the tree line to the north lay the once tranquil and ageless city of Thornwood, though Lucan knew that it, like all lands of Greater Tahr, was likely no longer serene, no longer at peace. Thornwood was the beloved home of the elf, he knew, but how he knew these things, he could not say.

A thousand paces separated the tree line and the river, and in that field lay an army of felled and falling elven warriors. To his left, the poisoned grey-yellow waters of the Trine thickened with the blood of elves and the ichor of the unnamable beasts they battled. The mighty river that had once been a pristine and shining sibling of the Morline was now a toxic vein of pestilence and blight, no longer giving life to the land of Tahr but stealing it away greedily. Lucan had never been to the Trine, yet he knew what it had once been. He could picture it in his mind not as an imagination, but as a memory. Beyond the river, Lucan witnessed a relentless surge of blackened, hairless, shrill and terrible creatures flooding the ashen Praër from the south. Many days' ride in that direction, Lucan's own city had once stood, the kingdom of Mor, the home of Man. He knew it stood no longer, yet again, he could not say how.

Lucan watched the battle play out before him, as he had a hundred times, and knew that the stories were not merely the artifice of frustrated parents, but rather an accurate portrayal of a horror that Tahr had once faced, and was facing again. Heroic tales of men, dwarves, and elves of the days of Fang's ascent were enshrined in ballads that Lucan had performed countless times to earn a meal in a tavern. He recalled his favorite, The Ballad of Mulgar, a hearty drinking song about a dwarven king who had fought the minions of Disorder and rallied the peoples of Tahr to final victory.

In the scene that he now witnessed, no such heroics were to be found. Only death, and a single source of hope and light that stood beside him, the beautiful elf, the ubiquitous and mysterious woman who had accompanied him to this hillside dream too many times to count. Yet Lucan was terrified to turn and look upon her, for he knew that when he did, she would vanish like smoke, and the nightmare would begin anew.

Lucan knew he was not *here*. The knowledge comforted him, for truly being here would mean that the things he saw were real, and they could not be. No, in no world where he wished to live would these terrors come to pass. Yet neither did he wish to awaken and return to his own world, a life in which he had no purpose beyond hustling his next meal, a life where he had run north, escaping the wrath of men he had offended. His true life was one in which his body most certainly lay dying, *somewhere*. Lucan allowed his hand to rest on the pommel of the sword at his waist, a sword with a name he could not recall, a sword he did not own, yet did. As his fingers gripped the weapon, he sensed again that here, in this life, he had purpose. Here, his life had meaning, value, *worth*. Yet the cost of living in this world was more than he could bear, for he knew his merit was inextricably tied to the monstrous terrors before him.

In contrasting the values of that life and this one, Lucan had decided that the only thing he truly wanted from either was to continue to share the presence of the elf. In this world, if only for fleeting moments, he could stand beside her. In the other, in his true life, he did not know her. Lucan decided then that, if he should ever awaken from this nightmare, he would seek out the beautiful elf; he would find her if it took a lifetime.

Lucan turned to look upon her, and again she faded like mist.

# I: MOR

"And here we have a rider, come through the rains to peddle the lies of Evanti."

Barris resisted the urge to launch himself at the king of Mor, prepared as he was to be baited. The disciplined knight willed himself to stillness in response, and successfully so, appearing by all measure to have not even heard the layered insult. Layered, as he was certainly no mere rider, and it was well known that to accuse an elf of dishonesty was a grave affront. More, a slight upon Queen Evanti was a dagger to the breast of any elf; even more so to Barris. A span of a dozen breaths passed in the drafty great hall, and despite the chill, a bead of sweat trickled its way down Barris' forehead, winding its way down from his dark hairline, pausing to gather momentum at each wrinkle in his bronzed brow, finally coming to rest in the corner of his left eye. Barris did not blink, nor did he wipe at his eye, for he believed that to do so would prove to all assembled just how truly vulnerable he felt. The elf was the only one of his kind present among hundreds of onlookers; their delight at watching him twist was barely concealed. If he could have straightened his travel-weary spine any further he would have done so, if only to convince himself of his own façade.

King Halsen's yellowed, rheumy eyes followed the droplet down the knight's face with dark amusement, desiring an early end to the

Game, yearning for this lackey from Thornwood to speak out of turn, knowing that he would not. The moments passed as Halsen beheld the knight. A bit tall and solid for his kind, unusually dark of hair, which he wore long and tied tightly at the back. He wore a light brown cloak, fastened at the neck with a hand-carved wooden brooch indicating his title of First Knight of Thornwood. Although the knight had ridden for days on end, the finely woven garment lacked a wrinkle, a smudge, or any sign whatsoever that the rider had been out of doors. His grey tunic and pants, unmarred by the elements...even his boots, made of soft leather, were laced to the knee with care and appeared as clean as the day they were first sewn. The weather had not been fair these past days, certainly not to the north, yet this wisp of a man—no, not a man—stood before the king as if he were entering a knight's dress parade. Rather than causing the king to feel some grudging respect for Barris, or at least for his noble presentation, the elf knight's cleanliness provoked Halsen to hate him all the more, to envy the pride (or more likely the enchantments) that allowed him to appear so... so *perfect*. As it became clear that the knight would stand there like a witless fool indefinitely without speaking, the king gloomily conceded the contest, his renowned bloodlust giving way to his legendary impatience. His excuse to kill the rider might still be forthcoming, he knew.

"Do you expect us to sit here all day, *knight*," Halsen bellowed, with a sarcastic emphasis on the last, "or are you planning to enlighten us as to why we must bear your presence in our halls?"

Barris glanced to either side of the great bronze and leather throne the king of Mor sat upon, perceiving slight movement as the heavily armored Defenders relaxed their grips on their halberds, if only by a fraction. *So he feels he requires an excuse*, Barris thought, knowing well the implications of such an observation and taking heart. Barris replied, his deep, resonant voice contrasting with the congested tones of the king's speech.

"Her Majesty Terrias Evanti of Thornwood bade me to bring tidings of the North, my lord. As you are most certainly already aware, there have been rumors of instabilities in and surrounding our lands, and strange omens, perhaps heralding distress within the very land of Tahr itself."

"We have heard the grumblings of the mystics and wizards, knight. About your northern wood, and a thousand other things over the years, that have come to no more than rat dung in the kettle. What of it?"

Chuckles then, from the assembly, and a smirk from the king, pleased with his vulgar expression. Halsen held out his bejeweled right hand; a goblet of wine was immediately placed within his chubby fingers by a servant Barris had not even seen standing behind the throne. Barris reminded himself to ignore the tone of the king's voice, recalling his objective and the warnings he had been given. *He is more than simply petty. Every part of him hates every part of everything else. Do not play into his hand, and do not underestimate him; he will try to goad you, and none is more treacherous.*

"You may not yet know the extent of the disruption, good king."

"Spare us the 'good king' nonsense, knight. I have not come to possess all that you see before you through benevolence."

Again, silence overtook the hall. The guards stiffened as Barris recognized that to speak here would assure his death, for he was not asked a question, and thus, again, was not permitted to speak. Such was the Game, enshrined in law, in the throne room of the great king of Mor. As the silence passed, however, Barris took notice that for the first time in the brief conversation, the maniacal king had referred to himself in the first person, as "I", breaking his habit of using the haughty and royal "we". *In the context of his possessions. Perhaps that is the way...*

After another moment, the king continued, holding out his goblet, which was immediately replaced with a full one. "By all means, rider, tell your tale so that we might shed our need to suffer this intrusion."

Barris nodded and told the king of all that his people had seen over the past few cycles. Ancient pines that had been tall before the oldest of his kind had been born, suddenly shedding half their needles overnight. A mass exodus of birds migrating south, a full cycle earlier than a typical year. Even the insects had begun to fade into winter early, while the temperatures had yet remained seasonable and mild. Most troubling, however, were the fires.

"When I left the Wood to begin my journey to your kingdom, King Halsen, I witnessed plumes of smoke from your own land rising in a dozen places. I have come to tell you that we of the Wood have experienced much of the same and that we, particularly Terrias Evanti, do not believe these fires to be natural or accidental. It is our Queen's position that, despite our differences of opinion on some matters, both our kingdoms would be well served to work together to root out the cause of these anomalies."

The king began to cough...or laugh, Barris could not be sure, as the phlegmy, rattling sound emanating from Halsen would most likely be the same in either case. Barris had come to Mor promising himself to not despise the man out of hand, despite his character, which was well known to the elven people. Yet this man was anathema to all that Barris was, in appearance, civility, and heart. Barris saw a slovenly wretch who, despite the finery of his clothing, the magnificence of his marbled halls, and the grandeur of his throne, appeared to Barris as nothing more than a gluttonous street merchant who could not be bothered to comb the locks from his own hair, nor wipe the wine that was slopping from his mouth as he coughed it out.

"Tell us, Knight of Thornwood," the king's voice was raised now, as he dropped his goblet to the floor for his servant to collect, "why Mor should concern itself with the campfires and hearthfires of its people? Do you think us so cowardly, that a few wisps of smoke should send us into a panic? You either come here to mock us, or to waste our time with the nonsensical ravings of that pointy-eared strumpet of a Queen you serve!"

Barris' right hand perceptibly quivered, longing to pull his sword free from its usual resting place in its sheath on his back. If the weapon had not been confiscated upon his arrival... none could be allowed to speak that way of his beloved Queen!

*No, Barris.* He heard a gentle female voice speak in his mind. *My pride is not worth the lives of our people. You must succeed.* Barris started; the voice that grazed his consciousness was truly that of his Terrias Evanti, not a thing of his own mind's conjuring. No sooner did he come to that realization than a warmth spread from his center to his extremities, calming him and bringing his mind and heart out of their agitation. *Forgive me, my Queen,* Barris thought to himself, wondering if even his very thoughts were known to her. *Is she listening even now?* he wondered, *or did she merely enchant me with a reminder, set to trigger in the event of my impending failure?* In either case, he quickly decided, he felt ashamed, both for his weakness and for his queen's lack of faith in him. Yet as he chided himself, he knew that even his shame was vanity. Too much was at stake for his pride to factor here.

With a deep breath, Barris brought himself back to the matter before him, and realized that he had been asked two questions during the king's outburst, but the king had not *ended* his speech with a question...should Barris reply? Would a failure to speak when expected to bring the same result as speaking out of turn? *Damn these games!* Barris thought for another moment, and settled on a strategy.

"In answer to your questions, King Halsen of Mor, the power and bravery of your kingdom and its people are precisely the reasons I have come." A slight pause, as the king slowly sat back a bit in his throne, the knight's delicate phrasing apparently successful. "And it is your wisdom we seek, as well. If, through investigation, you determine that these fires and other events are in fact nothing more than what is common and ordinary, then no harm has been done. If, however, you were to discover, as we suspect, that something unnatural is at work, you may rely upon the assistance of the elves of Thornwood to help do battle against their cause as your neighbor, and protect all that you possess." Another slight pause, to allow the covetous king to consider the risk to his fortunes. "We merely seek to openly share with you what we discover in our investigations, and to request the same of your sages and advisors."

A slight murmur began to spread among the merchants and councilors assembled in the hall. Barris assumed they were most likely discussing the wagers that had been placed upon whether or not he would survive his audience with the king. He watched the king's expression and demeanor, which did not exactly soften, but did somewhat relax, and for the first time since his sword was seized in the anteroom as he awaited his audience, he began to believe that he might survive the day. Halsen examined his ringed fingers as he spoke, doing his best to appear bored and dismissive.

"Your people are weak, knight. And that is why you have come to seek our help in the unlikely event that something odd is afoot." The king let the slur settle in the knight's heart for a moment, then raised his gaze to the knight's eyes. "But it would please us to prove your fears to be no more than the superstitions of a frightened and fragile people. Perhaps when we have done so, you will cease to disturb us with your babbling nonsense every time a swallow breaks wind in the wrong direction. Be gone, return in a cycle with your own report, and we shall have ours."

The knight had to force himself to bow, as law required, before the king as he began to take his exit, not only because the act was as distasteful to him as the king's choice of language, but because after riding for nine days and nights without rest, bending from the waist—and returning to an upright position—was truly a feat of strength and resolve.

"KNIGHT!" The king hollered as Barris had just turned away. Barris halted and turned back to face the man.

"It will be you, in particular, to return for audience with us. Do not think to do so beyond the next zenith of the Twins; we would be greatly displeased."

*Twenty-six days to the next zenith,* Barris quickly counted to himself, *eighteen of which to be spent riding without rest. This king is a bastard of the highest order.*

"As you wish, King Halsen." Barris bowed again.

# II: THORNWOOD

ith a slight wave of her hand, the misty vision dissipated like smoke before the elven queen, and she faltered slightly, exhausted from the effort of Seeing from such a distance.

"My lady, please, sit," said her Captain of the Guard, as he rushed to bring her wicker chair from behind her small oaken desk.

"Thank you, Mik. That was a bit trying."

Mikallis frowned, for Terrias Evanti rarely used his shortname in front of others, and even more rarely admitted fragility of any sort, even among her inner circle. Mikallis Elmshadow was the son of Queen Evanti's former and late Captain Jons Elmshadow, and had grown up alongside her own daughter. He was as close as anyone who was not directly related to the queen's family, yet propriety was almost never breached when official matters of the elven kingdom were being discussed, not once in the four seasons that Mikallis had served as Captain. This council was quite small however, as the queen did not wish to expose Barris' private perspective to anyone whom he did not personally call friend.

"*Trying*, my lady?" This from Aria Evanti, only daughter of the elven queen, and the newest member of the Society of the Druids of the Grove. "Seeing from such a distance has never been done before in our history, and certainly never throwing the Speech! How in the

Wood did you even–"

"Be calm, my daughter. When the need is great, the Wood has always answered. This much you know."

"Yes, Mother."

"And it has been done once before," the queen soberly added, "but only once that I know of."

This brought a bow of the head from the three others assembled in the small room.

The four were gathered in the queen's study, which amounted to a small apartment across a narrow hall from her personal chambers. Dark, exotic woods made up the floors and walls, oiled to a sheen and flawlessly clean. Several wide windows lined the top of the room on the west and north walls, each partially opened to allow the floral Thornwood air to circulate. Thousands of books, letters, and parchments lined the shelves on the walls, neatly, but without attention to organization, for but a thought from the queen would guide her to the needed material. Dozens of small mirrors built into the bookcases were angled to the center of the room, though their angle would change spontaneously to reflect towards the area of the room where the queen required light.

A large mahogany reading table sat in the center of the room, lined with comfortable padded wicker chairs, gifts made by the hands of friends and subjects who wished to offer a kindness to the queen. In Thornwood, to use one's hands to make a chair for another was considered among the highest personal honors one elf could bestow. It signified gratitude for a job done, or respect for a task accomplished, and said to the gifted, "You are beloved to me, and you have done well. I wish for you to rest." Such chairs would often take months, even years to make, for no magic was ever used in their creation, and often even the most nondescript chair was, upon close inspection, a marvel of design, engineering, and respect to detail. The wicker the queen sat upon now was not of the most sophisticated design –it was not even padded–but nonetheless it was among the most precious to Evanti, for it had been made by the children of one of the eastern villages, in gratitude to the queen for simply spending an evening around their fire, telling stories and sharing a meal.

The queen continued after the prolonged silence.

"Neral. Tell me what you saw."

Neral was the oldest member of the Evanti family, the brother of Terrias' own grandfather, and among the oldest in the entire kingdom of Thornwood. He sat upon his own padded chair, and was the only member of the Council of the Wood permitted to sit while the queen was in attendance (and not sitting herself.) While the Elves would hardly make such a rule into law, it had been a tradition kept to since before even Neral's grandfather had served on the council, nearly a millennia past. To disregard the custom would not bring punishment–yet it was simply not done. Such were the elven ways; one did as all were expected to do, for to upset the order of things would be to potentially cause discomfort to another. More than a matter of politeness or propriety, it was the simplest issue of morality to the elves; law and tradition first, their people second, and if both are served well, then the joy of the self would be inevitable. Failure to live one's life according to that principle predictably would cause chaos, and from chaos, turmoil. Traditions, if they are born of respect and kindness, serve all, and thus are upheld.

Yet Neral was granted exception, for not only was he a beloved elder of the elven people, he was once their most revered captain. It was Neral, foremost, who had made the first peace with humankind, a truce won both through his boundless heroism in a battle that cost him a son and a foot, and, eventually, through his forgiveness of the man who took both from him.

Despite his infirmity and age, Neral stood upon the address of his Queen. Terrias bowed her head as he used his splintered oaken staff to pull himself upright. It was not expected for Neral to stand, but stand he would, as he always had.

"It is good and bad, Lady. I saw what you saw. Halsen is an evil, frightened man holding on to his throne with naught but his fingernails, and eager to slaughter our own Barris for his own pleasure. Yet, I also saw that his fear may just yet cause him to align his purposes with ours." He paused for a bit, most certainly for effect, for Neral so did enjoy a bit of drama when his opinion was asked for.

"I see. Please continue, Goodfather." Terrias was skeptical here, but she knew better than to doubt Neral's instincts and wisdom.

"Why not simply kill Barris? He could have at any time. He could not know that you were Seeing this parley. He sought an excuse, to be sure, giving Barris plenty of opportunity to misstep, but if he wanted him dead, why not simply do the deed and be done with it, Game or no?"

"I'm not sure I follow your line of reasoning, Neral. Are you implying that he has some reverence for the elven people? That he sincerely wishes to unite with us? Or that he sees the looming threat as clearly as we do? Because if so, I disagree on all three counts."

"No, no, my lady. Not that; he is a shortsighted man with no love for his neighbors. But he does *fear* us. He knows you, my lady, or at least knows of you, and he knows that if Barris broke his senseless law of throne room etiquette, you would not avenge him."

Mikallis stepped forward at this, incensed. "What are you saying, Neral–that our Lady would ignore the murder of Barris, and let his death go unpunished? That is madness!"

Queen Terrias raised her palm to Mikallis, who immediately took a step back. "Please, Mikallis, allow Neral to finish. Go on, my friend."

Neral inclined his head towards Mikallis, and offered a gentle smile. "Ah, you are young for a Captain of the Guard, dear Mikallis, but listen closely and you shall gain wisdom. No, our Lady would never ignore the murder of an elf of the Wood. But it would not be murder if Barris, knowing the law of the land, wicked as it may be, broke that law. Do I misspeak, my lady?"

The queen sighed, her face drawn and downcast as she replied. "No, good Neral, you have it right. If we enter another's domain, we do so while accepting their interpretation of order, or we do not go at all. That is our law, and has been since the Truce." She lifted her eyes to Mikallis then. "And our observance of that law has served us well, despite the risk to good elves like Barris."

Mikallis bowed his head to his Queen, and then to Neral.

"I apologize, Goodfather; you are wise in this."

Neral smiled again, and nodded respectfully to the young Captain.

"I'm sorry, but this makes little sense to me," Aria Evanti said. "If he wanted Barris' head so badly—and as you say, Neral, had no way of knowing that he was Seen—why not just satisfy his lust, and claim a violation of the law when we came asking?"

"Why not, indeed? Mikallis, would you care to answer?"

Mikallis thought for a moment, looked to Aria, and shook his head. "I know not, Goodfather."

"I do not fault you on that, Mikallis, nor you, young Aria, for the intrigues of the courts of men would likely escape most elves. But to one as old as I, it is clear as the Trine."

"The Trine is not so clear these days, as you well know, Neral." Yet as Neral looked to Queen Terrias, he saw the glimmer of understanding dawn on her face. She nodded, bidding him to continue his lesson.

"Halsen kills without mercy, desperately trying to maintain control of his people through fear. He pretends to fear nothing himself, yet only cowardice could drive a man to do such things. If he fears that Thornwood would avenge Barris, and fear us he does, it is because he also fears what all tyrants eventually come to suspect—that he is besieged by spies."

"I thought you said it was good and bad, Neral. I hear only bad."

"The good, my queen, is that his weakness of heart and his paranoid mind will not allow him to sit long upon his throne. He is no threat to our people, if he ever was."

"Is not a wounded animal the most dangerous?" asked Terrias, still unconvinced. "Should we not be concerned that he will make war with us, if for no other reason than to unite his people against a common enemy?"

"If that were the case, my lady, we would already be mourning our Barris."

At that, the queen took heart, as Barris had done, when he had the same realization as he stood before the king. Mikallis and Aria, however, remained shaken by the idea that a man of such character could even exist, let alone rule a kingdom.

"The king of Mor is truly a rotten bastard," offered Mikallis.

The queen frowned. "No young Mikallis, a bastard he is not, for I knew his father and mother well."

"Rotten then, to his bones," added Aria.

"Alas, perhaps," said Queen Evanti with a sigh, recalling a young boy dancing and singing in the Grove beneath the light of the Twins, chasing conjured sparkflies. "But it was not always so."

# III: G'NAATH

ort Greykin slowly pulled away the leather curtain that hung before the private stony nook within which Shyla slept, and peered inside.

"To the brass. Again," Oort whispered to his wife Thinsel, referring to the candle Shyla had been given just the day before. It was fully melted, down to the base of her brass lamp. "Even knowin' what's to be comin' t'day."

"We're gonna lose 'er, Oort," Thinsel moaned as Oort let the drape fall and they stepped a few feet away to speak. "Oh, my Oort, you must do something, I canna bear it." Thinsel began to sob, tears flowing freely down her round, pallid face. Oort took her in his diminutive arms, his callused fingers drawing the yellow hair from her eyes.

"We'll not lose 'er, my dear. Not today," Oort vowed, unconvincingly. "Nuth'n fer it but to get her up then, and face th'elders."

Oort patted his wife's shoulder as he released her.

"Oh, Oort!"

"Girl!" Oort thundered, "Git yerself outta bed, yer sleepin' late again, t'day of all days!"

Shyla's eyes popped open, and she immediately felt her heart plummet into terror, knowing in her bones what this awful day would bring.

"I'm up, Papa, I'm up!"

"Well, git yerself down the tunnels then and quick, girl. Don't be dallyin', for yer own sake."

Shyla rubbed her eyes and gathered her wits, which were formidable wits indeed for a gnome, and began to formulate a plan that would get her through this ordeal. But even as she raced to pull on her breeches, she knew that she was out of excuses. She had been late to begin breakfast for the gnomes of her clan more often than not the past few seasons, and had been warned repeatedly—she must do her duty, or face expulsion from G'naath. Two days before, as she arrived to the kitchens late yet again, she had found the Elder waiting for her, parchment in hand, with orders to appear before the Court.

For there were few things, if any, more sacred to the gnomes of the Maw than the virtues of labor and duty, and Shyla had proven herself a complete failure on both counts.

"I shoulda never been a gnome," the girl said ashamedly to herself, for at least the hundredth time, as she prepared for what would certainly be the worst day of her life. "Ain't cut out fer it."

~

Shyla Greykin had come to understand her dissimilarity from other gnomes fourteen years prior, in a cycle that had cost the lives of nearly a dozen gnomes.

While the people of G'naath were not unintelligent—indeed, most were capable of reading and writing—the higher principles of mathematics and science had never been their strength. Yet Shyla had always been unlike the rest of her people, and before she had reached her tenth year, she had gone missing from her own slabs within the great cavern for hours, to be found by a panicked Oort and Thinsel explaining to a team of tunnelers, in great scientific detail, how and why their newest branch would soon collapse, to the uproarious laughter and derision of all who had been present.

Less than a quarter of a cycle later, eleven gnomes were buried alive under hundreds of tons of cold, hard stone.

Her troubles began that day, and had accelerated since, for many of the gnomes were not inclined to hear her explanations of mathematics and physics, which she could scarcely put into language in any case; no, they had already drawn their conclusions. The girl was a witch, created by the very Hand of Disorder, and would someday doom them all.

It was not that pronouncement, however, that led to the trouble she faced this day. *No, it's me own damnable obsessions,* she told herself, as she marched with her mother and father down the tunnels.

One night, not long after the cave-in, while Shyla was exploring the tunnels seeking a place to hide from the stares and glares and cruel remarks and worse, she found a driphole that had apparently gone dead, for the impression on the floor of the tunnel was dry as a bone. She looked up, wondering where the water had once come from, and saw a recession in the stone that seemed deeper than it ought to be. Setting down her candle, she climbed up the nearly sheer face of the tunnel wall, as far as she could, and peered up and over the lip of the recession, her pointy little noise barely clearing the rim—and smelled something wonderful! Even her pink gnomish eyes, accustomed to the dark as they were, could not see far into the hole, but she could tell that the wonderful scent was not coming from inside G'naath, but outside.

*Outside.*

She had never been Outside. Never, not once. Outside was for the hunters. Outside was for the other races. Outside was for the beasts and the orcs and all things dangerous. Generations of female gnomes had lived and died in the tunnels of the Maw, never once having been Outside.

Shyla Greykin, however, was the most curious of gnomes, and had decided then and there that she would make a plan. She would get herself a ladder, she would climb into that hole, and she would go where it led, if only to see Outside just once, just for a moment. She could have no sooner denied that call than she could have licked her own elbow. That *scent*! It was...it was like...oh, she just couldn't even *dream* of not finding out what it was!

And so she did, but not without ordeal. For it would not prove easy for this petite little creature to find herself a ladder, the *right* ladder, let alone conceive a strategy to carry it all the way from the miners' branch to her secret channel, and stow it covertly and neatly for reuse once her mission had been completed. Shyla, however, was no ordinary gnome. She took measurements using a piece of string from the bottom of her skirts, memorized those measurements, and began her search for the perfect ladder to use for her ambitious task. Finding the free time alone was not an easy thing, for even young gnomes were expected to toil, not frolic and adventure throughout the tunnels like some shiftless, unreliable Airie.

Ultimately, it became clear to Shyla that she would need to fashion her own ladder, and so that is what she did. Using tools she "found" in the miner's branch, and discarded pick handles from the tunnelers, over the course of several cycles and many nights with very little sleep she had managed to build herself an elaborate, jointed collapsible ladder, one that she could stow in her knapsack. One night, after the evening meal had been cleared, the dishes washed, and all good gnomes were settling onto their cots for a night of slumber, Shyla Greykin made her way stealthily through the tunnels to her private passageway.

Her ladder worked as intended. She ascended carefully, crawling through the crevice, inching her way upwards, discovering to her great joy that there was, in fact, enough space for her to continue her climb, as the channel did not narrow, but rather widened as she gained elevation. She had brought her candle along, and managed to keep it lit throughout her ascent, until a gust of sweet air finally blew it out—yet to her surprise the fissure was not entirely dark.

And then, she saw them. Impossibly, Shyla Greykin looked upon the glowing orbs of the Twins, surrounded by a blanket of hundreds— no, hundreds of hundreds—no, more!—of tiny little dots of light, hanging suspended in the air as if the entire world were covered by a faintly lit chandelier.

*Oh, how wonderful,* marveled Shyla, *how truly, truly magnificent.*

As the scent of her extinguished candle subsided, the aroma she had first detected those many nights ago replaced it, permeating her senses with an unfamiliar mixture of soil and plants and flowers and animals; together, they blended into a bouquet of life, deep and rich and poignant, and Shyla Greykin, for the first time, began to understand how very small she truly was.

The little gnome completed her climb and pulled herself out from the hole, now just barely two gnomes wide, and her sandaled feet stood upon the soil of Tahr, at the very throat of the Maw, savoring the sweetness of the life of the world.

She knew at that moment, at the very center of her being, that she was not like other gnomes. Yet she did not care.

Shyla wept.

~

Oort reached over to wipe the tears from Thinsel's eyes as they watched their daughter, their only child, stand before the Court of Elders. She batted his hand away, trembling, then thought better of it and reached for him.

The Court was held in the largest cavern in this region of the Maw, the size and shape of a small amphitheater. The floor sloped gently downwards, towards the center of the room, with tiers cut into the stone so that all could witness the pronouncements of justice. Rows of torches in intricately carved stone sconces lined the aisles and walls. Shyla was led down through the centermost aisle toward the floor of the Court, escorted by a pair of armored gnomish sentries on either side, their spears towering nearly three times as high as the little gnome, causing her to appear even smaller than she felt at that moment. She felt the eyes upon her from all sides, heard the quietly uttered oaths and prayers for justice to be done.

The flames of no fewer than a hundred foot-high candles burned near the stage area, arranged in concentric circles around the slightly taller dais upon which Shyla was bid to stand. If the desired effect was to make the accused feel as if they were walking into Disorder's own realm, the design exceeded its objective. Hundreds of gnomes stood in attendance, their duties forgotten for the moment, many more than usual for a trial, as the unusual nature of the charges—and the charged—were indeed rare.

Gnomes were not layabouts. This sort of thing simply did not happen. And Shyla Greykin was a name that had spread throughout the tunnels like wildfire those many years ago, as had the rumors of her witchery. Those who had opinions on either side of the matter held them strongly, a few in strong support of the girl, but many more adamantly opposed.

The Head Elder, Ky'rl Gypstone, rose from his seat behind a long stone table situated directly in front of the dais. The table sat only slightly more than four feet from the ground, yet Shyla could barely see the seated Elder's chin over the lip of the slab. The eight other Elders, seated four to each side of him, arose as one as he cracked his silver hammer three times, slowly and deliberately, upon the stone. The first rap was barely heard over the susurrating of the crowd; the third echoed for what seemed to Shyla like an eternity. Upon that final strike, a full platoon of gnomish sentries took one step forward in unison from behind the rearmost aisle, their boots clapping loudly together in concert, making their presence known to all in attendance. It was not a trivial gesture, as the restless gnomish people were prone to a mob-like mentality, and but for the threat of the guard, Order could not be kept. At the thunderous echo of those boots coming together, the Elders sat as one, and Shyla nearly swooned in terror.

Her mother did, and was caught by the gentle arms of her father.

"Shyla Greykin," the Elder spoke, his sharp, clear voice easily carrying the hall. "Yeh come yerself before us today to answer to the charges of indolence and dereliction of duty. To these charges, what say yeh?"

Shyla cleared her throat and willed her tiny body to cease its trembling, reminding herself that she must be strong today, for Ma.

"Yes and no, ah, that is, no and yes, me good Elder."

The crowd began its first whisper at this, as did the now seated elders, and Ky'rl Gypstone was quick to reach for his hammer, stifling the muttering of the gathering with a single whack.

"What do yeh mean, yes and no, and no and yes, girl? Speak plain before yer elders!" The old gnome was clearly already agitated, and Shyla recognized immediately that she was on loose granite.

"I meant no disrespect, me Elder, what I mean to say is, that I canna argue the charge o' dereliction, but indolent I ain't, nor have I ever been."

"They are one and the same, young lady, as yeh well know."

"Then why'd yeh make 'em two different charges, me Elder?"

Again, the murmuring began in the chamber, louder this time, and Shyla could almost see the cheeks of the Elders redden. At the end of the long table, a female she didn't recognize put her hand over her mouth to hide a giggle.

Ky'rl cracked the hammer again, loud as a stonesnap this time. "I will have silence!"

And silence he had, as all in attendance nearly froze. Shyla's mind raced, instinctively realizing at this point that winning over the old grizzled gnome would be impossible. *The granite isn't just loose, it's a damned slide already, and I ain't even said but a word yet.* But could she win over the crowd? Or perhaps even one of the Elder gnomes on either side of him? It seemed that at least one Elder in attendance here took a bit of pleasure from seeing Ky'rl Gypstone frustrated.

"I have here in me own hand, Shyla Greykin, sworn letters from the gnomes yeh work with, tellin' o' dozens o' times yeh showed up late fer yer work in the kitchens. Do yeh deny it?"

"Nope."

Ky'rl Gypstone's jaw dropped at this. *Nope?*

"Well, then, I think we've heard all we're needin' to hear, from yer own mouth, no less!" The thoroughly incensed gnome crossed his arms over his chest.

"Then whadja haul me down here fer, if I ain't to get a chance to speak up for meself?"

That did it. The crowd behind her didn't break out into a whisper, or a mumble, but into a raucous mix of oaths, laughter, and calls for the little gnome's head. It took more than a few bangs of the hammer to quiet the crowd this time. Finally, the little old gnomish woman at the end of the table stood and raised her arms, making a slight twisting gesture with her hands. After but a moment, for some reason, this calmed the crowd, and even calmed the frightened Shyla a bit. She looked into the kind eyes of the woman, who was gazing at her directly, and knew that some magic was at work there.

"Elder Gypstone, I wish to address the accused, please."

Ky'rl stopped banging his hammer, gave Shyla a glare that spoke volumes, and waved his hand dismissively at the old female as he sat down, yielding the floor.

"Shyla," the gnome spoke softly and clearly, "I am Cindra Sandshingle, do yeh know of me?"

Cindra Sandshingle! Shyla had heard tales of the magic Cindra had employed to save their people the last time the goblins had cross-dug their tunnels...but that was a century ago! No gnome lived that long!

"I, ah, yes me lady, er, Elder Cindra, I have heard o' yeh." Shyla was at a complete loss here, wholly off her guard.

"I would have yeh tell me what yeh have to say, Shyla Greykin, but do not dissemble, for as ye know, I have magic, and I will know if yeh lie to me."

"Yes, me lady." Shyla felt herself calming further.

"And with a tone courteous to the Court, I'll be addin'."

"Yes, me lady."

"Then go on, child. I'll be hearin' yeh."

Something about the way Cindra spoke to her, something in the crystalline quality of her voice, or perhaps the way she looked at Shyla, no, *into* Shyla, completely disarmed the young gnome, so much so that she immediately began to cry, not only out of sorrow for herself, but also out of a sudden sense of... something? Peace?

Release?

It all came rushing out of her then, before the hundreds of gnomes there in that room. From the day she spoke to the tunnelers, to the day she heard the stonesnap that began the crumble, hearing them die in screams of horror, to the day she found her secret route to the surface, to her private love of mathematics, and science, and astronomy, and how no one understood her, and how she wasn't a witch and could never hurt no one never anyhow, and oh how it hurt when she would see the staring eyes follow her, and the shame she felt when she awoke late and when she arrived late to work, how much harder she worked to make up for her embarrassment, yet the pull, the insatiable need she felt to climb her tunnel would not abate, for she *needed* to count the stars, and measure the progress of the Twins, and to learn, and to make the notes on her parchment, for didn't it matter? Weren't the mysteries of life and the elements and time important, to her people, to *all* peoples?

When she finished, there were many with moist eyes in the great chamber, yet Shyla looked at the sorrow in the eyes of the dear old gnome she thought to be her champion, and knew what the verdict of the Court would be.

The Elders retired to an antechamber for no more than a few minutes to debate their decision, and in that time, she looked back upon her parents. She saw pride in her Papa's eyes, but so much sorrow in Ma. She looked back into the crowd, at more than a few faces she recognized, and she saw pity reflected there in some, yet in others, the same hatred she had come to know during her whole life.

For she was not like other gnomes, she knew. Nor could she ever be.

"Shyla Greykin."

It was Cindra who spoke, not Ky'rl Gypstone, who was standing beside the gnomish sorceress with what looked like shame etched upon his face.

"We all, to a gnome, are sorry beyond words for the pain yeh have known. On behalf of we Elders, it gives us no pleasure at all to see one of our own suffer the cruelties yeh have, through no fault of yer own."

Shyla looked down for this last part, for she could not look into the eyes of this kind lady as she said these next words.

"But our law is our law child, and by yer own admission, ye've not pulled yer weight." Shyla could distantly hear the sobs of her mother, as if they were coming from down a long, empty tunnel. "So, with me sorrow goin' with ye, ye're to be expelled from G'naath–" her mother wailed now "–for a period of eight seasons."

*What? Eight seasons? Ain't banishment ferever?* Shyla was in shock.

"Me lady, I don't–"

"Quiet, child. Ye'll be required to leave at dawn three days hence, or the night prior if yeh prefer to leave by the light of the Twins. I bid yeh come see me afore yeh leave. This court is adjourned."

# IV: THE WHISTLING WENCH

hat's eight! Two to go, my dear fellows, and you'll be buying my dinner!"

Barris looked across the smoke-filled tavern over the heads of the two dozen or so patrons eating their suppers, watching the brash young man boast of his throw, and shook his head. "I wish to buy some provisions for the road, friend," the knight said to the burly innkeeper, who looked back at him with surprise.

"The general store's on Taper street, elf, and the butcher's right beside it."

"The stores are closed for the night, and I must be on my way this evening. Will you sell me some bread and cheese, and perhaps a bit of wine to fill my skin?"

The innkeeper leaned over the counter and glowered at the elf. "My food is for my guests, elf, and if you'll not be staying..."

Barris sighed, understanding the nature of the game. "Then allow me to pay for a room for three nights, good keeper, which you may still rent to another, only help me fill my sack with all the dried meats, cheeses, nuts, and whatever else you would part with for such a price."

A slight smile then, from the innkeeper. "If I'm to fill your sack, elf, it'll be five nights. And the wine'll be extra."

"*Pay up, boys, that's ten in a row*! Ha-hah!" Barris heard the young man holler with joy, clearly unaware that he would not leave the tavern unchallenged, no matter what the wager.

Barris leaned in over the counter, a hand's width now from the innkeeper's face.

"My name is not 'elf', keeper. It is Barris of Thornwood, and I believe you wish to make a more equitable exchange than what you have just proposed."

The innkeeper blanched and took a step back, only now looking down at the brooch that rested on Barris' collarbone. Recognition began to flicker behind his eyes.

"Ah, my apologies, good knight, I may have misspoke."

Barris lowered his thick eyebrows just a touch more. "You did not misspeak, friend, yet I would request that you reconsider."

"Of course, of course. Ah, three days' rent will be fair enough, although the wine..."

Barris did not blink.

"Ah, the wine'll be a gift from the Whistling Wench, we've always been a friend of the Wood folk, don't ya know. Uh, a scale and a half seem about fair to you?"

"I will pay two full scales, but your best and oldest wine if you please, in a new skin."

"Fair enough, el... ah, Barris. Sir."

Barris moderated his expression as the man took the four coins, and brought his sack back to the kitchens to be filled. He did not blame the man for seeking the best price, but he would not allow himself to be cheated, for an elf is nothing if not prideful.

He settled at the bar and turned to watch the commotion developing at the far side of the inn, where the young blonde-haired man had just thrown—and stuck—ten dinner knives inside a target not bigger than a human head from more than ten paces.

"You're a cheat, boy, and I don't know how ya did it, but I'll not be payin'!" This from the biggest of the five men now forming a semicircle around the youngster.

"And neither will I," said another.

"Nor I," remarked the third. The remaining two stood with their arms crossed, their words unsaid.

The young man only smiled wider at this, perhaps thinking to charm the men? *Not likely*, thought Barris, as he watched the drama play out.

"Aw, c'mon, fellas, I didn't cheat, I'm just really good with a dagger is all, always have been. Tell ya what, I'll give you all a chance to get your money back, and if I win, I'll ask nothing extra from any of you, only what I'm owed so far."

"Hmph." The big one spoke. "What's the bet, kid?"

"I'll bet I can hit that target ten times again, but this time while riding on big Earl's back."

They all roared with laughter at this, even big Earl, who was certainly the least merry of the quintet.

"You're gonna ride my back, hit that target ten times, and stick it every one? It can't be done."

"It can be done, my outsized friend, and I'll do it. And you can move around all you like. All I ask, though, is that you all put the money on the table before I try, so that I know I'm not being swindled."

"He thinks to take the money and run, Earl," this from the tall, wiry one. "Well good luck tryin'! I'm in, and I'll be standing over the money with my own dagger if ya try."

"To the Mawbottom with ya, boy, I'm in too, if just to watch you make yourself a fool." The money left the men's pockets, and sat there in a pile on the table. Wiry stood behind it, dagger in hand.

The boy sighed. "Well, let me get on up, then, Earl. Come on now, bend over a bit, you're a big one!"

The huge man bent down and let the boy climb onto his back as the innkeeper returned to Barris, full sack and new skin in hand.

"Here you go, sir Barris. I hope your travels...wait, what in Disorder?" The innkeeper started around the bar, seeing the boy struggle to climb onto the back of the massive Earl.

Barris raised a hand to stay the innkeeper, smiling mischievously. "You'll want to watch this, I think. I believe we're all in for a good show."

"Well, as long as it's not a show that ends with my tavern busted up! Hey, boy!"

"Be still, friend, I will not allow them to destroy your inn."

Earl spoke as he turned towards the target, the boy straddling his back with an arm around his collar. "I'll even be a good sport boy, and let you throw the first one with me standing still!"

"All right. Well, clear the target then, gentlemen, and one of you bring me the first knife!"

The innkeeper audibly moaned at this, and brought his hand to his head to rub the tension from his brow. "Aw, Fury, here we go."

The young man lined up his shot, and with a solid *thwack*, hit the target dead solid center. The tavern went quiet, and Barris saw a man at the far end of the bar put his head in his hands, as if the sight of it all troubled him greatly. *That's odd...*

"Yeah, yeah, good shot, boy, but try it now, with me dancin' all around!"

And Earl danced. Sliding left and right, spinning around, and his friends began to clap in rhythm as the boy struggled to get his aim. He timed his second shot to match the turn of the great dancing Earl...

And his knife missed the target completely, clanging harmlessly off the wall and onto the floor.

"Haaaaaaah! I knew ye couldn't do it, boy!" Earl laughed, and the men clapped, and they all danced around now, as if they couldn't be more pleased with themselves.

The boy slid off his back, turned to bow dramatically at the diners in the tavern, who were all clapping and laughing now, and finally turned to Earl.

"Well, I have to admit, my good Earl, you danced with much more spirit than I had counted on. You have bested me."

"You're a damned fool, boy, but I like you." Earl clapped the boy on the back as he smiled from ear to ear.

"Well, I'll give you a reason to like me all the more, friend." The boy leaned up and whispered into Earl's ear. The bulky man's eyes went wide as saucers as he listened, and his smile widened even further. He looked to the bar, then turned back to nod at the boy.

The young, blond-haired showman walked up to the man at the end of the bar, Earl and his entourage in tow.

"I'll be having that ring now, good merchant."

"No, you most certainly will NOT!" said the man, trying to appear taller in his stool than he really was.

"What's all this about then, Earl?" asked Wiry.

Earl just smiled and shook his head.

"You tell him, boy."

"Well, you see, gentlemen, when I arrived at this fine establishment, I made a wager with our merchant friend here, his ring against my dagger, that not only I would be riding our friend Earl's back inside an hour while he danced a jig, but that he'd be pleased as a peach about it."

The men nearly fell over each other laughing, and their great friend Earl, who could have easily considered himself the butt of the joke, saw the right side of it and laughed along with them.

"I will not pay!" the merchant insisted. "The boy cheated, and you all saw it!"

Earl stepped forward, edging the boy out of the way.

"The boy didn't cheat you, mister. He didn't cheat us, either. Turns out he's just damned good with a knife, and better with his head. The ring."

The merchant hesitated. Earl leaned in.

"Now."

Barris departed the inn, shaking his head, just as the boy bought a round of drinks for his new friends. The knight just failed to see the embarrassed merchant's gesture at another man at the far end of the bar.

# V: MOR, THE NORTHERN ROAD

he weary Barris circled Phantom, inspecting his mount as best he could under the light of the streetlamp, and determined that the care Phantom had received while in the command of the too-young stable hand was, in fact, excellent. His jet-black coat gleamed in the meager light, his silver mane and tail were brushed free of tangles, and his hooves were scrubbed clean. The spectacularly muscled horse was still clearly exhausted, to be sure, but he had rested some this day, and would rest again this night.

"You have done well, young man. Tell me your name."

The copper-haired boy beamed back at him. "My name's Nikalus, Sir Barris, and you can bet I done well! This is Phantom, I heard o' him, he's the best horse I ever seen or I ain't never seen a horse, and you can bet I seen some horses! I just knowed it were him when you brought him in this morning, I knowed it! I told Tam-"

Barris interrupted the boy with a smile. "You know of Phantom, Nikalus? Tell me, how many years have you?"

"I'm ten, Sir, but I'mma be eleven in a cycle, and everyone knows o' Phantom—well, at least everyone who ever cared about horses, that is! Is it true he can run for a cycle without a rest? Cause I heard some tales that..."

"It is close enough to true, Nikalus," Barris replied, gently stroking the muzzle of the great steed. "Though such exertion taxes him much more than is fair." The wide-eyed Nikalus tried to speak again, clearly a thousand questions on his mind, but Barris was too sorely fatigued to indulge the boy further, and held up his hand.

"You can be sure I will tell you more about Phantom when I leave him in your care again, Nikalus, less than a cycle from now. You shall be his only caretaker when I travel to Mor, from this day hence. But we must be leaving; tell me what I owe your master and we shall be on our way."

"'Tis but a quarter of a scale, Sir Barris, but you don't even have to pay if you don't wanna, I was happy to care for him, I even oiled your saddle and bags for ya but that didn't take no time at all and..."

"Hush, boy. Here, this is for your master." He handed the boy a halfpiece. "And this is for you," he said, reaching into a secret pouch within his cloak and withdrawing a currency of a different color.

The boy looked at the coin, and back to Barris, stunned.

"Your family shall reap the rewards of your hard work this season, Nikalus."

The boy did not quite frown at this, for he was too overjoyed with his gift to be saddened, but his expression did darken a bit. "Ain't no family, Sir Barris, 'tis just me, Master Argus, and his boy Tam, but Argus, he's a lot like a father to me, to be sure. But the crown, Sir Barris, I wouldn't even know what to spend it on..."

"Then I am sure you will find something, Nikalus. Perhaps a present to yourself for your last birthday, and something kind for your master and Tam. Do not spend it all however, for I shall return in a cycle with more to match what you have saved, if you will agree now to care for Phantom again as you did this day."

The boy's grin widened in admiration and gratitude as Barris climbed upon the great steed, and he proudly straightened. "Thank you, Sir Barris, and you can bet I'll take even better care of him next time. Ain't no one in Mor gonna care for Phantom never but yours truly!"

Barris made a soft clacking noise with his tongue, and the noble Phantom reared steeply on cue, as much to impress young Nikalus as to invigorate mount and rider one last time before they rode on to their camp to rest.

~

Barris was forced to bring Phantom to a skidding halt as he turned a corner onto the thoroughfare to the main gate, narrowly missing a horseman who had ridden past him with all speed. "Fool! Slow your mount!" yelled Barris, and a trio of riders sped past a moment later in pursuit. *A thief, to be sure*, thought Barris, but it was not his affair, and he brought Phantom back to a trot towards the gate. The road leading out of the city was paved in cobblestones, and to run a horse so speedily upon it was more than dangerous, it was cruel, for many a horse had broken a leg in such runs. Barris sighed and stroked the mane of the great Phantom. "They do not respect the sacrifices your kind make for us, dear friend."

He passed over a narrow moat and through the towering iron Northern Gate of Mor, hardly drawing the attention of the sentries on either side, who were peering through the darkness to follow the progress of the maddened riders that had just careened past. Less than a hundred yards beyond the gate, the cobblestone gave way to an earthen road, lined sparsely with young elms that had just begun to shed their first leaves. Barris willed Phantom to pick up the pace, for he was eager to cross the Morline, where he could properly rest

Phantom, pitch his tent, and finally fall into slumber. He briefly considered that he could have stayed the night at the Whistling Wench, and would already be at rest, yet the thought of the fleas and the stench of smoke and overfull chamberpots brought a scowl to his face. "No, my friend," he spoke softly to Phantom, "it is the river for us tonight, as I know you would have it, too."

The forest thickened and the road narrowed slightly as they rode on. The temperature dropped a bit yet still remained mild enough that Barris did not reach into his saddlebag for his gloves. Just short of an hour past the gate, they came upon the Morline bridge and a small guardhouse, with a trio of watchmen milling about. Barris slowed and approached the familiar men.

"Well met, gentlemen. How fares the evening?"

The tall, silver-haired Captain Storey reached up to stroke Phantom's neck and spoke first. "It fares well for us, Barris, but I'm not so sure about that boy that just rode past. Looks to me like he's in for a rough one."

"Might be his last one, if I were to wager," this from the dusky-skinned, hulking Sergeant Long.

"I wouldn't bet against it, Sergeant," said the Captain, shaking his head. "Thieves."

"Thieves," his men agreed, in unison.

Storey turned to the knight. "How was your visit with our illustrious King?"

"I was reminded why I rarely venture south of the Morline, my friend."

"Well, at least you're back with your head still attached," this from Guy, the greenest of the three sentinels, and the only one wearing his helm.

Long glared at the man. "Careful, Private, or it'll be you with a hole for a neck."

"Ah, it's just us four, Sarge, I'm no fool."

Barris sided with the Sergeant. "As far as you know, watchman. Agents of Halsen need not be present to hear. And so we should dispense with this talk."

"Agreed," replied the Captain, eyes leveled at the youthful Guy. "But tell us, Barris, did he hear you?"

"He heard, Captain, to the degree that he would, though whether he listened, time will tell. At the very least, he has agreed to meet again in a cycle. I must make haste to the Wood with news of our audience, for he has requested that I return personally for our next parley."

"The Mawbottom he did...," this from Sergeant Long.

"Mawbottom, indeed," Barris sighed, "but I am expected, Sergeant, and too much is at stake for me to worry myself with a bit of discomfort over the matter. Though I do pity Phantom, for I work him too hard." Phantom snorted at that, as if the prideful animal were offended by the idea. "In any case, I must be going. I wish to make my camp just beyond the bridge, and rest as soon as I might."

"Why cross the bridge, Sir Barris?" queried Guy. "There's little reason. You can rest and eat here with us. I was just about to light us a fire and—"

"No, private," the Captain interrupted, "though I would extend the same offer. But our friend needs to cross the Morline, so the air of his Wood can renew Phantom's strength."

"You have it right, my friend. Be well, gentlemen, and stay alert this cycle, for your own sakes. I fear that the signs we have observed do not bode well for the season, and perhaps longer still."

"Be well, Elven Knight. Take care of him, Phantom, he looks like Disorder."

Barris leveled his gaze at his friend. "On the worst of my days, Captain, I am a shining beacon of glory compared to you on your best."

Captain Storey's men laughed heartily at this, and the captain cuffed them each firmly in return as Barris urged Phantom to the bridge.

~

Barris had prepared his camp just off the Northern Road, in clear sight of the bridge and guardhouse along the northern shore of the Morline, before crossing the river on the way South that very morning. He did so partly to make it easier for himself and Phantom to quickly find their rest this evening, but more as a promise to himself that he would survive the encounter. *How sad that an emissary from a neighboring kingdom should fear for his life when visiting on business of the realm,* thought Barris, as he quickly lit his fire and unsaddled Phantom. Barris unrolled a blanket over the mount, who shied beneath it, stamping his front hooves.

"As you wish, willful creature. You are most rude when weary." Phantom whinnied softly and bumped Barris in apology as he removed the blanket, and the elven knight took a moment to stroke his friend's mane, nuzzling up to his neck. "Ah, but you have right to be, my friend. Rest well; we shall take it slowly tomorrow, and perhaps even rest once more in the evening."

Barris unrolled his own blanket under the small tent, and nearly crawled into it—remembering, however, as he reached to remove his boots that he had not set protection around the camp for himself and Phantom. He straightened and paced a circle around the camp, softly chanting the prayer in the ancient language of his people as he paused at each point of the compass.

"Fah ni yef Da, tah Nü shadda ni." *As we serve you, Father, so You shelter us.*

The spell would awaken both knight and rider if danger should approach, and unlike many elven spells, it did not draw upon the life energies of the petitioner, but was rather a gift from the First Father himself, its power proportionate to the faith and service of the one delivering the appeal. Barris did not doubt its effectiveness.

*I was afraid this day,* Barris thought to himself as he inched nearer to the fire and finally lay upon his thin bedding, remembering the long hours spent in the antechamber of the throne room, exhausted yet too frightened to close his eyes. Only in dark, quiet moments such as these would Barris admit to himself his anxieties, for to do so in the light of day, he believed, would make them plain upon him for all to see. *Yet I am not ashamed. It is not I, nor my people, who caused Halsen to become the tyrant he is, no matter what he may believe in his heart.* This brought a sigh from the knight, as he considered his lovely Queen. *Ah, how I wish you were here beside me now, my Terrias. I fear I shall see you seldom in the seasons to come.* Barris chided himself immediately, for she was not *his* Terrias by any means, though he would wish it so with every fiber of himself. *It is enough to serve you, my Queen. In that I take much joy.*

Barris rolled away from the fire in time to glimpse three riders heading south at a canter over the bridge. *Three only. Perhaps there is one less thief in the world this night.* And with that, Barris slept.

# VI: G'NAATH

hyla returned down the wide tunnel with her head down, Oort and Thinsel hovering protectively at either side. Oort's menacing expression and fierce gaze fended off any dared comments from the gawking gnomes they passed along the way back to their family's stone recesses. She marched numbly along, incapable of thought or reason or speech, so heavy was her heart for her parents, so petrified by the prospect of her looming expulsion. After what could have been an hour or a minute, for in her daze Shyla had lost all sense of time, they turned up the passage to her parents' stony hollow, and Oort pulled back the drape to let her mother pass. He seized Shyla's arm, however, holding her back for a moment.

"Ye'll be strong for yer mother, girl. Yeh can cry in me own arms whenever yeh like for the next three days, but in front of yer Ma, ye'll be brave. Do yeh understand me, Shyla?"

Her father never used her name. She was always "girl," or "child," or "Nugget," or any number of other affectionate titles, but never Shyla. The sound of her own name established just how afraid her dear Papa was at this moment, and Shyla's heart managed to sink further, so deep into her belly that she palpably felt her chest hollow out. Yet she wiped her tear-stained cheeks and fixed her pigtails, smoothed her blouse, stood up as straight as she ever had, and looked into her father's cloudy green eyes.

"I know, Papa. I'll not be causin' her more pain, of that yeh can be sure."

Oort beheld his daughter's own pink, clear eyes in return, his chin trembling for a moment, but then straightened himself as well. "Then come on in, girl, and let's comfort yer Ma best we can."

There was no comfort to be had for Thinsel that day, and Shyla's promise not to cry lasted less than a minute. Mama pulled Shyla into her arms and her great, heaving sobs shook Shyla to her very bones. Oort looked on uncomfortably for a moment, suddenly unsure what to do with his hands, until Thinsel stretched her tiny, wrinkled fingers from behind Shyla's back towards him. Oort reached for the small hand, and took his wife and daughter into his arms. He joined them in their weeping, his own broad shoulders slumping and rocking now, as he tightened his arms around the two broken-hearted lights of his life, his tears flowing as freely as theirs.

After a long while their moans began to recede, yet they continued to hold each other, none of them speaking, as if letting go now would be a final, irrevocable acknowledgement of the fate they confronted.

It was Thinsel who broke their shared embrace first, squeezing and patting them each as she did, stepping back to straighten her dress and her spine. She quickly turned away and reached for the bellows to breathe new life into their small hearth, its embers still glowing from her morning meal with Oort. Her husband looked on at this, one arm still around Shyla, whose face remained buried in his chest, and he thought how strange it was that so much in life could change in less than the time it took for a hearthfire to burn itself out.

"Yeh'll be needing to eat, child, and eat well, as much as yeh can stand afore yer leaving us." Thinsel placed another pitch-dipped dunglog onto the fire and leaned into their cupboard, gathering ingredients for a stew. "Yer father's hard work has got us a hollow with a chimney, and we'll put it to good use these few days, on that yeh can count."

Shyla turned her head enough for one eye to watch her mother shuffle about, and her shame deepened. *Me father, workin' extra shifts fer a year to earn us a nook with a chimney, me Ma, even now putting her sorrow aside to cook me a meal...why in Tahr could I not be more like them? All they have done, all their years, all for an ungrateful layabout like meself...*

Shyla's tears began again, and her mother turned when she heard the sobs return. "No more o' that, Shyla. Ye're to be facin' the wide world in naught but a tenth of a cycle, and the time fer pityin' yerself is past. Git over here and help yer mother with the stew, or ye'll catch me spoon on yer backside."

"Yes, Mama." Shyla dutifully joined her mother.

"And find som'n to do with yerself, Oort, for yeh sure ain't no help in the kitchen no how."

Despite his broken heart, Oort couldn't help but smile at his resilient wife as he stepped out from their home, looking back on his ladies as he pulled the curtain shut. *Sure, we'll comfort your Ma, we will, girl. As if she ain't the pillars o' the whole stinkin' cavern already.*

Oort meandered along the passageways, oblivious to the stares and whispers of the gossipy gnomes he passed, replaying the morning's trial in his mind. *Cindra Sandshingle herself,* he thought. *Now there's a twist. And eight seasons, not a lifespan...I ain't never heard o' such a thing, long as I been a gnome.* He turned a corner, then another, as he wandered and puzzled it over.

*Could be the law's been changed, and I didn't hear none about it?* he considered. He dismissed the idea out of hand. *Naw, canna be that, for as deep as G'naath goes, news flies from one end to th'other like a cloud o' dungflies.* Oort continued his walk and his conjecturing for a brief while, until he nearly tripped over a gnome that had suddenly appeared in his path.

"Well, hello there, Oort. It is good that you came."

Oort looked down at the elderly female gnome, and was stunned to be looking into the bright, smiling face of none other than the silver-haired Cindra Sandshingle herself.

"Uh, I ah, I weren't meaning to..."

"Of course you were, yeh silly old gnome, now come in afore the whole of G'naath finds me door."

And there *was* a door, and Cindra held it open for Oort, grinning all the while, and Oort stood there in the middle of the tunnel, jaw hanging open. He looked down the tunnel, and behind him, and back, rubbing his bald, pale head, baffled.

"I been down this tunnel a hunnerd times, and I ain't never seen no door..."

"Well didja not just hear me, ya daft old gnome? 'Tis a secret door, now git yerself in it!"

Cindra shut the door behind her, and motioned to a stool on the near side of the circular table that sat in the middle of the small, cluttered room. Oort sat down obediently, if slowly, and Cindra walked around the table, taking a seat across from the bewildered gnome.

She leaned forward, cheerfully watching Oort watching her as she rested her chin on her miniature knuckles.

"Such pretty eyes yer daughter has, and so unlike your own."

~

"Yer to have one job and one job only, me daughter," Thinsel said gravely, as she stirred the kettle and Shyla set the table. "That's stayin' alive Outside, and make no mistake, the Outside is no friendly place to a gnome."

"Yes, Mama," Shyla replied absently.

Thinsel turned and glowered at Shyla, the expression on her mother's face the most severe that Shyla had ever seen.

"This ain't the time fer 'Yes, Mama', child."

Shyla nodded, sensing her mother's intensity and trying her best to clear her mind and focus on her mother's words. Thinsel set the large stone spoon down on the counter and pulled up a stool beside Shyla, placing her hands on her daughter's knees.

"Now, yeh listen, girl, and yeh listen well. Yer a smart one, there's no denyin', and maybe the smartest gnome in all G'naath. Don't look at me like that, yeh know it and yeh always have. But there be bad people in the wide world, worse than the meanest gnome you ever met, and beasts and monsters alike, and the worst part is, ya won't be knowin' the good from the bad most times until it's too late for yeh. Yeh got to be wary, child, wary of all yer seein', all the time, and yeh can't let yer guard down never, not fer a minute."

Shyla listened as her mother continued, and as she did, she felt a tickle of understanding develop in the back of her mind. *Mama has been Outside. She must'a. How could she know these things if she ain't?*

She waited until her mother took a breath, and interrupted.

"Mama."

Thinsel heard her tone and knew a grave question was coming. She hoped it was one, and not the other.

"Yes, child."

"Have yeh been Outside yerself?"

Thinsel sighed, relieved. She paused for a moment, looking to her hands and gathering her response, then looked back to meet her daughter's eyes.

"Yes, Shyla, your father and I have both been Outside."

Another pause.

Shyla looked at her mother and Thinsel looked back at her. Their unblinking eyes locked, and Shyla knew that there were things she could ask at this moment, and things that she should not. She recognized that their conversation was at a tipping point, a crossroads of sorts, and she instinctively turned away from the latter direction, the deepest part of her terrified of what she would find at the end of that path.

*I know that if yeh wanted to tell me more of it, Mama, yeh would have afore now. But yeh can tell me what yeh know to help me survive this trouble, and I'll not ask more than ye're willing to tell.*

Thinsel nodded as if she had heard every word in Shyla's mind, and continued to teach her what she could, skillfully avoiding the truths she could not speak aloud.

~

A bit more than two hours had passed, and Oort returned to their home, just in time to see his Greykin ladies clearing the table.

"There's more stew in the kettle, Oort. Girl, git yer father a bowl and a spoon, would yeh? And some bread, if there be any left."

"Yes, Mama."

Oort and Thinsel exchanged a look then, and each immediately knew that the other had just undergone something profound.

*Later,* mouthed Thinsel, glancing sidelong at Shyla.

Oort sat down to eat his meal, and the three of them talked lightly for a bit, not quite as if all were well and normal, but not quite as if the world were ending, either. The conversation inevitably led to the trial, however, and Oort leveled his eyes at his daughter.

"I dunno if yeh heard at the time, but the Lady Sandshingle asked ye to visit her afore ye go, girl."

Shyla stiffened at this. "I intend to do no such thing, Papa. She spelled me to spill my guts afore all o' G'naath, and that's a fact."

"That ain't how I see it, Nugget."

The girl was nearly disarmed by his heart-name for her, but quickly steeled herself.

"Papa, I felt it. She raised those wrinkled old arms o' hers, and my whole speech I had planned out fell apart in me own mouth, and next thing yer knowin', I'm blubberin' and spittin' out things I didn't never mean to say."

"I don't doubt yeh, girl, but that still ain't the way I see it."

"Well if ya don't doubt me, Papa, then how –"

"Listen to your father, child."

Shyla's anger only intensified at that, mindful now that she was being talked down to, and by both her parents.

"I'm no child, Mama, at least I better not be, seein' as what I got afore me."

"Yeh speak true, me daughter, yer no child no more, but to yer Ma and me, yer the only child that ever was or ever will be. Now, will ye hear me, or won't yeh?"

Shyla sighed. She was no less angry, for the shame she felt at emptying her heart before all of G'naath ran deep and hot, and she blamed the sorceress chiefly for it. Yet she could not find it in her heart to defy her father, not now.

"I'm sorry, Papa. I'm listening."

"Good, then, and listen well. The Lady saved yer hide today, child, don't yeh doubt it fer a minute. Sure, yer mad at 'er fer makin' yeh spill yer guts, and make yeh she did, we all saw it. But if ye hadn't done just that, just what do yeh think ol' Ky'rl Gypstone was gonna do with yeh?"

"I coulda defended meself, Papa, it weren't fer sure what woulda happened–"

Oort interrupted. "Think, Shyla. And tell yer father why that ain't true."

Shyla paused, irked that her intellect should be tested, as if she weren't capable of reasoning it all out on her own...and not a blink later, her head drooped in resignation.

"Yer right, Papa."

Oort nodded. "Why am I right, Nugget?"

"Because the Lady has magic, and even if I had convinced the whole cavern of what I was wantin' to say, she woulda known the truth, probably the whole of it, and woulda told th'elders as much when they went back to decide me fate."

"And?" Oort urged his daughter to continue.

"And I woulda been shunned forever, not just fer th'eight seasons, and wouldn't nobody have been carin' a bit, once they heard that I weren't tellin' the whole truth."

*But how did Papa reason the whole thing out?* Shyla wondered, for she loved and respected her father, but...

As if on cue, her father spoke. "There's no denyin' yer smarter than me, Nugget, and fer that I'm proud as can be. But ye ain't as wise, not yet, and there's a sickness only age can cure, and twenty-three years ain't yet enough. And smart as ye are, yeh canna think straight when yer mad or scared, can't no one, and when yeh lie, yeh need two brains–"

"One to manage the lies, and one fer hidin' the truth." Shyla completed the moral for him, a lesson he had taught her more than once.

"Yeh'll be seein' the Lady Sandshingle then, me girl, if not by yer own desire, then fer me and yer Ma."

Shyla nodded her head in resignation. "Yes, Papa. But, Papa?"

"Yes?"

"How did they only expel me for eight seasons? Ain't the law s'posed to be that I'm out fer life?"

"Like I said, girl, see the lady."

The little pigtailed gnome looked at her father with suspicion then, and it dawned on her that this driphole she was in descended much deeper than she had supposed.

# VII: THE WHISTLING WENCH

o coin, boys, and heaps of it!"

"Heaps of it!" replied the men in chorus.

The golden-haired young man tilted his mug and took a drink. Earl drained his own in three enormous swallows, finishing with an ear-splitting belch.

"Now, that's a talent, Earl!" said the boy in honest admiration. "You could earn a decent living, wagering on your drinking prowess!"

"I already earn a living, boy, though it ain't so decent."

"Doing what?" he asked, not really caring, but more to further ingratiate himself to the colossal man.

"Earl here is a wagon loader, and us four work on 'em," this from Stubs, whom the boy had learned was missing three fingers "on account of a dice game gone bad."

"Wagon loader, huh. Is there much work to be had doing that?"

"This time of year, there's plenty, but winters can be a bit rough."

"Same for fixin' em," added Pike, the tall, thin man who had stood over the pile of coins during Earl's nimble performance. The boy wasn't sure whether the man's name had been given at birth, or assigned later, as his long, lanky build did very much resemble a pike.

"And how about you, boy?" asked Earl. "How do you earn your keep, and hey, what's your name, anyhow?"

A voice spoke up from behind the four. "His name is trouble, and you'll not want to share it."

The young man and his new friends looked up at the three severe-looking men who had just made their way to their table. The one in the tight black jerkin on his right was the spokesman; the other two, in dark grey cloaks, were just now maneuvering behind the boy's chair. *Mawbottom. Here we go...*

Earl was the first to respond. "Well, right now Trouble over here is buyin' the drinks, so unless you wanna get the next round, you can take a walk."

The man who had spoken nodded at the other two, who pulled back their cloaks to reveal long, wide scabbards at their hips.

Earl's boys looked at him, unsure, and Earl addressed the speaker.

"We don't want any trouble now, mister..."

"As I said. I expect, then, that you will be returning to your homes. It's getting late, and you'll need to be to work at dawn, Earl. As will you, Pike, Stubs, Han, and Kendrick." The man glanced at each in turn as he named them.

From Pike, "How in Tahr do you—"

"Now."

Earl stood, and for the briefest of moments seemed to consider his options, but then grabbed the boy's shoulder and gave it a squeeze. "Good luck to you, kid. Looks like you'll need it. C'mon, boys, work in the morning." The four made their way to the door. Earl looked back once at the young man, shaking his head.

The spokesman took a seat at the table beside the boy, while his men remained in place.

He leaned in and flashed a hungry smile. "Hello, Lucan."

"Lucan? I don't know any—"

A flash of pain nearly knocked the boy to the floor of the tavern, as he was struck on the ear from behind by something a lot more solid than a fist. His hand went to his head as his vision cleared, and he saw the first splatters of blood drip onto the table.

*Get it together, Luc, this is bad. Really bad.*

He blinked away his shock and pain, and decided that his first order of business would be to do whatever was necessary to avoid being struck again.

"Lucan, sir. That's my name. Whatever it is you think I have done, I am sure—"

"The ring."

*Huh? For Tahr's sake, this is about the ring?*

"It was a fair bet, friend, but if it matters that much to the man..."

"The ring means nothing. Though the pride of Vincent Thomison means much."

*Aw, Fury.* Vincent Thomison was known to be among the most ruthless merchants in all of Mor, the term "merchant" being applied loosely. He was rumored to be the leader of a small army of thieves, thugs, and mercenaries, though his legitimate businesses peppered the streets of the city, from arms to armor to magical items and more.

"I'm sorry, friend. I did not know that the man was Master Thomison. I am happy to give the ring back, here." He pulled the chain from his neck and began to remove the ring, and one of the men behind him snatched both chain and ring from his hand.

"The man you cheated was not Master Thomison, fool of a boy, but rather his brother. And he would like to have a little conversation with you. Outside."

Lucan Thorne willed himself to think, and think fast, for if these men got him outside, he was fairly certain that his last meal would, in fact, wind up being his last meal. He closed his eyes, bowed his head, and feigned resignation, as he tried to quickly recall every detail of the last few minutes.

*We ordered another round of drinks, and I heard the horses approach the tavern. Earl did as well, I noticed, as he turned his head towards the entrance. Talking, drinking, the sound of boots on the porch...a man outside telling another to move along, the trio enters, the wagon men leave, words, pain, a laugh, a sliding stool behind me at the bar...he should just be getting to his horse now...*

Lucan exploded out of his chair, his legs flinging it behind him, overturning the table onto Master Thomison's man. He leapt high and to his right, directly onto the long dining table beside him, and ran right along the top of it towards the door, nearly reaching it before he heard the shout behind him.

"STOP HIM!" Black Jerkin shouted.

The boy burst through the door, bowling over a waitress on the way, and there was the ringless brother of the infamous Thomison, the reins of his horse in hand, the mount already untied from the rail as Lucan had hoped, and thankfully facing the center of the street. *Well, there's a bit of luck, then,* thought Lucan, as he launched himself off the porch, levelling a kick at Thomison's chest. Lucan missed his mark, but was not off center—the kick caught the man square in the groin, dropping him like a stone. Lucan mounted the horse in a graceful vault, faster and more cleanly than he had ever mounted a horse in his entire life. He grabbed the reins, and kicked the animal into motion. Shockingly, the horse did not throw the boy, but instead obediently took to a run, just as Lucan heard the steps of his pursuers on the porch.

He had to veer the mount to the right as he reached the first cross street to avoid another rider that had made the intersection at the same time, and he heard the man shout at him as he rode past.

*Sorry pal, but I promise you're not in as much of a hurry as I am.*

He heard the galloping of his pursuers behind him as he neared the gate and cleared the moat bridge, silently praying to no one in particular that the sentries at the wall would not be too alert. His wish was granted, as they were milling about several yards from the cobblestone path, and as he flew past the walls of Mor he felt hope's faint spark, followed shortly thereafter by the returning pain in his ear as his initial adrenaline rush began to fade.

His escape was not a yet foregone conclusion however; far from it. He urged the mount on, and wished he had a whip, or spurs, or *something* to inspire the horse to find more speed —although he had to admit, this was quite a horse. While he had ridden many times growing up, Lucan was acutely aware that he was no horseman. He was familiar enough with the saddle, at least, to know that it was extremely rare, if not unheard of, for a strange horse to accept a new and frantic rider so quickly, and respond so effortlessly to his command. Yet Lucan began to realize that even his good fortune in acquiring this quick, compliant mount might not be enough, for the sound of galloping hooves behind him was getting louder as minutes turned to miles.

*Cursed bastards, can they not relent? It was just a damned ring, and they got it back!*

On they rode, fast approaching the Morline. Lucan managed to coax bursts of speed from the horse on occasion, but it was becoming clear that the beast was flagging, nearing the limits of its endurance.

*Just a bit more, get me across the bridge and they'll surely give up the chase!*

The horse responded yet again as Lucan leaned across its neck, lowering its head and throwing earth behind them as powerfully as its great legs would allow. They sailed past the Morline guardhouse and over the bridge, yet still the trio came on, showing no signs of slowing.

*Dammit, think, Lucan, think!*

They weren't going to give up, Lucan was sure of that now. They'd run their horses into the grave, and if Lucan's estimation was correct, his own mount would collapse soon, its heart exploding from the chase. If he'd felt that his mount might outlast those of his hunters, he might have decided to risk it, but he knew his own luck— or lack of it. *It's only a one in four chance my horse survives them all, and the way my fortune runs, it might as well be one in a hundred.*

Lucan decided then what he would do.

*For Tahr's sake, horse, please run true for just a bit more*

Lucan climbed partway out of the saddle, preparing to jump off the horse and make a break into the forest. It was dark enough, and the trio of riders just far enough behind, that he believed he could make it beyond the tree line unseen. His only hope, however, was that his horse would keep running and lead his pursuers on, for if it did not, it would just be a matter of time before the trio found him.

*Run like the wind, horse, you've been good to me*

Lucan jumped out of the saddle, rolling into the brush to his left, immediately cracking his head on a thick root in the precise spot where the thug had struck him earlier, his next roll slamming a rib against a stone. Hot, searing pain brought a howl up to his lips as his roll concluded against a sapling, but the wind mercifully tore the breath from his lungs, for he knew that to make noise now would ensure his death. He clenched his fists and squeezed his eyes shut against the pain, trying to get as flat as he could among the knee-high grasses where he had come to rest. He could not see, nor really hear, but he *thought* he could just make out the sound of his horse's gallop, far ahead, as the trio of riders passed him.

Gradually, his breath returned, and he could no longer hear his charging doom. His head and side now began to throb in time with his fast-beating heart, and he took a moment to count his injuries. The ribs were the worst of it, one or more almost certainly cracked. The still-bleeding wounds on his ear and head were painful but not debilitating. Everything hurt, but to a tolerable degree, as long as he did not take more than a quarter of a breath. He rose and began stumbling into the woods, almost hoping that a bear would come eat him and end this miserable night.

Almost.

# VIII: BELGORNE

ull, ye arselickin' sons o' dung, pull like ye got a pair!" shouted Kelgarr through the horn, lamenting the slow progress of his kin.

"If I pull any harder, Boot, me pair's gonna swap places with me guts!" replied Gritson, his face purple and his arms shaking from the strain on the thick rope.

"Ain't none of ya got no guts, nor a pair to speak of besides, now PULL!"

The gargantuan boulder finally began to roll again, at last beginning to clear the lip of the cavity in the stone. Kelgarr– "Boot" to most–dropped his horn and ran to help his men finish the monumental task, its conclusion now in sight. He faced away from the boulder, bent low and sprang up from the knees, slamming his broad shoulders into the underside of the twenty-foot high rock. A cracking, snapping sound came from behind him, but it wasn't his back–the pulleys were starting to come off the walls, and if they didn't get it over on this try...

"*Stonarris!*" he howled, and his company of kin took up the call.

"STONARRISSSSSSS!" they roared in refrain. The boulder found balance on the lip just as Kelgarr heard the last of the three pulleys separate from its anchors in the ceiling. His sturdy legs and back were now the only force being applied to the massive round rock, and if someone had entered the cavern just then, it would have appeared as if two dozen dwarves were standing around watching one of their number singlehandedly plug a volcano with a mountain.

At long last, the ruddy light from below was extinguished. The boulder's great bulk settled onto the aperture of the pit, seamlessly closing it and, more importantly, sealing off the cavern from the sulfurous smoke that had been rising from the pit for nearly a cycle.

As the echoes of the thundering report of stone-on-stone faded, Boot faced his incredulous comrades, breathing heavily. "Hmph," he snorted. "I shoulda rolled the damnable thing here myself." A groan issued from the exhausted band of engineers. "Mud the seam and roll these ropes, boys, and back to the halls for a mead or three!"

The groans turned to cheers as the bone-weary company raced one another to shovel the mud, roll the ropes and gather the remains of the ruined pulleys.

"Dunno why in Fury we're down here bustin' humps, Boot might just have rolled that bastard rock here himself!" said Gritson in awe, after waiting for the dwarf to turn a corner.

None dared argue the suggestion.

~

Boot was finishing his first horn of mead to the sound of his men's merriment at the bar behind him when his king's young firstson straddled the bench beside him, two tankards in hand.

"Took a bit longer this time, Kelgarr," said J'arn Silverstone as he handed a mug to Boot. "Though from what I'd seen, t'were a mammoth job indeed."

"Bigger hole. Bigger rock." Boot looked down at the tankard J'arn had brought him, and back to the prince. "Not mead."

"Not mead," J'arn agreed.

"Ya ain't never drank but mead with me, J'arn."

"Ye speak true." J'arn eyed the tired but perceptive dwarf.

Boot returned J'arn's gaze as an understanding passed between them.

"How long?"

"Not long. Mayhap a cycle, two at the outside."

Boot quaffed half the contents of the pungent moonjuice in a single gulp. "How can ye be sure?"

"Well, your own reports for one, the dig reports from Beezle for another, and then this last from the priests." J'arn slid a folded parchment across the bench to Boot, who took it in his hands and brought a thick monocle out from within his vest. He stroked his greying beard and leaned back, pulling a face, arm outstretched, clearly struggling to make out the writing.

"Gahhh, damned priests write too small. What's it say?" Boot handed the parchment back to his prince, who folded it immediately and shoved it into a pocket.

"In short, Boot, it says what we suspected. First off, it's no ordinary tahrcracker. Second, it's no ordinary mawflow. It's coming from the heart o' Disorder itself, and it's not just happening here."

"Where else?"

"Everywhere. Thornwood, Mor, the Sapphire Sea, even. Somehow G'naath ain't seen much yet, but they will."

"The Sapphire? How could anyone know that?"

"Well, supposedly there have been maelstroms here and there, running the southern coast over the summer, and unlike the usual ones they see in the spring, these ain't goin' anywhere. If anything, they're gettin' bigger."

"But what've the priests to say about it?"

J'arn stroked his own thick, burgundy beard and kicked his leg over the bench, facing the table now, shoulders slumping.

"Ye cannot tell the men, Kelgarr. Not a word."

"Goes without saying."

"Say it anyways."

Kelgarr reached to his belt and put his hammer on the table, one hand grasping its head, the other its handle. "I'll not tell a soul, my prince, on my seat in Stonarris' halls."

J'arn nodded, and continued. "The priests say, Boot, that we're about to face the same damned thing the dwarves of Mulgar Silverstone faced."

Boot paled. "Mawbottom, no."

"Not just Mawbottom, Boot. Mawbottom we might could handle. This runs deeper."

"Dammit, J'arn, in a *cycle?*" Boot exclaimed.

"*Keep your voice down,* damn ye! Aye, in a cycle, maybe two, never more than three."

The friends sat there in silence as the moments passed. Boot looked back on his men, watching them harass pretty young Kari as per usual, while she laughed, and dodged, and swatted them with her towel. His eyes examined the whole of the stony subterranean inn, appreciating for perhaps the first time the fine workmanship that had built the benches, the great wooden bar, the staircase, the elegantly carved hearth, the dozens of lines of brass tubing leading to the great casks in the cellar, the faded tapestries and chiseled reliefs on the walls, all of it...

Boot brought the remainder of his drink to his lips, hands trembling. "Where will we go, my prince?" he asked quietly into his mug, his reddened eyes moist.

"My father has not told me, Boot. I do not think he yet knows."

# IX: MOR

kingdom of Mor sprawls centrally within a wide, gently sloping valley just to the south of the Morline, nearly a cycle's ride south of the elven kingdom of Thornwood (upon a typical mount), roughly equidistant from Thornwood and the southern Sapphire Sea. Its fertile land rises again onward to the west, through the farmlands to the dense forests of Eyre, within which sits Eyreloch, home of the Airies and the great lake which marks the convergence of the Morline and the great river Trine. Beyond Eyre lie the deserts of the west and its tribal peoples. To the east of Mor the great peaks of the Maw rise, and many cartographers have exaggerated the relationship between Mor and the Maw to make it appear as if the kingdom were nothing more than a pending meal for the Beast of the East. Little artistic embellishment was required to convey the effect, however, as a true representation of the terrain was not far removed from the interpretations.

From along the balustrade of the topmost level of the Keep of Kehrlia, situated in the absolute geometrical center of the city of Mor, one could walk the radius beneath the parapet and look upon the entire city and many of its nearest surrounding villages. On a clear autumn day such as this, one could barely make out the gentle plumes of smoke rising from the Fang, an extraordinarily tall volcanic mountain marking the westernmost teeth of the upper jaw of the Maw. Today, however, some effort was required to differentiate the more commonly seen cloud of volcanic ash from the numerous thin trails rising throughout the kingdom.

Sartean D'Avers, master of Kehrlia, chief advisor to King Halsen, head of the Fraternity of Incantors and one of the most powerful wizards in the recorded history of Tahr, looked out over the railing and for one of the few times in half a century knew fear.

Sartean did not fear the smoke, nor the fires, nor what the accelerating changes in the lands, or even the very Order, might portend. He did not fear the powers of opposing kingdoms, nor any man, elf, dwarf, or beast. He did not fear the tribal peoples, individually or as a whole, nor their witchdoctors and soothsayers, nor all the swords and spears of all the peoples outside the walls of the city of Mor combined.

He feared that his wretched fool of a king would continue in his reckless and violent ignorance, and the very subjects of Mor would soon rise up against Halsen, and when they marched him to the square and tore the very flesh from his bones, Sartean D'Avers would be watching it all from the stocks, awaiting his own turn for justice at the hands of the filthy, avaricious mob.

His terror at this notion was neither baseless nor overstated, for he had seen that very scene unfold in a vision not a quarter cycle past.

Which was not to say that the course of destiny could not be altered, for to a wizard's mind, that was the very function of the art of divination—to foretell that which was impending, and to modify fate's course before the possible became the inevitable. While many naïve and craven practitioners of magic would argue that to attempt to rework providence was foolish at best, disastrous at worse, and impossible most often, in Sartean's estimation this view was nonsense. A great wizard must acknowledge no restraint upon his power, neither tangible nor ethical, and the greatest of wizards had accomplished much, much more than a simple amendment to a divined possible outcome. For after all, could he not simply dive from this very tower to the street below, at this very moment, and render the vision moot?

Sartean would do no such thing, of course, for he had a much more agreeable answer in mind.

He turned and walked to the stairwell at the center of the balcony, his practiced stride and long, flowing black robes lending the illusion that he was not walking, but floating. He descended the marble stair and as he made his way onto the landing in his luxuriously appointed private library, the room began to glow with light, not from one point, but from all, as if it the very air were luminescent.

In the center of the room on a low glass table sat his favorite diversion, a fist-sized uncut diamond, resting within the grasp of a sculpted jade talon, its three pointed nails chiseled so sharp that one had to look closely to be certain that they were in fact holding the gem, and it was not merely hovering above the claw. *Perhaps a bit of fun, then, before I return to my work.*

Sartean sat cross-legged upon an outsized plush velvet pillow before his toy, and, closing his eyes, made a barely perceptible gesture towards the stone with the fingers of his right hand. The enchanted diamond was empowered with the life energies of an entire pack of dire wolves, whose hearing was well known to be unparalleled in the animal kingdom, and was attuned to the frequency ranges of the human voice. The sound he listened for, using the powerful gem as a conduit, would not be audible in the room, but rather within his own mind, and he was presently assaulted by the noise of every word being spoken at that instant in and near Mor. The initial sensation was always unpleasant, but he was practiced at the endeavor and within a few moments, the cacophony of muttering filtered down to his intended target, the sound of his own name.

Three hundred thousand men, women, and children lived within the city of Mor, and during the day, the streets could fill with many more, as merchants and visitors from around the kingdom and beyond entered the walls of the city to conduct trade or other business. He had discovered one day (with great satisfaction to his considerable sense of conceit) that at any given moment, dozens could be in a conversation about the wizard, either in passing or in earnest. He also discovered, however, that the discussions were often unflattering, though Sartean D'Avers relished the sound of own his name on the lips of the masses, no matter the theme.

Well, the theme *mattered*, as one would no doubt discover this day.

He allowed his attention to flit among the various conversations until he found a suitable target, and with scarcely a thought, the scene appeared within his mind, as if he were present among the men's discussion.

"*The rotten old drunk is gonna work us all to death or starvation, and that's a fact. You know it and I know it.*" The emaciated youngish man was digging a hole for some reason alongside another man, older and thinner.

"*It won't be the work that kills us, James,*" the older man replied, leaning on his shovel. "*That smoke rising up all over the damnable city will choke us all out well before then, mark my words. It's devilry, boy, I know it. Something awful is coming, and that old pickled fool doesn't have a clue.*"

"*Well, like I said, why doesn't old Sardine Cadaver do*

something about it?" James asked, wiping sweat from his eyes with his forearm. "The man's supposed to be some all-powerful sorcerer, why in Tahr can't he put out a few fires?"

Sardine Cadaver. Ah, how the fools loved their little jokes.

"He probably lit the damned things himself, boy. Why don't ya just go ask him? And while you're at it, ask him to wizard us up a few lamb steaks and a cask o' wine."

"Don't drink wine, but I won't be asking him a thing anyways, that's for sure. And while we're at it, let's talk about something else. They say he listens, ya know. Might be that he decides to turn us into toads for speaking his name."

"You're already ugly as a toad, boy, won't be much work."

"No, James, I won't turn you into a toad," Sartean said aloud as he allowed the vision to dissipate. "Though I expect you shall find yourself the victim of a most unfortunate accident tonight." The wizard smiled to himself and stood, walking over to his desk where he would begin the work of divining where the boy lived, to whom he was related, and if time allowed, what his deepest, greatest fears consisted of.

*Oh, how I do enjoy my hobbies,* Sartean thought to himself, when a single knock interrupted his thought.

*Damn!*

"Enter!"

A young apprentice opened the door and peeked into the room, his eyes darting about, clearly anxious.

"I said enter, fool, not reconnoiter my library for goblins. What do you want of me? Speak quickly!"

The boy entered and addressed the floor.

"Er, ah, I'm sorry for disturbing you, Master, but you've been summoned to the king's residence, with all haste."

"'All haste', boy? Your words or those of the messenger?"

"Ah, the messenger's words were more colorful, Master."

"Were they," said the wizard rhetorically.

"Shall I tell him—"

The air left the room for a moment, and the frightened young apprentice looked up to see that his master was no longer behind his desk, nor in the room at all. He did not have time to register the wizard's departure before he found himself back in the hall, facing away from the library. Disoriented, he turned around in time to see a glow under the door of the wizard's study fading to blackness.

*Fury.*

~

King Halsen sat at his dining table within his expansive bedchamber, his silken nightrobe hanging loosely about him, light streaming in from behind him through the open window beside his enormous poster bed. A knock came from the door, and he nodded to his manservant Yan to allow the visitor entry.

Sartean passed the threshold of the bedchamber. Halsen had only recently begun inviting Sartean to his private chambers, after two decades of service. The wizard was pleased to see that King Halsen had honored his request from their last visit in this room, and had a cloth draped over the table, for no sight was less appealing to the wizard than King Halsen's open robe. He glanced at Yan and back to the king, who dismissed the man with a wave.

"Enjoy your meal, my liege. I shall await your command," and the man closed the heavy gilded door behind him with a bow.

"Ah, Sar, what a fine day, is it not? Join me for breakfast." Halsen motioned to a chair across from him, which the wizard did not immediately take, where a plate of poached eggs, ham, and potatoes steamed invitingly.

Yet *Sar-tee-ann* was not in the mood. *Why must he insist on calling me Sar?* thought the wizard, full well knowing the answer.

"It is past noon, my lord."

"One of the advantages of being king, mage. I eat what I want when I want, and awaken when I am no longer asleep. Wine, then?" he offered as he filled his own golden cup.

"No thank you, Sire."

"Ah, but you are sour today Sartean, and I even had Yan cloth the table for you, though I know not why you would shy from the sight of my royal dangly bits." The king roared with laughter at this, egg and ham spilling from his mouth. "Have I stolen you from a task of great importance, then?"

"Not so important, my king. How may I serve you today?"

"Well, you may begin by telling me why you did not attend the visit from the woodie."

"My apologies, my king. I was required at the keep, though I did witness the meeting."

"Good, for it is that meeting that I wish to discuss. How do you see it then, Sartean? What are your thoughts on the matter?"

Sartean paused to consider the best approach here. Halsen poured himself another glass of wine, and the wizard immediately regretted not having accepted any himself, for now the king would drink the entire decanter, and that could make for a most trying meeting, if not the entire day.

"I pray that I may speak freely, Sire."

"You've never prayed a day in your life, Sartean."

"That is nearly true, my lord."

"Nearly? Do you mean to tell me that you once carried the spark of religious fervor?"

Sartean thought back to his childhood for the briefest of moments, very nearly remembering his mother's voice...he dismissed the memory immediately.

"Only in passing, my king."

"Well, in any case, rarely do you not speak your mind, Sartean."

"Only when I sense your permission, Sire."

"And what do you sense today?"

Sartean sat now. "I sense that the people of Mor grow dangerously restless, my king."

"Bah, tell me something I don't know."

*Fool.* "I am aware that we do not see this matter through the same lens, my king. But I implore you to hear me, and at least consider that I may have valuable insight..."

"You *implore* me, do you?"

Sartean knew he had chosen the word poorly. He had crossed the line already, however; no sense retreating now. *Perhaps this is the day that it comes to a boil,* he considered. *As good a day as any other.* He continued.

"My king, there is no way to express the depth of my concern here without arguing against the position you seem to hold on the matter. But as you rely upon me to advise you, I humbly ask that you allow me to do just that, without fear of reprisal, this one time."

Halsen poured himself another cup of wine, but did not yet drink. He reached for a napkin and wiped his mouth and beard, something Sartean had rarely witnessed. He regarded the wizard silently for a moment before he spoke.

"Never have you been this direct with me, Sartean. I do not like it." A pause. "However, I am wise enough to appreciate that you must feel strongly compelled to do so. You may continue, for now."

*A small victory,* thought Sartean.

"You are aware of my Listening stone, my king?"

"The whole damned kingdom is aware of that thing, Sartean. It's not been a secret for many years."

"Then you are also no doubt aware that I employ it regularly, and through its use, I have come to suspect—no, to know—that the seeds of a revolt are taking root."

"You know this, wizard? And you have not had the upstarts arrested?"

"There has yet to be a specific threat, nor any organized gatherings, my lord. However, I have access to extensive notes and journal writings in Kehrlia from my predecessors, from times far gone when similar rumblings have been heard among the masses, and I tell you with certainty, revolt is coming, and soon. I will present to you all of my evidence if you wish to see it, though to review it all will be a considerable task, one that I hardly enjoyed, and I am sure your highness would find quite tedious."

The king sneered at this. "I do not require your parchments and books, Sartean, I have you. Tell me, then, how do we stamp out this spark before it becomes a flame?"

"I fear that it is already a flame, my king, and I do not believe that stamping it out is the best approach."

"You would have me sit back, then, and allow my throne to be overturned?"

"Certainly not, Sire. I would have you address the chief complaints of the people, to their satisfaction."

Halsen's eyes widened, and a sarcastic smile turned up the corners of his mouth. "You jest, wizard. Are you softening, truly?"

"I believe you misunderstand, Sire. Or rather, I have not sufficiently explained myself."

"Certainly that. Go on."

"There are three primary issues that require resolution. The first, and most easily rectified, concerns the rations of food allotted to your soldiery."

"Then I shall instruct my generals to increase them to the necessary degree. I care not."

"Well, the difficulty there is that your treasurers do not feel they can pry open the purse sufficiently to do so."

"Then I will arrest my treasurers and replace them. Simple enough."

*And where will the new treasurers find the gold, you fool, when no one wishes to trade with us as a result of your bloodlust and greed?*

"I believe, with your permission, that I can save you the grief of hiring new bankers, and can solve the problem more efficiently, which brings us to the second matter."

"Do not assume my permission just yet, wizard, but do continue."

*This is going much better than I had hoped*, thought Sartean, willing his face to remain impassive.

"The second issue is a matter of labor, Sire, as many of your subjects, particularly here in the city and in the direct employ of the kingdom, are worked for more than fourteen hours each day, and in some cases, eighteen or more, with–"

"How many hours in a day do you work, Sartean?"

*Like a fish on a line,* Sartean thought. "If I am not asleep, my king, I am engrossed in my work. I sleep little."

"Then why should it not be the same for all, Sartean? Are you possessed of some strength of character that the people of Mor lack?"

"Character no, Sire. Magic, yes."

Halsen chuckled derisively. "So, you enchant yourself with a work ethic then, mage?"

"Not exactly, Sire, although you are near the mark. Magic allows me to tolerate more discomfort, perhaps, and certain enchantments and potions can empower me to require less rest. Although I will say honestly that I do very much enjoy my work, Sire, not only because I am passionate about the tasks, but because it allows me to serve you and your–"

"Spare me, Sartean. You serve me to serve yourself, and I would have it no other way. But tell me more about these enchantments. Could you, say, ensorcel my laborers to work longer, or faster?"

"Well, that was not the idea I had in–"

"Can you do it or not, wizard?"

Sartean hesitated for effect. "It would require some thought and research, my king, but I believe it would be possible."

"Then I shall expect you to focus on no other task until you have found the solution."

"As you command, Sire. Although there is one other matter..."

"The fires."

*Let him believe it is his own mind that leads him...* "Yes, my king As you have certainly deduced by now, they are far from ordinary."

"I have deduced that, have I?"

"Forgive me, Sire, I did not realize that we were in disagreement."

"Relax, Sar. Of course I have concluded as much. How do you propose we address them?"

"I have not yet found their cause or a solution, Sire, although, I fear that the real threat is not the fires, but rather their effect on your subjects. I worry that if we do not quickly address the matters of rations and labor, the fires and other oddities will turn the current flame of discontent into a full-fledged conflagration. Superstition and fear have been catalysts for many a war, my king, civil and otherwise. Perhaps, however, if we can find answers to the first two problems, it will buy us enough time to find a solution for the third."

"So, then, Sartean—food and labor, gold and magic, and you believe you can deliver me all of it?"

"Without meaning to boast, my king, have I ever failed you in the past?"

"Do you still draw breath?"

"I do, my king." *And so, Sartean D'Avers' station is enhanced,* the sorcerer told himself. Sartean finally allowed himself a small smile.

"Then let us hope your flawless record continues, wizard, for both our sakes. You have my leave to do as is required. There is one additional matter, however."

"Yes, Sire?"

"The elf knight will return in less than a cycle, and an assessment is expected, upon my word."

"I shall prepare it myself, Sire."

"You shall do no such thing. Assign the task to your subordinates. I wish for you to dedicate yourself exclusively to these matters discussed today."

"I will not disappoint you, my king." Sartean rose from his chair.

"No, you will not. Tell Yan to bring more wine on your way out."

"At your command, Sire," replied Sartean with a refined bow to his mighty king, and glided from the room.

*The drunken fool doesn't even know he just delivered me his own throne. And with enthusiasm.* The wizard beamed as he cast the incantation to return to his library. *Now what was that young man's name? Ah, yes, James. Perhaps I shall grant you a reprieve, James. Of a sort.*

# X: THORNWOOD

hy the hurry, Mik?" called Aria melodically, as Mikallis hastened down the flagstone path leading from the elven castle. She had not spoken to him at all the previous day, nor at all this day.

He halted at her voice, and turned to regard the elven princess as she caught up to him. "Your mother has requested that I gather her councilors, and so I do," he replied, a chilled tone in his voice.

"She said she wishes to meet this evening, Mik, not an hour ago. Why the rush? What troubles you?" she asked, taking his arm.

"Do you not know?"

Aria led him ahead at a lazier pace. "Ah, Mik, your pride will be your undoing. Neral chided me as well, you know."

"He did not reproach you yesterday, Aria, as an overly young officer with the wisdom of a buffoon. And rightly so, for I had no notion of his insights until he laid them bare. Fury!" His arm stiffened in Aria's grasp. "He and your mother must surely consider me witless!"

"You overestimate your mistake, Mikallis, or perhaps underestimate the affection they hold for you."

"It is not a matter of affection, Aria, it is a matter of respect."

Aria sighed, knowing better than to debate the topic in more depth, but instead offered, "Will you not enjoy this fine walk with me, friend? The leaves turn so colorfully now, the air is mild, the sun warm on our faces. It is not a day for such cares."

Mikallis softened at this as they continued silently, his head rising to survey his surroundings. A beautiful autumn day it was, he found himself admitting, perhaps one of the few remaining before winter set in. The path gently rose and fell as they walked on, the diverse foliage dyed in tints of bright orange, leaves and plants displaying shades of red from pink to scarlet to deep crimson, the still-blooming violet lilacs and white peonies on either side scenting their route in sweet perfumes. No imaginable color was underrepresented, for the elves of Thornwood tended their land with talent and care, favoring the natural beauty of Tahr above most other worldly pleasures.

They reached a small vale within which sat the homes of the foremost families of the 'Wood, segregated somewhat from the rest of the populace. The division was not out of a sense of oligarchy; rather it existed merely as a natural evolution, as here lived the oldest of the families of Thornwood, and their homes had been built first, when the Castle of Evanti was erected more than a millennia past. Indeed, these homes were humbler than those of some of their woodland kin, not much more than cabins in some cases, but they were certainly the oldest and comeliest, and none had suffered the passage of time.

A fountain lay in the center of the cul-de-sac, a life-sized, petrified wooden likeness of two elves, one male, one female, at its center upon a stone dais, engaged in eternal embrace. The Lovers, it was called. Upon reaching it, Aria turned Mikallis towards her and took his hands in her own.

"Mik, you are dear to me. It saddens me to see you punish yourself for such small matters. You are a decade my senior, and I have no right to condescend, but promise me you will try to take your lessons from your elders in the spirit in which they are intended. Please?"

Mikallis was not certain of the nature of that spirit, but looking down into the bright azure eyes of Aria just then, he could find no unpleasant feeling in his heart. He brushed her long platinum hair from those eyes, and planted a soft kiss on her forehead.

"Thank you, Aria. Only you can bring me from my gloom."

"That's what I'm here for!" she said cheerfully. "Now go, I wish to walk the gardens a bit more before we assemble at dusk."

Mikallis inclined his head to her slowly, still keeping her gaze, and turned to complete his task.

~

"Ah, but she leads him so," observed Neral, as he and the elven queen watched the pair depart the castle from the wooden balcony.

"Do you think?" replied Terrias. "It appears to me as no more than two friends sharing a stroll."

"It appears the same to me, Terrias, though we both know it is more."

"I do not believe she plays him as you say, Goodfather," rejoined the queen. "She is not wicked."

"No, far from it, dear— but perhaps she does not recognize the depth of the young man's affections."

The queen regarded Neral at this, objection clearly displayed on her features. "Do you think Aria simple then, Neral?"

"Blissfully so in some cases, my queen, as we all were at that age."

Terrias smiled at this. "As always, you are wise, Goodfather."

"Not always wise, my queen, but certainly old, and these eyes have seen much."

"Well, let us rest your old eyes then, Goodfather," she said, as she took his arm and turned him into the castle. "I fear it will be a late night, and you have not had your doze today."

"Hmph," replied the aged elf in feigned outrage. "I find that age is much like infancy."

"With your kin always urging you to take a nap?" asked Terrias teasingly.

"That, and the need to relieve oneself twice per hour."

The queen chuckled at this.

"Perhaps I should install a bed in my privy, and save myself the walk."

"Or a privy in your bedchamber," replied Terrias.

"Fury no, child, could you imagine the odor?"

~

The assembly of elves in the council chamber, situated at the end of the central hall of the citadel, included a representative from each of the sects of the kingdom. General Tobias, leader of their regular army, stood at the opposite end of the long table from Queen Evanti. On his left stood the lithe and lethal Nishali, head of the Rangers of the Northern Wood, and on his right Captain Mikallis, representing the Guard. Along the queen's right side, in order, sat Neral first, followed by a standing Margris, the queen's principal advisor on matters of trade, then Malkam, from Treasury. On her left stood the druid Pheonaris, Mistress of the Order of the Grove, then Kender, Hand of Justice, and beside him stood Sir Marchion, Second Knight of Thornwood, present in Sir Barris' stead. Beside Queen Evanti on her left, on the corner of the end of the Father's Table, Aria stood with her hands folded before her respectfully, her task to listen and learn as the young Princess of Thornwood.

The queen raised her hands slightly at her sides, bowed her head, and prayed aloud tunefully.

"Kar enna spen ai den bestu Nü glahr ai blei."

*May our words and deeds give You honor and joy.*

"Glahr ai blei," answered the elves in chorus.

"Please be seated, my friends," said the queen as she took her own chair.

One elf did not immediately sit. "Before we begin discussion of Barris' parley, my Queen, I would ask to speak," this from Sir Marchion, whom had been in attendance at these meetings more often of late.

"Of course, Sir Marchion, please do." The queen nodded at the noble brown-haired elf, who was, by the measure of all, the most physically imposing of any in the Wood. Even seated, many elves would only meet his height, and now, standing above all those seated, he was most magnificent indeed. Tall and strong as he was, however, he did not lack humility.

"Thank you, Lady, and I request your pardon for the interjection," he said with a slight bow. "As we all are aware, Sir Barris has been active and engaged in the South often this past season, and the Knighthood is poorly represented at this conference without him, particularly as it is his very experiences that we come here to debate."

"Your voice is equal to his in his absence, noble Knight, and none here regret it," said Neral.

Marchion nodded towards the wizened elf. "You do me honor, Goodfather, though it is not from a position of modesty that I speak. I only wish to say that if there are to be decisions reached here today, that I be permitted to withhold the vote of the Knighthood until Sir Barris' return, for his insights into these matters are born of firsthand experience, and my own would merely be judgments inspired by supposition."

Terrias Evanti regarded the proud warrior as he returned to his seat, and through her peripheral vision considered the pensive expressions of her councilors. *They share his concern*, she thought to herself, *all but Neral*. Despite this, she addressed the Knight.

"Sir Marchion, you speak with logic and thoughtfulness. However, I respectfully deny your request." Eyebrows rose on both sides the table. "I fear that time will not allow us the luxury of awaiting the return of Sir Barris, and I have the utmost confidence in your wisdom and care. Should a poll be required this evening, I will require the voice of the Knighthood." The queen allowed her gaze to briefly settle on those present, particularly Nishali. *A subtle nudge here, perhaps.* "Yet I believe we all share similar opinions on the difficulties we face, and I do not expect much division. I thank you, however, for your deference to Sir Barris, whom I am sure honors your loyalty and reverence."

"As you wish, my Queen."

Evanti continued, speaking now to all. "As you know, Sir Barris met with the king of Mor yesterday morning, and by now I suspect that you have learned that four of us here bore witness to that audience."

"Four, my lady?" queried Nishali.

"Yes, four. Myself, Neral, Princess Aria, and Captain Mikallis."

All eyes turned to regard the young captain, who visibly reddened. Nishali immediately turned back to glare at the queen.

"Do not regard me so, Nishali. Would that I could have invited all of you here to witness the vision, but I did not wish to overly intrude on the privacy of Sir Barris." She did not have to add that Captain Mikallis was as a son to the knight, for all well knew how close the two were. "Four to bear witness was enough, I believe, in order to ensure that no detail was overlooked."

Nishali lowered her gaze, leaving it at that.

"Three things were learned from that meeting. First, that the kingdom of Mor is vulnerable from within, and Halsen's hold on the throne is perhaps quite tenuous. Second, that while he sits the throne, he does not wish to use these latest portents as an excuse to make war upon us, despite his hatred of the elven people."

"The Order sensed as much, on both counts, My lady," said Pheonaris. "It is a great relief to have the second belief confirmed." All nodded, with the exception of Nishali.

"Indeed, it is a great relief, Pheonaris. Though the third revelation is most troubling. It would appear that the disturbances we are experiencing are also well known to the king, as well as to his wizards and sages."

This sobered the room, as all were mindful of what that truth foretold.

"Does this confirm anything with certainty, my Queen?", asked Margris. "We still cannot know that these signs all point to any particular doom, can we?"

Margris was the most psychologically delicate of all assembled. Her gentle, methodical nature rejected the very idea that her world could be overturned by forces unseen.

"Nothing is ever known, dear Margris," this gently from Neral. "But much has been observed, and we cannot afford to be optimistic when so much is at risk."

"Nishali, would you share with us what you have witnessed this past cycle?" asked the queen. Evanti did not expect new details from the ranger, but sensed that Nishali felt an overwhelming need to speak.

"My Queen, it is as I have stated. The very land itself is breathing heavily, and the creatures of the wood flee in anxiety, yet they do not know where to run. The Pinestroke bed is as deep as one's shins with needles, the Trine yellows, and the Rangers are stretched to our limits in addressing the fires that seem to come from everywhere."

"Can you explain 'everywhere', Nishali? Do you mean from the ground itself, in numerous places?" asked Malkam, the treasurer.

"Not only from the ground, Malkam. Some fires seem to start in the soil, yes, but others..." Nishali paused, her eyes falling to the table.

"Go on, Nishali," prodded the queen.

"My lady, some of the fires...they seem to be igniting from within the trees themselves, from the center of their very roots, and in some cases, their trunks! It hurts them, my Queen, I sense it...it is so difficult to witness, and we can do little to help, for by the time we are aware that a tree is burning, its life is nearly spent! It is a horror, akin to the saws and hatchets of the damned humans..."

"Peace, Nishali," soothed the queen. "Our brethren have not yet learned how to balance their industrial needs with those of the land, and they do not hear as we hear. They cannot be hated for their ignorance–"

"It is not a matter of hate, my queen! It is a matter of witnessing the suffering and being instructed to remain idle!" The elf stood then, heated tears welling in her green eyes. "My lady, I would ask for a moment."

"Of course, Nishali. Please return as soon as you are able."

"Thank you, my lady," the ranger replied icily, long strides removing her from the council.

The elves sat silently for a moment, no one wishing to be the first to speak. Pheonaris broke the stillness.

"To be a Ranger of the Wood is a burden none of us should

envy," the strikingly beautiful druid began. "Nishali must patrol the boundaries of our kingdom, witnessing the abuses of man, dwarf, orc, and gnome, with a soul more keenly attuned to their impact on the life of the land than any of us."

Pheonaris settled her eyes upon Queen Evanti. "I see judgment in your eyes, my queen. Or perhaps wounded sensibilities at Nishali's outburst. You must not allow those feelings to take root, my lady, for they are of the self, and they disregard the sacrifice of Nishali and her Rangers." She glanced at Kender, who saw his word was required.

"The Mistress of the Order speaks justly, my queen."

Only Pheonaris could speak to the queen so, or rather, only Pheonaris would. As Druid of the Grove, her chief responsibility was to serve as a reminder to the conscience of the elven people, for her very life was dedicated to existence as a conduit to the will and wisdom of the First Father. While it was true that in council, no words spoken could be punished, it was not the accepted place of any but Pheonaris to chastise the Elven queen. The confirmation from Kender made it clear that it was not only the empathic druid who sensed the queen's feelings.

Queen Evanti bowed her head for a moment, and appeared to be in prayer. After a minute or so had passed, she spoke again.

"You guide me, Mistress Pheonaris, and for that I thank you."

Nishali returned to the room at that moment, and the queen rose, as did all at her cue, including Neral. Nishali returned to her place at the table, guarded, conscious that all eyes were on her, readying herself to defend her statements, if need be.

The queen bowed deeply at the waist to Nishali. "Your sacrifice is great, Ranger. *Nü glahr ni.*"

The council repeated the homage. "Nü glahr ni," they spoke as one.

Nishali did not soften at this, for her pain was not lessened, but she returned the bow with sincere humility, knowing that the rare grace she had just received was equally sincere. The council returned to their seats, and Queen Evanti directed her attention to General Tobias and Captain Mikallis.

"We have not heard from the brave elves of the Guard, nor the Army of Thornwood."

Mikallis shifted nervously in his seat, and glanced at the general, who returned the young elf's gaze.

"My lady," replied Mikallis, "it is not for me to opine on such matters. The Guard shall do as instructed, as always."

The General nodded his agreement and approval. "As will the Sword, my Queen. The mysteries of such omens are beyond the experience of elves of the soldiery."

At this the queen nodded to Neral, for the time for his voice had arrived.

"My brothers and sisters, there is much you do not know," began Neral soberly, "and I regret that it falls upon me to enlighten you."

# XI: G'NAATH

otwithstanding Thinsel's declaration of family bravery, the tears fell continuously in the Greykin household throughout the rest of the day. For the first time in many, many seasons, Shyla did not look to escape to her crevasse that night, but rather fell into a restless slumber, interrupted by nightmares and an overwhelming sense of melancholy. She awoke the next morning, unrestored, in plenty of time to make the kitchens.

Yet there would be no work for her today, would there? The day before, her mistress of the kitchens, Merne, came calling, to generously inform Shyla that she would be free to do as she pleased during her remaining two days in G'naath. Merne never had the chance to apologize to Shyla, however, which she had sincerely intended to do, for Thinsel begin flinging kitchen implements at her well before she could get the words out. Only when the irate mother ran out of spoons and pots, and reached for her carving knife, did Merne finally leave, more than one angry welt rising from her head.

Shyla was sitting on the side of her cot with her head in her hands, feeling the pangs of the first sobs beginning to well within her, when her mother slid open her curtain.

"I knew yeh wouldn't be sleepin', child. Come along'n have

breakfast with yer Mama and Papa."

"Yes Mama, just let me get dressed."

"Don't dally, dear, I made yeh sommin' special." Her mother left her candle in Shyla's hollow to help Shyla prepare for the day.

Shyla looked around and saw that she had no clothes lying about besides a pair of leggings and a tunic, laid neatly at the foot of her bed. Her Mama had clearly come and collected the rest in the middle of the night, washing them for the distressed gnome. *Oh, Mama, how will I survive without yeh?*

She dressed quickly and made her way to her parents' nook, drawn by the scents of fresh bread, tea and...something else? Her father smiled at her as she sat down at the table, and passed her a towel-covered basket.

"What is it, Papa?"

"Open 'er up, girl." He nodded to the basket, still smiling.

She pulled the towel open to see a whole steaming applecake, her very most favorite thing in the entire world to eat.

"But Papa, how did yeh-", she tried to ask, with an open-mouthed grin, for fruit of any kind was the rarest of things in G'naath.

"Quit with the questions, girl, and fill that gapin' maw o' yours with some cake afore I eat it meself."

"Here Papa, have some, you too Mama-"

"Listen to your Papa, girl, don'cha worry, we done already had a share."

Shyla knew this was a lie to beat all lies, but she also knew better than to say so. She greedily dug into the cake with abandon, for despite her desire to be generous, it was *applecake,* for Tahr's sake!

They enjoyed their breakfast together more than what was imaginable, Papa again recounting the tale of her mother's hurled kitchen missiles from the day before, the three laughing hysterically and mocking the hypocritical Merne, who had filed many of the original reports against Shyla.

When the silliness died down, it was Shyla who spoke first. "Ah, but we can't fault her Papa, 'twas me own foolishness that made 'er report me. 'Twas her duty, is all. I ain't mad at 'er."

"Fault or no, child, it sure felt good to see her wet 'erself when I grabbed fer that carver!" The three laughed uproariously again—for indeed, when Thinsel had reached for the carving knife the other gnome had in fact wet her skirts, and Thinsel had made Oort swear, on pain of no supper, that he would make sure the whole cavern knew about it before the day was out.

The horns sounded down the tunnels then, a single blast passed from one end of the G'naath to the other, signaling the start of a new day. The horns Shyla had so often slept through these past seasons. Her smile nearly collapsed then, until her mother rapped her in the behind with her spoon.

"Hey! What was that for, Mama!"

"Fer good measure, girl. I won't be gettin' ta whack ya for eight more seasons, and yer usually in need o' at least a few per cycle!"

Shyla smiled at this, knowing her Mama was just trying to keep her from feeling sorry for herself. She decided then to do her best to stay upbeat, but a heavy question was weighing on her mind, and it was time to ask it aloud.

"Papa?"

"Yes, Nugget?"

"Do ya think I'll make it?"

Silence.

"The eight seasons, I mean?"

No one spoke for a few moments, then Oort stood. "It's time to go see Cindra, child."

"Oort." Thinsel eyed her husband. He nodded and took Shyla by the shoulders, looking into her round, pink eyes.

"Shyla, me dear sweet Nugget, ye'll make it. Of that I be sure as stone."

"Truly, Papa?"

"Truly, Nugget. On me life, I know it to be true."

"But how can ye *know*, Papa?"

"As I told yeh, child. 'Tis time to go see Cindra."

~

Oort stopped in the center of a tunnel just as the second horn blast sounded, two blows in rapid succession, signaling the beginning of the first work shift of the day. Shyla stopped beside him.

"Do yeh need to work today, Papa? Will they not let yeh stay with me for me final two days?"

"No, child, I ain't gonna be workin' t'day nor t'marra."

"Oh. Well, why're we stoppin', then?"

Oort looked around, unsure.

"The Lady asked that yeh come alone, girl. I'll be headin' back to yer Ma now. Yeh come right back when yer finished, yeh hear?"

"Uh, yes, Papa, but how do I git to the Lady from 'ere?"

"You're already here, child," Cindra Sandshingle announced from behind them, startling them both considerably. "Come, girl, come sit with an old lady fer a bit." She reached out for Shyla's hand. The girl pulled away, looking at her father.

"'Tis all right, Nugget. Don't ya be fearin' the Lady."

Shyla allowed Cindra to grasp her hand then. Her father was already making his way back down the tunnels.

"Quickly now, dear, we won't be wantin' a line at old Cindra's door." She gently pulled the young gnome into the waiting door, closing it behind them and shuffling to her seat at the table.

"Tis a grand day, is it not?" asked Cindra, her smile warm and inviting, yet Shyla's jaw was firmly set. She crossed her arms over her chest, trying to appear menacing, but only elicited a warmer smile from the elderly gnome.

"Ah, yer afraid I'm gonna spell yeh, is that it, child?"

"I ain't afraid," said Shyla defiantly.

"Did I not already tell yeh, child? Do not dissemble now, for I'll know when yeh do. Though, the truth be plain on yer face. Ye're scared as a stuck tunneler, ye are."

Shyla could not lie to the Lady, but neither did she need to be submissive. "Yeh made a fool o' me yesterday, me Lady, and I ain't meanin' to be nasty, but I ain't pleased none about it, neither."

Cindra sat back, crossing her own arms now. "I made a fool o' ye, did I? Tell me child, how'd I manage that?"

"You cast a spell on me to make me spill me guts, Lady, and ye know ye did!"

"Yer guts, yeh say. Yeh're meanin' that I made ye speak the truth?"

"Yup."

"Hmm," replied Cindra, "and ye're angry at me fer it?"

"Yup."

"And yeh think I made fool o' yeh, then?"

"Yup." Shyla was prepared to 'yup' at the old lady until the guards of G'naath dragged her out into the daylight.

"Seems to me, Shyla, that the truth made a fool o' yeh, not me spell."

Shyla frowned at this.

"Yup," continued Cindra, nodding mockingly, but not unkindly.

The two gnomes stared at each other then for a long while, when finally Cindra spoke again. "Yeh can stand there lookin' at me ferever, Shyla, or yeh can sit with me and we can git to figurin' out how to save yer skin. Now which way will yeh have it, fer my eyes get dry when I be starin' so hard?"

Shyla did not want to relent, but she knew that this Lady before her was not her enemy, no matter the pronouncement of justice she had asserted the day before. She let her arms fall to her side and took a seat before the table, feeling both as if she had lost some battle that she desperately needed to win, and as if she had been a fool for battling with the old gnome to begin with.

"I'm sorry, me Lady, I'm just angry is all. I don't wanna leave, and yer the one who said I'll be needin' t'go..."

"I asked yeh not to lie to me, girl. I'll not ask again."

Shyla looked up, confused.

"Don't look at me, girl, yer the one that wants t'be leavin'."

"Wait, wha-"

"Not a third time, child, or we'll be done here, sure as stone."

Shyla stopped, heeding the Lady's warning, and closed her eyes, taking inventory of her heart and knowing in the space of a beat that the Lady was not only right, but that there was an unacknowledged part of herself that was in fact *overjoyed* at the prospect of leaving G'naath.

Cindra leaned in a bit, speaking softly now. "What am I thinking, Shyla? Right now, what am I thinking?"

"That I'm a fool, and no doubt, me lady."

"Don't guess, Shyla. Tell me. Tell me what I am thinking."

Shyla cocked her head at Cindra, noticing for the first time the ruby red irises of her eyes, not very unlike the pink color in her own. She felt something inside her...a tickle? Something...odd, yet not unpleasant, and the Lady spoke again, as Shyla noticed her accent had changed somehow, becoming more...well, less *gnomish.*

"Tell me, Shyla. Tell me what I am thinking, at this very moment," more softly this time.

"My lady, yeh be talkin' strange."

"Ah, yup. Would yeh prefer I be talkin' like this here, for yer ears t'be made happy?" Cindra beamed now.

That tickle again...and Shyla knew. She knew precisely what Cindra Sandshingle was thinking at that very moment, and the realization shocked her.

"You are thinking that you love me, my lady, and that you are proud of me."

Cindra smiled then, a smile not unlike her Mama's smile.

"Why, Lady? Why do yeh love me? Yeh don't know me from—"

"Peace, child. I know you are confused, and with good cause. I will explain all to you. But first, a question. Do you believe that I enchanted you, allowing you to read my mind just now? Think now, do not answer without consideration."

Shyla withdrew into herself and reviewed the past few moments, allowing her memory to come to rest on the instant that she recognized the Lady's feelings...

"No, my lady. I do not think yeh spelled me."

"No? Are you certain?"

A slight hesitation, then, "Certain, Lady Cindra."

"Hmm." The Lady leaned back to an upright position. "Then how, my dear, was it accomplished?"

Cautiously, but with confidence, Shyla replied. "I did it, me Lady."

"You did what, child?"

"I read your mind." *Fury, but I did, did I not?*

"And how, my dear, did you do that? Think now, Shyla."

Shyla thought. And knew. Her eyes widened and her pupils dilated as the truth dawned within her.

"I...I think I've always known how to be doin' it, me Lady! I just...oh, Fury, Lady, how could I notta known I could *do* that?"

Cindra laughed musically, gleefully. She stood and clapped her hands together, and began to dance around her chair, moving quite well for a gnome over a century old. Shyla smiled and laughed, too, a part of her terrified at what she had just discovered about herself, but the biggest part elated, filled with wonder and awe. *How...how amazing! How truly, incredibly marvelous!* She looked at Cindra then, a question forming on the tip of her consciousness...and then an answer, one that brought her immense joy and profound sadness in equal measure.

"My lady, I know another thing now."

Cindra stilled.

"I know you are me Grandmama."

# XII: HIGHMORLAND

ucan awoke to the meager overcast light, shivering and aching, wincing at the stinging stab of pain in his right side as he gingerly rolled himself upright to a sitting position. The root upon which he had laid his head the night before was covered in dried blood–but, he thought with gratitude, at least it was dry. He felt behind his ear at the wound, but his hair was too matted with gore to allow him to evaluate it thoroughly. He could tell, however, that it hot and swollen, and he would need to wash it soon or risk infection.

He stood slowly, rubbing his arms in a futile effort to warm himself, and accepted that he would need to get moving, and quickly, if he wanted to stop shivering. He was still too nauseated to be hungry, but quite thirsty. He considered walking along the road back towards the Morline, then quickly dismissed the notion.

*Won't be going back south anytime soon, Luc, that's for certain.* His options were limited. North lay the Elven wood, safe yet far from civilization, and making the trek all the way to Thornwood without a mount was out of the question. The elves would likely not turn him away, but neither would they wish him to stay overlong in any case, and the walk would take the remainder of autumn and much of the winter besides. To the East lay the Maw, completely out of the question. A day's ride or so to the west of his position lay the farmlands of Mor, and he felt his best chance might be to take on work as a farmhand in some dale, but the thought of slinging horse manure and sleeping in a barn was more than offensive.

*Where exactly to you plan on sleeping otherwise, smarty?* he asked himself. He looked at the forest surrounding him, trying to discern any sign that might help him get his bearings, and felt his thirst deepening. *First things first, then. Water.* No sooner did he have the thought than a crack of thunder resonated around him. *Well, that little problem might just take care of itself,* he thought, and at nearly the same moment heard the whinny of a horse not far to his right.

He swiveled his head at the noise, instinctively knowing to be still, and through a thicket of trees he could barely make out the swinging tail of a horse. *How about that,* he thought, certain that this was his mount from the previous night's frantic ride. He made his way slowly, careful to avoid sticks on his path, but to no avail, for he could see the horse start at his approach. The mount remained in place however, and he drew near to within a few paces of the animal.

"Easy now, friend, easy...," and a report of thunder made him cringe as the horse reared in protest, but remained upon the spot.

"It's all right now." He began his approach again stealthily, humming softly to soothe the spooked mount, his left arm out, back bowed, taking first note of the gender of the animal, his fingers now brushing the reins...

*Ha!* Lucan thought to himself, grasping the reins. As he did, the horse shied away from him, suddenly uncertain of his intent.

"Shh, shh, easy girl, it's all right, shh..." He reached up to stroke the horse's neck, and over the course of a few moments, the chestnut mare began to settle and accept Lucan as her companion, for the moment at least.

Lucan knew that he needed to mount the horse now, before the next stroke of lightning sent her racing into the forest. He grasped the horn of the saddle despite his rib's insistence that he not do so, then stepped into the stirrup and somehow threw his leg over without passing out from the agony.

He swore upon and against the whole of Tahr then, trying to combat the pain with vulgarity, or at least to offend it, but failing miserably. *Son of a whore, but this is unbearable!* Yet bear it he did, and turned the mare around, facing what he believed to be the direction of the Northern Road.

His instincts were correct, and he and the mare reached the trail–for beyond the Mor it was no longer much of a road–just as the first of the rains began to fall. Lucan considered his choices then. North or south?

He could not recall passing a trail leading to the western farmlands since passing the Morline Way just this side of the river, and he had no intentions of heading that far south if he could help it. He was certain, or at least terrified, that his pursuers would be out in earnest again this day, and it was just his luck that he would pass them on the road. Lucan had not been this far north before, however, and did not know how long it would be before a western route became available.

"Well, I believe we'll choose the devil we don't know this time, my great friend," he said, turning the mare to the north. The rain was falling heavily now, and he knew that it would be rough going this day if his analysis of the black skies was correct, but he did not consider finding a place to wait out the storm, for now he had cause for hope that he might get far enough ahead of his enemies to survive the day.

Lucan and the mare ambled on for some time, and Lucan reached for the saddlebag on the mare's left flank. He had hoped beyond hope that it would contain something useful, perhaps even food, but he had been afraid to look before now, fearing disappointment. His growing hunger finally took hold however, and to his utter joy, his fingers recognized the shape and texture of dried meat. He held a slice before him, letting the rain moisten it a bit before he devoured it. *Oh, but that's good,* he thought, and considered reaching for another piece, but knew that it might be some time before he would find another source of food. He felt around then in the right-hand saddlebag. This one contained a skin, among other objects he could not immediately recognize. He found the strap and hoisted the skin out of the bag, discovering that it was nearly full, and stained purple at the mouthpiece. *Wine!* He opened the spout and took a long swallow, and his mouth tingled with the sweet flavor of fermented green grapes, oranges, and some other berries he did not recognize.

"Damn. Good stuff," he said aloud, and good it was—better than he had ever had occasion to sample, certainly. *Perhaps my luck changes,* he thought to himself, the notion immediately followed by the reminder that he was without coin, roof, nor even clear direction. He sighed in resignation, taking another drink of the fine wine. *I'll take what I can get.*

The soggy day wore on, the rain mercifully halting just past noon, and he became aware that his mount was beginning to act a bit disorderly, clearly filled with thirst and hunger. "All right, then, friend, let us find you a place to drink, and perhaps there are some oats in one of these bags..."

They continued for another hour. The sun began to shine again, and Lucan caught the sound of a nearby brook. He did not need to direct the mare, for she was already pulling at the reins to go left. They left the trail at a muddy crossing, and Lucan worked up the courage to dismount, knowing that to do so would renew the pangs of agony in his side.

It did, and the young man fell to his knees as he slid from the saddle.

The mare continued without him to the creek a dozen paces ahead, and Lucan rose from his crouch slowly, the pain worse than it had been the entire day. His vision began to narrow, yet he fought against the dizziness that had tried to overtake him, knowing that he would, at the very least, need to tie the mare up before he allowed himself to collapse. He made his way clumsily down to the waterline, and searched the saddlebags for a waterskin and something for the horse to eat. He found both; three small apples and an empty skin. He eyed the apples greedily, but knew that he would not make it far without the horse, and fed them each to her when she finished her drink. The horse nuzzled against Lucan then, perhaps in gratitude, perhaps to coax more apples from the young man, but shied away fearfully when her nostrils neared the wound on his ear.

"It's all right, girl. Here, now, I'll wash it." He leaned down into the trickling stream, dunking his head as best he could, and washed the dried blood from his scalp. It stung deeply, but not nearly as bad as his rib as he bent low. Satisfied that he had washed the wound as best he could, he drank as much as he was able from the brook and filled the waterskin. The cool rinse had refreshed him somewhat, and he felt a bit more human without the globs of dried blood falling from his long golden hair.

A quick inventory confirmed that he was not suddenly a wealthy man, unwittingly carrying a bag of jewels and coins. What he did find, however, was somewhat encouraging. Enough food to last at least another day, two if he rationed it. Along with more of the dried meat, he found a wax-wrapped wedge of goat cheese, still fresh, and a small loaf of bread to go with it. *The merchant was on his way somewhere,* he reasoned, wishing wholeheartedly that the man's intended destination would take him south, not north. There was nothing more for the horse to eat, however, so he knew he would have to find somewhere for her to graze no later than the next day, for the healthy mare was clearly used to eating regularly. A blanket was also packed neatly within the bags, just about the right size for a horse, as well as a fine violet cotton mantle. Lucan examined the cloak, and saw that it was embroidered with a large "T" upon one breast. *Well, that won't do,* lamented Lucan, for wearing the Thomison family emblem would certainly not earn him any friends. To his dismay, he found neither flint nor tinderbox, and began worrying about how he would light a fire that night. He sat down to eat some cheese and bread and considered the problem, then paused to admire the fine mare that had brought him here.

"What shall I call you, horse?" Lucan asked, through a mouthful of bread. She ignored him, sniffing a plant. Lucan chewed and mentally listed off a series of horse names he had come across, and then it came to him. "Ah, of course, none other would do. I shall name you Hope, for that is truly what you are to me, my hope to live another day. How do you feel about that then, Hope?" The horse raised her head and eyed Lucan, suddenly disinterested in her meager leafy meal. Hope snorted loudly, stamped one hoof, and returned to her snack.

*If I didn't know any better, I would swear that silly horse just answered me,* Lucan thought, smiling despite the absurdity.

~

A few miles farther down the path from where Lucan and Hope rested, Sir Barris of Thornwood and Phantom were taking it slowly.

Although Phantom had finally gained a bit of rest the night before, the Highmorland air refreshing his spirit, Barris knew that it would not be until they reached the Grove that Phantom could truly be renewed. The Grove served as the first significant landmark that indicated one had passed from Mor territory into Thornwood, and was still five days ride ahead at a human pace, three for Phantom in his current state, and two or less required a murderous pace . Fortunately, such a pace was not necessary, for he was not in a hurry to bring the news of his audience with Halsen to his queen. She had been present in his mind at the parley, and had heard all that he had heard. His task was not to deliver news, but to receive it, and report back to Mor. Part of him hoped that Terrias Evanti would send a messenger to meet him, saving him and Phantom much of the ride, but a greater part of him hoped otherwise, so that he could see his beloved queen again sooner, if only for a day or two.

*Fool,* Barris chided himself. *You must not entertain such notions.* Yet he could not help himself, for Barris of Thornwood was hopelessly in love with his Queen. Hopeless, for he did not sense his emotions reciprocated; nor could he be the first to approach the queen romantically, for to do so unsuccessfully would result in a necessary resignation of his position. The queen would not ask that of him, never, Barris knew, nor would she willingly accept his resignation, but he could not remain in service at her side, day in, day out, living with the knowledge that she did not love him, knowing that she had left him unrequited after he had laid his heart bare.

*Is it not nearly the same now, nearly as unbearable?* Barris asked himself, the circular argument beginning in his heart again, but always he came to the same conclusion. *No, it is not the same. For I need not possess Lady Terrias to love her. To serve her is enough, and should I not remain silent, I might forgo even that honor.* The possibility of that was beyond unacceptable to Barris, so silent he remained, and would remain, unless the unlikely day came when the queen approached him with love in her eyes.

Barris had fantasized about that day a thousand, thousand times, and doing so did not sadden him, but brought a warmth to his heart. For elven lives were long, and many a romance had sprung between two elves well into their second century of life. Barris was barely a century and a half old, Terrias Evanti born not three seasons past the day of his own birth. Elves of the Wood could bear children as late as two and a half centuries into their lives, and so Barris took heart, knowing that Order would guide their lives as the First Father permitted, and that to give in to despair before its time was to choose to disregard the joys present in the here and now.

Phantom brought Barris out of his daydream, tossing his head in eagerness for Barris to pick up the pace now that the rains had ended. "Impatient to reach the Grove, my friend? Ah, I can appreciate your enthusiasm, but we must take it slow, today at least, for you are not as invincible as you would pretend." Phantom whinnied in response, and Barris sensed the great stallion's offense.

"Just today, friend, and I will give you your head tomorrow, once the ground has dried a bit." Barris looked up at the skies, clearing now, and took note that the wind had turned southerly, warming the air more quickly than he would have expected after the brief storm. "The Father favors us, Phantom. With luck, we may not suffer a freeze until after we have started our journey home from Mor." Barris knew this was possible, but not likely, for the Reapmoons had set the night he arrived in Mor, signaling the waning of autumn and the coming of winter. But a southern breeze this time of year would do much to lengthen the season, and to whatever degree that might be, Barris was pleased.

They continued at a lazy pace and made camp early that evening before dusk on a grassy bed they had camped at many times before, surrounded by a thin copse of trees. Phantom was grazing, or should have been, and Barris was cooking water for tea when the horse stamped anxiously. Barris had not heard anything to give the steed reason to be so alarmed, but trusted his companion's superior senses. He stood and walked back to the trail, facing south as Phantom had been, listening intently.

Hearing nothing, Barris was about to dismiss the horse's behavior as a false alarm when he glimpsed what he thought was movement far back along the trail. Even with his acute elven vision, however, the day's light was nearly gone, and he could not be sure. Closing his eyes and centering himself, Barris attempted the ranger's trick he had learned from Nishali years ago, listening not with his ears, but with his bones. He was never particularly good at it, his innate abilities more attuned to horsemanship and weaponry, but he felt as if he *could* almost sense a presence...*two perhaps? Beast and man?* He continued to listen, with bones and ears alike, but could not make out more detail.

Nevertheless, he returned to his camp and began his ritual of protective enchantment, for even if only one or two approached, if their designs were malevolent he would prefer to avoid conflict if possible. He would scout back along the trail after his meal, and determine if it were best to break camp and continue, or remain and rest.

~

"Shh, easy, Hope. We'll not want to alert anyone."

Lucan had noted the smoke rising ahead, and now, as the evening darkened, he could see the glow of the campfire. Hope was clearly uneasy about something, and that was all the warning Lucan needed, for he was not expecting to make friends along this trail.

*It could very easily be your pursuers, Luc,* he thought. He believed it unlikely, for they would have had to pass him either at morning's light or when he and Hope had rested for their noon meal, but it would not hurt to be overly cautious.

He climbed from the saddle, wincing with agony as he did, but he had managed to discover a method of dismounting that at least left him able to draw breath. He led Hope into the wood on the left side of the trail, opposite the campsite ahead, silently pleading with the mare to tread as softly and quietly as she could. It seemed that the horse was familiar with the game, for she stepped gracefully and gently through the leaves and deadwood at his side until they found a suitable patch of grassy ground upon which to camp.

*Not exactly camping,* thought Lucan. *No tent, no fire...* but he forced himself to see the positive as he ate a bit more cheese and bread, and drank a bit more wine. He brought Thomison's cloak from the saddlebag, and covered Hope with the blanket. His stomach no longer growled, there was a bit of grass for Hope to graze on, he still had fine wine to drink... it could be much worse, he decided.

As the light of the day finally faded to black, Lucan lay snoring upon the still damp ground, and neither he nor the sleeping Hope took notice of the elf that had approached from the north, and now stood watching.

# XIII: G'NAATH

ama, Papa, come in, hurry!" said Shyla, opening Cindra's secret door upon Oort and Thinsel, who were standing in the center of the tunnel, and nearly startling her parents out of their shoes.

Shyla took their hands and pulled them into the small room, and Cindra closed the door behind the three.

"Hello, dear Thinsel. It has been so, so long." The smiling Cindra reached over to embrace the uncertain gnomish woman, and pulled her in despite her stiffened demeanor, whispering gently into her ear.

*"Do not be angry with me, child, it was necessary to keep my distance."*

Thinsel replied at normal volume. "I be not angry yet with yeh Lady, but yeh'll have some explaining to do, sure as stone."

"Of course. Please, all of you, let's sit. Tea?"

Oort began to nod as he took a seat, but a glance from Thinsel changed his mind. "Not fer us, Lady. Maybe Shyla." He looked at his daughter, who was already pouring herself a cup. Oort looked around the room, confused, failing to see how the tea could have possibly been heated...there was no fire...

Cindra sat at the table to the left of Shyla, who had settled across from her mother and father. Cindra's wrinkled fingers caressed the rim of her teacup as she looked up at Thinsel.

"I have told Shyla some bit about her heritage, Thinsel, but her mama should be the one to tell her all."

Thinsel nodded, and turned her eyes to Shyla. Her features were stoic, not betraying a hint of the dread she was feeling, for she had known this day would come.

"Me girl, me sweet, sweet girl, yer gonna be mad at yer mama now, but know that I be lovin' ya, with all me heart."

Shyla reached out to touch her mother's hand. "Mama, I'll not be mad. I think I knew in me heart that ya were me Mama and Papa by choice, but not blood. Somehow all me twenty years I been knowin', but not knowin' all the same."

Thinsel nodded again, and squeezed her daughter's hand, and told the tale of how a young Oort and Thinsel would deliver food and other provisions to the hunters at the Mawgate each morning, as was their duty. She told her wide-eyed daughter how they had fallen in love over time, and would sneak Outside whenever they could to be alone with one another, keeping close to the gate, where their friend Rak would let them back in upon hearing their secret knock. For a just over a year they did so, until Oort had saved enough through working to earn himself a nook, and to buy Thinsel's hand in marriage.

~

On the morning after their wedding night, they had decided to go one final time Outside; final, for privacy was no longer a struggle, and the risk of being caught was no longer worth taking. When they reach the gate, however, a nervous-looking Rak told them they would not be going out that day.

"There be things happening outside the gate today, and yeh'll not want t'be goin'."

Oort and Thinsel pressed their friend for more details, but he would not answer. Not to be so easily dissuaded, however, they waited around the corner until Rak was distracted by the arrival of his noon meal, then sneaked out the gate. Giggling and holding hands and running into the daylight, the pair made their way to their usual spot beneath a great pine, where their ears were assaulted by the cry of a newborn gnomeling.

There at the foot of the tree, wrapped in tattered rags and bawling to raise the dead, lay a pink-eyed babe, totally and completely alone. The two looked at the babe, then at each other.

"Ain't but a wee nugget, Thinny," whispered Oort. An unspoken understanding passed between them—they would not abandon this child.

~

"Yeh were as loud as a gang o' miners, Nugget, and yer cheeks were as pink as yer eyes from yer yellin'. We waited off to th'side for hours n'hours, but didn't nobody come for yeh. It started gettin' dark, and yer Mama was gettin' cold, and there was nothin' fer it, so yer Mama took ye in her arms and we knocked on the gate. Rak about wet his breeches when we tried to bring yeh in, but Mama pinched his nose so hard his eyes watered and that were that."

The three ladies were each shedding tears now, but bravely, as Thinsel continued to explain how they had managed to hide Shyla for the three cycles that were needed to pass Shyla off as their natural born daughter. At the announcement of the birth however, Cindra had been called to the blessing, and the truth was immediately known to her.

"Your birth mother was my daughter, child, and her name was Scinty, and I cannot say which of the two of you was more beautiful."

Cindra's bravery was faltering now, her shoulders beginning to heave. "She did not survive long after your birth, however, and your father was too torn with grief to raise you himself. You were given to the elders, and they decided that your birth was a bad omen, and you were to be wolved."

"Wolved? What's that, Lady?"

Oort spoke up. "It means they were t'do what they did, Nugget, wrap yeh up and leave yeh Outside fer the wolves or whatever else t'git ya."

Shyla was first confused, then horrified. "But..., why? Why would they do that to a babe? Fury, Papa, but that's *wrong!*" Shyla was standing now, her eyes wild, and she slammed her fist on the table in rage...

...blowing a fist-sized chunk of stone through the table, leaving a hole the shape of a tiny hand.

Oort and Thinsel froze. Shyla yelped. Cindra sighed.

"Oh Lady, I'm so sorry, I didn't–"

"Peace child, 'tis but a hunk o'rock," Cindra had slipped back into her gnomish accent. "But yeh'll be needin' t'get hold o'yerself, or yer liable t'cause a Tahrcracker!" Cindra was giggling now, and the three Greykins looked back and forth between this ancient, giggling sorceress and the broken stone table in stunned disbelief.

Cindra shrugged. "We'll git to that soon enough. Now about them cursed elders..."

Cindra continued the story, completely ignoring the fact that the young gnome had just punched a hole through three inches of solid stone. Cindra explained how her legendary status as a sorceress was both admired and feared among her fellow elders. Due to her outspoken nature, despite the great things she had done for the gnomish people, she was not particularly well-liked. It had thus been decided that she would not be allowed to participate in the hearing to decide her granddaughter's fate.

The wolving of a motherless newborn gnome was a practice that had faded out of use decades before, yet the law had never been altered. And so it was that the council had decided to weaken Cindra politically through grief.

"But Lady, yeh have magic, why did yeh let 'em do it? Yeh were my grandmama!"

"Shh... easy, child. You must know that I would never have let harm come to you."

Shyla stayed her tirade, but did not take her fierce gaze from Cindra's face.

"I had two options, child. One, to destroy the council in a maelstrom of fire and death, and go to war with all of G'naath, and I tell you true, I had prepared just such an enchantment." A brief pause. "But I found my senses in time to avoid such a tragedy, and chose instead to look Forward, and see what would become of you should I not intervene."

"Look *forward*, Lady, you mean, into the *future*?"

Cindra smiled. "Yes child, it is a talent we both possess."

Shyla's eyes widened, as did those of her parents.

"'Tis a little trick I picked up from the elves of Thornwood, child, and I suspect that's where you shall learn it as well, but we will discuss that shortly. Now, Oort, and Thinsel, you deserve to know why I have not come to you these many years. But I suspect you already see, do you not?" Cindra concluded her story, explaining her decision to keep her distance from their family, for their own safety and peace.

"Know that it was painful to be apart from you, Shyla. Look into me, and tell me that you know."

Shyla regarded her grandmama, calmed her mind, and listened, with that secret, powerful part of herself that, she had just this day discovered, could listen *deeply*. After a long, silent while, she nodded at Cindra, and again to her mother. Thinsel did not quite understand what had happened between the old and young gnomes, but she knew from the tears in each of their eyes that it was profound and honest.

Oort had laid his arm over Thinsel's shoulders, and the two parents considered their daughter, worry and love equally apparent in their anxious expressions. Shyla looked back to Cindra, her features suddenly courageous.

"Lady?"

"Yes, child?"

"What are wolves?"

# XIV: BELGORNE

'arn Silverstone closed the door to his father's chambers quietly, and made his way through the stone halls to the Hammer, where he assumed he would find Boot. The walk was quite long, considering that the entire dwarven kingdom of Belgorne lay beneath the peaks of the Maw. J'arn considered this as he made his way past the king's personal halls, past his own smaller rooms, through the libraries, kitchens, and dining halls. He crossed the central passageway that led down to the forges on the right and to the living quarters of the dwarven people to the left, and continued on towards the common halls, where most dwarves would find themselves after a day's work, feasting and drinking and telling tales. Today would not be a day for such things, J'arn reminded himself, and as he walked he considered that each step he took represented the labors of dwarves millennia past, shaping the finely crafted halls he walked, the hands of countless laborers digging into soil, mining raw rock, turning the stony, unyielding Maw first into passable tunnels, then into stone-lined halls, and eventually into what they were today–true works of art.

Each passageway was intricately fashioned, nothing left raw. Expertly chiseled stone, brick, and mortar lined the floors, walls, and ceilings, and rarely could one walk more than a few paces without passing murals sculpted into the stone, depicting wars long ago won or lost, famous dwarves of old, or simple scenes of hearth and home.

Ages past, as the First War of Tahr was coming to a terrible close, the last of the dwarven people found themselves cornered in the throat of the Maw, besieged on all sides by every manner of hateful creature–trolls, orcs, goblins, and other tribal races long forgotten. Lacking the numbers to fight their way clear, but too fierce and stubborn to yield, they began to dig. At first, they sought shelter in ancient caves, and expanded them into makeshift homes. They found sources of water, underground rivers that led deep into the mountain. From these clear spring waters they found sustenance, and they continued to dig. While fighting on several fronts, their numbers dwindling, they dug. In time, over the course of many seasons and under the leadership of Brenn Blackhammer, they had succeeded in withdrawing completely into the Maw, and had built a defensible perimeter at the entrance to their new home.

Their enemies begrudgingly relented–more as a result of their own thinning ranks, as they spent their lives against the dwarven fortifications, than from any sense of mercy–and in time the dwarves were left in peace to expand their subterranean fortress inward. Centuries passed and the dwarven people flourished, discovering great veins of precious metals, mastering the science of purifying raw metals, forging alloys, and crafting fine weapons. They developed trade relationships amongst themselves, men, elves, and eventually even gnomes, who, seeking to emulate the dwarves, dug out their own homes within the rock. The two races were not completely dissimilar, both being diminutive in size compared to the other races, and while the gnomes had historically been more easily persuaded to make common cause with evil allies, they did not lack strength or a work ethic, and their leaders discovered that they, too, could marshal their people to toil and work the stone, much as the dwarven people had. The similarities ended there, however, as the gnomes were satisfied with digging themselves out of the rain and peddling the gemstones they discovered through their own tunneling, whereas the dwarven people had quickly developed a calling to make their homes and halls magnificent and grand in every respect.

Brenn Blackhammer was named king of the dwarven people soon after they closed their gates for the first time, and upon his installation, his first act on that first day was to name their new kingdom Belgorne, honoring Shan Belgorne, the last heroic dwarf to lose his life outside the gates.

The legends and histories of the dwarves vary significantly in their discussion of the days before Belgorne, as many histories, oral and written, were lost to the decade-long diminishment of their people in the Battle of the Maw. On the day the gates closed, however, all tellings agree without variation that as their new king first pronounced the name of their kingdom, a great gust of air swept over the dwarves assembled in the entranceway, extinguishing all flames and light. When the confusion settled and the torches were again lit, bare minutes later, the middle-aged Brenn Blackhammer was on his knees in tears, his long hair and luxurious beard no longer coal black, but now platinum-grey, and the square marble section of floor upon which he knelt was no longer marble, but pure polished silver. The dwarves silently and reverently knelt to the king as one, and he stood, speaking of a vision of an underground kingdom more grand and magnificent than even the wildest dreams of the most ambitious engineer, a vision of the dwarven kingdom of Stonarris. At the conclusion of his sermon, an elder dwarf declared that Brenn Blackhammer should be henceforth known as Brenn Silverstone, and the thunderous chanting of that name shook the very Maw.

When a dwarf thinks of life beyond this life, they think of Stonarris. For that, said Brenn Silverstone, is where the true kingdom of the dwarves lies, and their people must continue to dig, must continue to expand their halls, for one day, they will break through the stone and clay and soil and find themselves in their true ancestral homeland, where they will be reunited with loved ones lost, and finally find rest.

Faith in the promise of Stonarris is universal among the dwarves, but today, as he walked alone through the majestic home the dwarves had made for themselves, J'arn Silverstone found his faith tested. For the promise of Stonarris rested upon a premise that he now knew to be an uncertainty–the idea that the dwarves, and the world, would survive long enough for his people to reach the fabled halls.

~

Kelgarr sloshed down the last of his mead and saw J'arn enter the Hammer as he peered over the rim of the horn. He wiped at his long dark beard and motioned the prince to join him at the long bench. As he approached, Boot nodded to Gritson, seated at the bar, who returned the nod. J'arn seated himself across from the dwarf.

"You look grim, J'arn, more so than typical."

"Aye, Boot, grim times."

"Aye." Boot waved over to Kari, and held up two fingers. J'arn glanced around the tavern nervously, leaning in to speak.

"Not good news then," Kelgarr stated matter-of-factly.

"Not good, Boot. Not good at all. I just came from my father, and Fury, but things are bad."

"Well, don't honey it over, J'arn. Tell me plain."

"No honey to be had. He'd just spoken with the priests, the forge master, and Jansen from engineering–"

"Bah, the forge master Garlan? He's a damned fool and a liar besides. And Jensen? That ol' gearbuster ain't got a brain in his head."

"Brain enough to see what we're all seein', Boot. We've all looked at this thing frontways and sideways, and there ain't no denying it." J'arn leaned in closer, almost whispering, "Dammit, Boot, if we don't figure this thing out, the whole cursed Maw's gonna come down around us!"

Kelgarr dropped his voice to match the prince's volume. "Now how in Fury is that gonna happen, J'arn? We been cutting through this rock for ages, and we don't go an inch without shoring up a foot behind, and you know damned well that our shorin' is stronger than the blasted rock was to begin with."

"It ain't the tunneling, Boot, and ye know it." A pause, as Kari brought the two fresh horns of mead.

Boot lowered his gaze to the table. "So it's true, then. All of it."

"Far as we can tell, 'tis true, Boot. I wanted to be the one to tell ye sure, so that ye can be the one to tell yer men before word spreads."

"To Fury with word spreading, J'arn. Yer father needs to call an Assembly, and tell Belgorne himself."

"Aye, and he will, but ye know how these things go. By the time we gather all of Belgorne for an Assembly, won't be a dwarf left who doesn't already know what's what. Anyhow, I'm to head out tonight, and take a company with me to go speak with the elves, and see if we can't put our heads together and think of something."

"And Mor?"

"Halsen's a damned fool, but after we talk with Evanti, we're making our way to Mor and see if we can't get the old bastard to see sense. Best to secure some help from the elves first."

Boot nodded soberly. "Well, I supposed it's settled, then." Boot gulped down the remainder of his mead. "*Gritson!*" The younger dwarf rushed to the table, and set a pack on the floor beside Kelgarr.

"Just like we talked about it, son."

"Aye, Boot. Just like." Gritson nodded at J'arn, then Boot, then brought his fingers to his lips and whistled. As one, the team of twenty-three engineers stood up and walked out of the Hammer in silence.

"What in Fury was that about, Boot?" demanded J'arn.

"Ain't no sense in waiting for dark, J'arn. Might as well be getting' on with it. Besides, Gritson's ready. He'll make a good foreman, once he learns to kick a little butt."

J'arn was at a loss for a moment, then put it together. "Boot, you're needed here, you're not–"

"Fury, I'm not, ya fool of a prince. Who's gonna save your scrawny hide from the monsters and such on the way to Thornwood?"

"There ain't no damned monsters, Boot, and I'll have a regiment. I don't–"

"And I suppose that regiment's gonna just fly to Thornwood?"

"Well, no, Boot, dammit, we'll ride and march–"

"And come back to a pile o' rubble. You ever been to Thornwood, J'arn? Dunno if ya did the numbers, but it's a hell of a long ways."

J'arn rose at that. "Don't doubt my strength, Boot, I'm a Silverstone, damn you."

"I don't doubt ye, lad, but ye ain't got wings!" Kelgarr stood as well, facing the prince defiantly.

J'arn lowered his tone. "Keep your voice down, fool!" He glanced around and saw, thankfully, that the tavern was nearly empty already. "And I suppose you're gonna engineer me some wings then, are ye?"

"No, not wings, lad, but I can damned sure engineer ye a boat."

When J'arn did not respond immediately, Kelgarr continued. "I'm gonna walk out on a shelf here and guess that ol' Jensen didn't volunteer himself for this little trek."

J'arn sighed. "No, Boot, he didn't."

"Then ye ain't got no engineer, and yer gonna need one, no mistake. Now listen, me illustrious prince, ye can't make it to Thornwood and back in time without takin the Morline, and fer that, ye'll need a boat. And once word o' this nightmare gets around, won't be no boats to be had. Yer gonna need a sturdy raft, maybe two, and fer that, yer gonna need an engineer. And if yer gonna need an engineer, who in Fury else ya gonna take with ya?"

J'arn sighed again, this time in resignation. "Yer not gonna like the company, Boot."

Kelgarr grabbed his sack and headed out of the tavern, calling over his shoulder. "I ain't worried about the company, J'arn, so long as you don't bring that lyin' jackwit Garlan! See ya at the gates!"

Again, J'arn sighed, and waved the waitress over. "I'll be needin' one more, Kari."

# XV: MOR

artean chose to walk back to Kehrlia rather than travel magically, deciding that he would benefit from observing the comings and goings of common men along the way. It had been some time since he had been out of doors and among the subjects of Mor, for he found the stench of the city distasteful. *Perhaps that unpleasantness will soon be rectified,* he thought to himself, and smiled. *Well, one way or another.*

The walk to Kehrlia was a bit over a mile from the Palace of the People where the king resided—a truly ironic name, for while the people of Mor built it, a common man would not wish to have business there. A visit to the Palace these days by a common citizen was unfailingly made in chains and concluded in the stocks at least, in the digestive track of carrion birds at worst.

Sartean considered this, as he made his way across the palace moat, through the gates and onto Kings Way, the mile-long circular thoroughfare surrounding the palace. On the inner side of the street, spaced no more than a pike's length apart, stood soldiers in rusted and battered armor, standing at loose attention. In times past the position of Palace Defender was a temporary and ornamental one, and meant as an honor to the soldiers who were assigned to the division. They would serve at full parade attention for two hours per day, and would be allowed leave at the end of their daily service to do as they pleased. The assignment was considered a reward for excellence, or bravery, or sacrifice of some sort, and would last for a cycle, after which they would return to their battalion or, often, be promoted into a more senior position. Many of the men serving as Defenders would have been recovering from injuries in battle, and their time in the division gave them an opportunity to regain their strength before returning to full service.

The men who received assignment to the Defenders, however, were often of a character that disallowed them from enjoying the idleness between shifts, and unless they were convalescing from injury, typically would return to their usual duties upon completion of their daily stint as sentry. The Defenders had been a source of pride for the Army of Mor and its people, uniformed entirely in bleached white with a shining steel breastplate indicative of their excellence, bearing symbols of either the Order of Blood, for wounded soldiers, or perhaps The Blade of Mor, reserved for warriors who had shown great valor and courage. If a man fell in battle, a surrogate would serve in his stead on the Way, nearest the main gates to the palace, and was free to tell any who would listen the tale of how the fallen warrior met his courageous end. People would visit the carts and shops and markets that lined the opposite side of Kings Way, and be reminded that their way of life was made possible by the blood and honor of gallant men. Boys would walk the Way and admire the brave men, formulating tales of how they, too, would one day earn their place among those ranks. Young women would shop one side of the street for provisions, and the other for husbands.

Today, the uniforms of the Defenders could only be described as "once-white", and rather than remaining at parade attention for two hours per day, Palace Defenders would be made to serve for a full half day, receiving relief only once per day in order to feed and relieve themselves. Upon taking the throne, one of King Halsen's first orders of business had been to dissolve the original tradition of the Defenders, and replace it with one of his own design. A shift on the Way was to no longer be a reward, but a punishment for some infraction or another, for to Halsen's mind, why waste good soldiers in idleness? The result was inevitable; instead of being a source of dignity for the people of Mor, the rank of Defenders became populated with the worst sort of soldier, no longer notable for cleanliness, presentation, and pride, but rather for sloppiness and poor discipline. Eventually, due to their proximity to the centers of trade, a disorganized system of harassment, extortion, and abuse developed, eventually establishing itself into a hierarchy of organized crime. The corruption spread throughout the regular army, and Halsen turned a blind eye to it all, only intervening when the corruption negatively intersected with his personal ambitions.

It was those ambitions that Sartean weighed carefully as he made his way through the markets, not completely oblivious to the terror he left in his wake as he drifted through Mor. *The stone will tell me much tonight, I suspect,* thought Sartean, aware that his passage on foot through the streets would inspire rumors and nightmares in abundance. The more pressing matter at hand, however, was Halsen. His meeting with the king had been substantially more successful than he had imagined, and he had parted ways with the fool in possession of a mandate to reshape the kingdom as he saw fit. Of course, the king had not quite used those terms, but he might as well have. The power in Mor, as in any great city, was concentrated within the treasury, and by extension, wielded by the treasurers. For so long as they controlled the distribution of wealth, they controlled all. The status of the kingdom's finances today, however, was atrocious, as the king had spent a lifetime enriching himself at the expense of his subjects. As a result, the system of finance was on the verge of collapse. This left the treasury managers in a state of disarray, as they were soon discovering that their ability to wield power was dwindling in proportion to the coffers of the kingdom.

Sartean had foreseen the inevitable societal decay decades ago, in part through his own considerable intelligence and reasoning skills, and in part through his (also considerable) powers of divination. The wizard had spent the better part of twenty years preparing for this day, and had found the solution much by accident, while disciplining an apprentice several years before.

~

A beautiful young woman was Mila Felsin, intelligent beyond measure, gifted with an inherent understanding of all things magical, and as ambitious as any apprentice Sartean had ever tutored. Her only real flaw was her insatiably competitive nature, and to Sartean's mind, this was no flaw at all. Mila was part of a class of a dozen apprentices who had been serving and studying at Kehrlia for over three years, and fewer than half of them would graduate in the coming spring. There had been one hundred to begin training three winters prior, but the process of earning the title of Incantor was, by design, brutally competitive. In reality, any of the applicants who had successfully made their way into the initial class of one hundred would have made talented wizards or sorceresses, but there was more to serving Sartean than mere talent—and to become an Incantor was, above all else, to dedicate oneself to a lifetime of service to Sartean D'Avers. Five of the initial hundred would succeed in obtaining their Title, no more, and perhaps fewer.

Mila's skills and talents related to sorcery were equaled only by her exceptional beauty, and she had no qualms about using both to advance her position and standing. The young apprentice was blessed with nearly perfect physical features. The first thing one noticed about Mila was her eyes, intolerably green, wide, and bright, resting beneath a perpetually curious brow, and above high cheekbones that were at once soft and severe. Her face was purely symmetrical, aside from the slight smirk she always seemed to display with her full, delicately painted lips. Naturally silky and thick hair, the color of richly brewed tea, carefully maintained to hang on the swell of her ample bosom, accentuated her alluring figure. Long, slender arms ended in delicate hands, one usually perched on the shelf of flesh between her slim waistline and her just-wide-enough hips, the other playfully teasing her hair, or the locket she wore, drawing even more attention to her endowments. Her legs, thin but muscular, while not disproportionate to her body as a whole, managed to seem impossibly long, an illusion created by the cut of the dresses she wore, slit to dangerous heights along one side, one luxurious leg always managing to slide out from beneath her silken gowns. This was the view of Mila Felsin from the front, and whenever the class was expected to walk any distance at all, there would inevitably be a fight for the right to walk behind her.

The first three years of training at Kehrlia consisted of what one would expect. Rigorous academic instruction in their first year was followed by a gradual introduction to practical concepts in the second year, by which time more than half of the initial class had already been winnowed out. Those who possessed the discipline and talent to survive the second year would be immersed in magic in their third year, expected to complete all tasks and duties purely through the use and application of sorcery. An observed transgression as simple as reaching for a pen when one could instead have used psychokinesis could be sufficient for expulsion. The objective of a third-year apprentice was to develop magical instincts, and to overcome fully the limitations of the flesh. That was not to imply that the flesh no longer had any use, as Mila had demonstrated in her acquisition of political standing among her peers. As with most competitive ventures, becoming an Incantor was as much about politics as about talent and effort, for to make the wrong enemies or show vulnerability was to assure one's failure. While many who began as apprentices to Kehrlia did so with idealistic ambitions, the altruistic among them quickly fell victim to the machinations of the ambitious and unethical. This was by Sartean's design, for he had no illusions about his own ethical nature, and could not suffer an idealist to gain power within his ranks.

Mila succeeded in all, and enjoyed her position at the very top of her class at the end of her third year. Unlike her classmates, however, in her ascent among her fellow students, Mila Felsin did not attempt to endear herself to Sartean. Those who did quickly learned that their efforts were wasted– and some of the clumsier attempts at ingratiation resulted in immediate expulsion–but all had tried. All, that is, except Mila. This was a curiosity to Sartean. Like any man, Sartean did not completely lack a certain lust for the seductive apprentice, and more than once he had fantasized about exactly how she would one day attempt to secure his support. Being possessed of inhuman internal discipline however, and even greater ambition, the wizard was not put out by her neglect, but rather assumed it to be a masterful display of power by the young woman. For, after all, most men of power are quick to discard their sexual conquests, and perhaps Mila Felsin felt that to keep herself distant from Sartean would enhance her mystery and allure, assuring herself a continued place in Kehrlia while the fantasy of her continued to burn unquenched.

It never once dawned on Sartean that perhaps she simply failed to favor him; a woman such as she could not resist a man with his power, and it would only be a matter of time until he would possess her. If he so chose.

The studies that made up the fourth year of apprenticeship at Kehrlia were impossible to master. Truly, and by design, impossible. Complex and monumental tasks, beyond the power of any one individual to accomplish on schedule, were the norm. On the morning of the first day of the first session of the fourth year, Sartean himself instructed the prospective Incantors to assemble at the steps of Kerhlia.

Their assignment was simple. Each apprentice was required to team up with another student. Each team was given the task of travelling to two different points on the compass in the area surrounding Mor, and to retrieve various objects of power that had been skillfully hidden. None of the students yet possessed the secrets of teleportation, and it was, in all likelihood, impossible for any usual means of travel to allow them to retrieve both objects in time. Each objective, however, was assigned to a single member of the team, meaning that they would have to work together to obtain both, but one of them would likely fail. Failure, as always, resulted in expulsion. Splitting up was not an option; the incantation required to free the targeted object from its hiding place required two wizards to execute. The teams would have two days to return with their objects, and whoever was not present at the entrance to Kehrlia by dawn of the third day would be expelled. The only rule was that they could not enlist outside help; horses would be allowed, assistance from others would not.

The unspoken purpose of the exercise was to determine which

individuals among the teams would possess the power of will and persuasion to ensure that *they* were the member of their team to obtain their trinket. Some would try to obtain both in time, but in the history of Kehrlia, no team had succeeded. They were given the remainder of the day to form their teams and strategies, and would be expected to leave together at daybreak the next day.

The commencement of the contest began as a race for the stronger and wiser apprentices to recruit the weakest, attempting to ensure that they would be able to convince the weaker apprentice to go after their token last. Sartean had barely turned to withdraw into the keep when the infighting and arguing and pleading began. Noticeably absent from the fray, however, was Mila, who had quietly left the gathering and followed Sartean into the keep.

Sartean waited at the steps leading to the second level for Mila to catch up, suspecting that this would be the day that she decided to exercise her sexual allure to secure herself some assistance. Instead, however, she entered the keep, nodded politely to the wizard, and made her way to the laboratories in the chambers beyond. Sartean returned her nod and watched her slip away, perplexed.

Later, after evening had fallen and the wizard walked his private balcony, he saw the young woman leaving the keep and walking towards the apprentice's sleeping quarters, seeming to be in no hurry whatsoever. *Curious*, he thought to himself.

Dawn arrived the next day, and the students waited in mounted pairs at the entrance to the keep for Sartean to make his appearance. He made them wait fully one hour, knowing that his delay would increase their desperation, and reduce the amount of time they had available to make their journeys. As he departed the keep and walked into the sunlight, he saw that not *all* pairs were mounted—waiting at the front of the class, without mounts, stood Mila and the second most promising student in their year, Kynneth Ansel, a well-built and intelligent young apprentice whom Sartean had expected to graduate with ease.

*Interesting*, Sartean thought. He distributed sealed envelopes to each pair which contained the locations of their objectives, with instructions to not open them until he gave the word. Once all the envelopes were distributed, he announced that the race had begun, and the six pairs dashed off towards the gates. Mila and Kynneth did not immediately depart. Instead, Mila reached into her pack, and pulled out two small vials of brown liquid. They each quaffed them down, nodded to one another, and raced off on foot at a speed that allowed them to overtake their mounted opponents in seconds.

*So that is her plan,* thought Sartean. *A shame, they will never survive the journey.*

The common name for the potion the pair had just appeared to drink was Speedsap, a powerful drug that could instill the imbiber with strength and speed and endurance, a potion that had once been used primarily in battle when facing the direst circumstances. In addition to being highly addictive, it was also quite unstable, and would affect its users differently. Some would tolerate it well, for a time at least, until their hearts exploded. Others would fall dead at the first taste. Others would become crazed, disoriented, and violent. The preparation of the potion was as much the cause of the variety in effects as was the metabolism of the user. The ingredients for the cocktail were a mixture of rare plants and roots, boiled and steamed and pressed and juiced, and not only was it difficult to obtain the ingredients, but it was nearly impossible to make one batch match the potency of the last.

The creation and use of the potion had long been outlawed, though this did not matter at all to Sartean. He did not specify in the rules that illegal substances would be forbidden in the exercise, so they were not. What he did find interesting, however, was that not only had Mila taken the risk of using such a powerful and dangerous drug, but that she had somehow convinced the second-best student in her class to abandon the traditional strategy of the contest and follow her lead. *Perhaps she has somehow perfected the potion?* he surmised. No, not that. Many a wizard, himself included, had attempted the pursuit. It was not possible.

The day wore on, and the next, and dawn was near on the third day when Sartean arose from his rest. He called for tea and breakfast, and asked it to be readied for him on his balcony, so that he might watch the weary students make their way to the keep as daylight approached. He did not often participate directly in the supervision of his apprentices' tasks; he had dedicated instructors for most of the necessary training. This one, however, he enjoyed taking a personal interest in, for much can be learned about a person under such conditions.

He made his way to the balcony and could see the black night sky giving way to lighter violet over the peaks of the Maw. He looked to the southern and eastern gates and saw no sign of his students yet. He considered contests past, and the ways in which various apprentices had attempted to succeed at their tasks. One pair had given a crude counterfeit of Speedsap to their horses, only to be thrown and trampled before they made it to the gates. Another had attempted a complex incantation to manipulate the fabric of time, resulting in their disappearance at the steps of the keep. His most vivid memory was of one of his first classes, when a pair had attempted to enchant a sparrow to enormous size, hoping to ride it to their destinations. The bird grew, certainly, and pecked half of the class to death before Sartean intervened. Only one student graduated that year, and with only half of a face.

No, the contest was usually won much more simply. Horses, minor enchantments, and treachery. The primary challenge was this: few wizards are great equestrians, and almost none are capable of riding at speed while leading a spare mount. The secondary challenge was where the treachery came in—what happened along the trail when it became clear to one apprentice that hope was lost, and that he or she would not obtain their trinket? More than one pair of wizards had fought to the death at this point, neither to achieve their goal.

Sartean pulled himself from his musings, and looked down to the base of the keep...to see a young woman curled up in a cloak, sleeping on the steps of the entrance to Kehrlia. With a thought, he stood beside her.

"Good morning, Mila."

Mila opened her eyes and smiled at Sartean, stretching slowly and tossing off her cloak. "Good morning, Master D'avers. It is a fine day, is it not?" She stood to face him. "Pardon me please for not rising immediately, it has been a difficult–"

"I see you are alone," Sartean interrupted.

Mila stood and bowed her head convincingly. "I am sorry to say, Master, that dear Kynneth may not make it back in time for dawn."

"Tragic, I'm sure. How?"

"How, Master?" she asked innocently.

"How did you do it girl? Spare no detail."

"Certainly, Master. As you saw, when we departed on our journey, Kynneth and I took a potion..."

Mila wove a tale of how she had, over the course of the past two years, managed to discover a manner to combine Speedsap with a variation of a common sleeping potion, in just the right proportions to predictably stabilize the volatile concoction. She had tested it over time, initially in small doses on herself, then eventually had shared it with Kynneth, who for all practical purposes, had acted as a voluntary human laboratory for her experimental potions. How he had been persuaded to volunteer was not discussed, but the implication was clear. He was not privy to her recipes, only allowed to enjoy the benefits of the alchemical formulae she created. Mila had been preparing for this contest, a rumored event among senior apprentices, since she had first been accepted into training and learned of the challenge. Gaining access to highly secret information about the fourth-year challenges was "not overly difficult", as she delicately put it.

"I do not care how expertly you altered the Speedsap potion, Miss Felsin. Stabilizing it sufficiently to complete this task is not possible, for like all potions, it is limited by the strength of the user, and the energies required to travel such distances are beyond the capabilities of mortal man. There is much you are not telling me."

"You are wise, Master D'Avers, and correct as to the science. However, with the right combinations of rest and exertion, it is possible for one person to cover the distances required."

"Except that one cannot rest enough to complete the task, and still meet the prescribed deadline. You must be moving at all speed, at all times, to even have a chance."

"Also true, Master. However, if one spent a portion of that travel time resting..."

Sartean stared at the young woman, losing patience. "Enough, Mila. Tell me how you did it."

"It was simple, Master. After reaching our first objective–the Book of Silence you had hidden near the Morline–I had, ah, suffered a minor twist of my ankle, and had persuaded Kynneth to carry me on his back to the second objective–"

Sartean interrupted her. "There is no way I will believe that you could have convinced that young man to carry you thirty miles on his back, potion or no. He would have known the risks to his health. More to the point, Kynneth is nearly as ruthless as you, and he is certainly intelligent enough to know that your plan required an exertion of energies much too great to succeed in the first place."

"Convince him I did, Master, and it did not even require the use of my, ah, most unique talents. A simple alteration to the Flightfluid left him quite eager to be of assistance."

"Flight...fluid?"

"Yes, that is my name for it. Clever, is it not?"

"Hardly. So, this...alteration...there is no such thing as a mind control potion, Mila. And any concoction that would make him so mentally pliable would also make him too physically weak to carry you."

"Yes, Master. But a love potion would not."

"Foolishness. A love tonic must be given continuously over the course of many seasons, and it cannot in any case create love, only enhance—"

Mila smiled mischievously.

Sartean's eyebrows narrowed skeptically. "So, you would have me believe that you have been courting the infatuation of this man for three years, and perfecting the Speedsap potion—"

"Flightfluid, Master," Mila corrected cheerfully.

Sartean sighed. "Flightfluid, then. In any case, you would have me believe that this little plot of yours has been in the works...for *years?*"

Mila straightened, and leaned in closer to Sartean.

"I very much wish to be an Incantor, Master."

Sartean narrowed his eyes at the young apprentice. "Your tale has gaps, Miss Felsin."

"Oh?" she asked innocently.

"Yes. Why not simply return back directly to Kehrlia once you had obtained the Book? Why the charade of seeking the ring that Kynneth was tasked to find, when you knew his strength would never persist long enough?"

"Oh, Master! I am not *entirely* wicked! Here, I have brought the Listening Ring as well. I had hoped that once you had seen the industriousness of our efforts, especially since no student team has *ever* successfully returned both items, you would declare our tasks complete, and allow dear Kynneth to advance. I promised him I would do my very best to persuade you." Mila beamed at Sartean expectantly.

Sartean laughed at this. "Child, you are a fool. You know very well that I do not grant exceptions. Ever."

Mila Felsin leveled her gaze at the Master of Kehrlia, all impishness and innocence vanished in an instant.

"Pity."

~

So it was that Sartean discovered the manner in which he would usurp the kingdom of Mor. A guarantee of graduation to Incantor given to Mila Felsin ensured her cooperation in further development of the Flightfluid, with particular attention to certain properties. First, the rarest of ingredients must somehow be synthesized, or the manufacture of vast quantities of the substance would be impossible. Second, the potency must be further refined to a fully predictable and reliable measure, though Mila's efforts had nearly solved that difficulty already. Third, one of the more undesirable effects of the potion—its addictive nature—must be addressed.

Mila was shocked—at first—to learn that Master D'Avers did not wish to eliminate the addictive properties of the drug.

*No, not eliminate.* Sartean wished to enhance them.

# XVI: HIGHMORLAND

arris stood silently within the darkened forest, watching the young man wrapped in a cloak, slumbering upon the damp ground. Black as the moonless night was, Barris' vision was extraordinary, and he could clearly make out the details of the man's campsite, or lack of campsite, as it were. No fire, no tent, two small saddlebags, no weapons. This was their thief from the night before, Barris was certain, and he had somehow narrowly escaped capture by his three pursuers. Barris was not one to suffer thieves, but neither could he afford to take the time necessary to question the man and bring him to justice.

*You do not know that he is a thief, Barris, in any case,* the elf knight thought to himself. More than once he had found himself pursued unjustly by men, and he did not have the necessary evidence here to shape an informed opinion. Satisfied that the weaponless traveler was no threat to Barris, thief or no, he quietly made his way back north to his own camp.

The two travelers slept in their respective camps, and Lucan awoke just before dawn, shivering. He assessed himself quickly, and decided that his chill was not simply due to the conditions; the morning was mild enough that sleeping without a tent should not have been so unpleasant.

"Damn it all, I've got myself an infection," Lucan cursed to no one in particular as he rose. He felt beneath his scalp at the wound behind his ear. The swelling had subsided somewhat, but the warmth remained. The cut, however, felt dry; he could not feel or smell any discharge, which meant that either he had come down with the world's most untimely cold, or the injury to his rib was more serious that he had feared.

*Got to get moving,* he told himself. He was much too stiff, and it was much too early, and all he wanted to do was climb back beneath his cloak and sleep away whatever sickness he was experiencing, but he knew better. There was no guarantee that his hunters were not still looking for him, and if he was in fact severely injured, he would need to find help, and soon. He fastened the mantle around his neck and approached Hope, who was alert and had already grazed bare the patch of ground near where she had been tethered. Lucan himself did not feel hungry, but knew that he must force himself to eat something if he was to maintain his strength. The notion did not last long, however, as he soon discovered that he could not hold down the dried meat he attempted to eat for breakfast.

After a brief bout of retching that left him breathless with pain, he abandoned the idea and decided that the best he could do was mount up and ride on. He gathered up his meager supplies, saddled Hope, and led her to the brook for a drink.

"I surely cannot thank you enough, Hope," he spoke through gritted teeth to the mare as she drank her fill. "I'd be a goner already if it wasn't for you. I'm gonna need you a bit more, though, friend. I'm not feeling so great today." He waited in painful silence as the horse finished watering herself, then cautiously began to climb into the saddle. It took more than a few tries, as his ribs protested fiercely, but Hope was tolerant of his clumsiness, and eventually he made his way atop the horse, just as the sun crested the horizon.

Each stride Hope took was agonizing; Lucan felt as if his insides had been shattered, and were being shaken like a cup of dice. After a few miles, however, he managed to again find a way to sit in the saddle that was not so punishing, though a ride at more than a trot was out of the question. He drank his water, ate tiny amounts of bread, and looked desperately for a path leading west, so that he might find his way to the farmlands. Midday had come and gone when he began to feel himself lose consciousness for the first time, yet he was unsure still if he had just dozed off for a bit, or was in fact becoming more ill.

It was then that he first saw what appeared to be a fork in the path up ahead. He resisted the instinct to urge Hope into a more hurried pace, but allowed himself to feel optimistic. As he approached the fork, however, his mood diminished, as the two paths seemed to both veer off at merely slight angles to the road behind him. Both of them still headed roughly north, at least by his estimation. The one on the right had clearly been taken by a rider recently, but as he had determined earlier in the day, his trio of pursuers had most certainly not come this far north, not yet. He had at least that much to be thankful for.

A decision then. By his calculation, he had come too far north for there to be a simple western route leading to the farmlands. If he were to take the path to the left, there was no guarantee that he would find a route west, nor eventually back south. It was clear, however, that the path bearing northwest had been untraveled in some time, at least since before the recent rains, and perhaps longer still. It was entirely possible that the path would taper and disappear into the dense forests, where he could not hope to find help, let alone keep his bearings.

The northeastern path would certainly not bring him any closer to the farmlands, but it was possible that he would encounter the rider who had passed that way today. That was an idea with both threat and promise, since he could not know the nature of that rider, his destination, nor his disposition. *At least there is a destination that lies that way,* thought Lucan, for the rider before him must have been heading *somewhere.*

A closer look at the tracks leading up the northeastern path left Lucan discouraged, however, as he could tell that the length of the horse's stride was much longer than his own tracks, leaving Lucan to reason that the rider had come this way at a gallop, or at least at a considerably higher rate of speed than his own.

"Ah, don't be downhearted, Luc," he said aloud. "At least you figured that much out. Look at you, never tracked a thing in your life, and you're already calculating the traveling speed of a rider long gone. Hah!" *I'm talking to myself. That can't be good,* he thought. *Nah, you always talk to yourself, Luc, you're great company!* Lucan laughed at himself then, and decided quickly that he would be better off taking the northwestern path. His original plan had been to make for the farmlands, why change it now?

Lucan began to urge Hope to the left, but she was having none of it. "Hey, girl, come on, we're gonna find you some food and a nice place to rest." He gently kicked at her flank and pulled at the reins, but the mare wouldn't budge.

"Now, listen here, Hope, we can't stay here arguing about this all day...whoa!" Hope reared slightly, took the bit in her teeth, and began to trot up the path leading northeast, and there was no amount of coaxing Lucan could do to stop her. Finally, after they had gone about half a mile, he finally gave up the argument. "Okay, horse, you better know what you're doing." Hope whinnied in response. *I swear this damned beast understands me,* he thought for the second time.

Hope continued on, and Lucan fought to stay alert. It was a comfortable afternoon, yet his shivering had returned, and he was certain now that he had developed a high fever. The more they rode, the more he shivered, his pain and nausea increasing. He felt his strength leaving his body with each mile that passed, yet he would not leave the saddle, for he was certain that if he did, he would not be able to mount up again. Dusk drew near, and Lucan began to lose all sense of time and direction, only distantly aware that he was riding a horse, until suddenly, Hope stopped in the middle of the trail.

"Oh, come on, girl, we can't stop here..." Lucan objected weakly, but Hope just stamped and snorted, having gone as far as she was willing this day. Lucan sat there in the saddle for a long while, wishing he were somewhere else, wishing he was some*one* else, feeling utterly alone and terrified. He knew that if he dismounted, and Hope took it to her mind to abandon him, he did not have the strength to stop her.

*It's not much better than you deserve, Luc,* he thought to himself ashamedly. *It's not like you're some great boon to the world, anyhow.* Resignedly, he decided that if Hope wanted to go, she had earned the right, and so be it. He had the presence of mind to first untie the saddlebags; then he dropped from the saddle like a sack of beans, crumpling on the trail in agony, and began to sob, not altogether from the pain.

The light of day was just beginning to fade as Lucan lost consciousness.

~

After a hard ride for a half day, less than a mile after passing Widow's Fork, Barris noticed Phantom start in midstride and begin flagging, quite unlike the great stallion. Many a rider would not have noticed the stress the horse had been experiencing, but Barris was no ordinary rider, and Phantom was no ordinary horse. They had shared more miles together than perhaps any rider and horse alive, and Barris had always been possessed of an acute bond with all animals, foremost among them his great friend Phantom. He eased the pace, brought Phantom down to a walk, and eventually dismounted, speaking gently to his companion as he did so.

"You are not yourself today, Phantom. Are you yet weary from our ride south?" He walked around the animal, inspecting him from hoof to mane. "No, not that. You are far too strong for that." He continued his inspection, and finally saw what he believed to be the cause of his friend's distress. An insect of some sort had stung the horse, on the inside of the hock of his right hindleg, and the bite had begun to swell. "Ah, that must pain you so! What foul creature dare sink its stinger into you, mighty beast?" Barris continued to speak to his friend, knowing that the cheerful tone of his voice was more important than the words. On closer inspection, it appeared that it was not a stinger that had pierced the great horse's flesh, but rather the fangs of a large spider, or perhaps a small snake. A spider seemed more likely, and preferable, for as a general rule, the smaller the snake, the deadlier the poison, whereas larger spiders could pack a punch, but their venom was rarely lethal.

"Let us get off the road, friend, and I will make you a poultice. We'll rest the remainder of the day, and I'll have you back to yourself in no time." He led Phantom off the path, then stood listening carefully, with his ears and his bones, for sources of water, and quickly located a small brook. Slowly they made their way through the foliage, and as Phantom drank, Barris went off in search of the plants he would need to lessen his friend's discomfort.

The search took most of the afternoon, and by the time Barris had returned, Phantom's wound had swelled considerably, though it was apparent that it the venom was not sufficiently strong to cause the stallion more than discomfort. "There now, friend. Just a few moments, and we'll have you on the road to recovery." Barris lit a small fire and boiled the roots and leaves of the plants he had found, then carefully laid them upon a stone to grind them into a poultice. Tearing off a piece of Phantom's blanket, he prepared a bandage, and moved to rub the poultice into the injured leg.

Barris began softly chanting as he worked the mixture into his companion's flesh. "Fah ni yef Da, tah Nü herra ni." *As we serve you, Father, so you heal us.* Barris had no doubt of the effectiveness of the prayer, which was much like the incantation he used to protect his camp, nor of the poultice. While the poultice alone would heal the wound in a matter of days, Barris knew that the power inherent in his prayer would hasten the healing, and by morning, there would be little if any trace remaining of the bite or its venom. Unlike the prayer of protection, however, the power of this spell would not come as a gift from the First Father, but from Barris' own life energies. *No less a gift, though*, thought Barris, as he marveled, not for the first time, at the grace his people had been given to be able to accomplish such things. Barris was not simple, by any means, and he knew where the limits of science ended and divinely granted power began. *Perhaps this is merely science of another sort*, thought Barris, but he did not doubt that it was a science rooted in faith and devotion, for among the elves, the degree of each had always determined the power of such things.

He finished bandaging Phantom, who had patiently allowed him to do so. A willful being was Phantom, as Barris had learned on more than one occasion, but his trust in Barris was absolute, as was Barris' trust in him. *So strange,* thought Barris, *that such a bond could exist between members of entirely different species, when men and dwarves and even elves so often find themselves facing each other with murderous intent.* He thought back to his meeting with Halsen, and the bloodlust of not only of the king, but of the crowd, wagering on whether or not he would survive the Game.

"These are terrible times we live in, my friend," he said to Phantom.

They could have ridden off after Phantom had been bandaged, but Barris decided that his friend more than deserved the time to rest and heal. In truth, Barris was not eager to return to the road. There would likely be very little time, if any, for him and the great stallion to simply enjoy one another's company before the storm the people of Tahr now faced rolled in. If one afternoon of his life should make any difference, Barris considered, that would mean he was far more important than he knew himself to be. A justification, he knew, but one that satisfied him. Barris and Phantom spent the remainder of the afternoon wandering just off the path, looking for a suitable place to make camp. They found several, but Phantom seemed to also enjoy the walk, so walk they did.

Twilight had fallen when the pair settled on a campsite, a patch of dry grasses that had been trampled not long before. There was no sign of passage aside from the flattened plant life, leading Barris to conclude that an elven Ranger had camped here recently. "Well, that certainly means it is good enough for the likes of you and me, dear Phantom. Let us rest here." Barris began to make camp, deciding to save the oats he had brought for Phantom, as the horse had eaten more than his fill of grasses throughout the afternoon. He had just covered Phantom with his blanket, which the stallion accepted this night, when he heard a rustle nearby, coming from the direction of the road. Phantom snuffled and tossed his head. "You heard it as well, friend."

Barris did not delay; he found it unlikely that he and Phantom would be threatened here, certainly not by an ordinary animal, but a rabid creature or a traveler could bear them ill intent, and his instincts told him something was amiss. He bounded towards the sheath on his saddle, withdrew his sword, and silently made his way to the source of the noise.

Reaching the path, he could just make out in the meager light a chestnut horse grazing a few dozen paces south of where he stood. No rider, though the horse was saddled. The horse shifted position to face Barris, revealing a lump of arms, legs, and blond hair in the middle of the narrow trail.

# XVII: THORNWOOD

he elven advisors assembled in the council chamber sat and listened attentively as Neral shared much of what he knew about the dangers the elven people now confronted. Not all, for some truths were too horrifying to yet give voice to. It would take time for even the wisest and most even-tempered among them to accustom themselves to the imminent perils the world now faced. While Neral knew that no amount of preparation would sufficiently prime the elven people for the threats ahead, the gentle nature of his people would not enable them to easily come to grips with the whole of it too suddenly. *We again live in a time for warriors*, thought Neral, *and the tender among us may not endure long.*

Neral had once been such a warrior, though centuries had passed since he had wielded a sword or led elves on horseback. This war would be fought by the young.

"All of you here have studied our histories to some degree," began the wizened elf. "Do not worry; I do not wish to lead you all to slumber with a recitation of the history of Tahr, though we will return to subject of the past shortly. It is the future I wish to discuss with you, not of the people of Tahr, nor of the elves, but of *your* futures, of your lives beyond this one." Neral surveyed the hall, his eyes settling for a moment on each of the elves assembled, and addressed the daughter of the queen first.

"Aria. Would you tell me dear, if you will, where will you go when draw your last breath on Tahr?"

Aria blanched, stunned by the inquiry, for the question was the most private of matters, a question reserved for lovers to share before their Joining night, or among closely bonded friends and family, in equally intimate moments. Certainly not publicly, in an assembly.

"It is all right, child," said Neral kindly. "I will not force your answer, though I would ask you to share this gift with us today, for the good of your people."

Aria was confused, but pride would not allow her to withhold her answer. "I will answer, Goodfather. On my last day, I shall go before the First Father and ask Him to allow me to continue to serve my people, in the manner He deems fitting."

Neral nodded his thanks, and measured the expressions of those seated at the table. Queen Evanti's demeanor was severe, doubtlessly upset by the intrusion into her daughter's deepest heart. As he eyed the others assembled, it was clear that all were uncomfortable, save Pheonaris, Mistress of the Order.

"Pheonaris," Neral began.

"Beyond, Goodfather," Pheonaris interrupted cheerfully. "I shall ask the First Father to go Beyond."

Glances were exchanged at this, and Neral allowed a moment to pass before speaking again.

"Thank you, Pheonaris. I know you are all perplexed, and I shall not make you each expose your eternal path. I do not wish offense or discomfort to you, Aria, nor you, Pheonaris. I do, however, require your candor, for I wish to demonstrate how, even among us, the chosen leaders of an enlightened people, discussion of Eternity is met with strong emotion. Think of how each of you are feeling right now.

We talk of the pain of the land, of impending wars and death, and we feel anger, and remorse, and pity, and grief. Yet when we speak of Eternity, our emotions sharpen even further, and we begin to understand a bit more of what the abstract concept of death truly means. This is unsettling, is it not?"

Nishali spoke. "Goodfather, death is a part of life. It is not to be feared."

"Ah, brave Ranger, but you are mistaken in this."

Silence rang like a bell. Neral let it ring.

"I do not believe she is, Neral," this from the queen. "All here know that while our bodies are not immortal, our spirits will persevere. I do not believe any here would fear to lay down their lives for another."

"Of course, my Queen. But that is not what Nishali said. She said that death is not to be feared. That is most certainly untrue. Perhaps those of us here do not fear our own deaths. Perhaps." Neral glanced along the table. "Nishali, why do you not fear your own death?"

Nishali replied without a hint of discomfort. "I have given my life in service to the land, to my people, and to the First Father. My place is assured. I made my choice long ago, and I have not reconsidered."

"Of course, of course, Nishali. Let me ask you however, when do you believe you will die?"

Nishali was uncomfortable at this. "I don't understand, Goodfather."

"Of course you do, dear. How long do you believe you have left on Tahr, before you are called to the Next?"

"I cannot know that, Goodfather."

"True. You cannot know. Tell me also, please, Nishali, in the days or decades or centuries you have remaining to you, where shall your path take you?"

Nishali began to redden. "I cannot know that, Goodfather."

"You speak wisely. You cannot, Ranger. So tell me, Nishali, though your life to this day has been in service, who is to say that some tragedy will not befall you in the future that will alter your path, leading you to a place of darkness, where your place in Eternity is no longer so certain?"

The elves in the room all looked to Nishali expectantly. The Ranger was not known for her patience and tolerance. Her reply, however, was insightful.

"You speak of things I pray about daily, Goodfather. If you wish to ask if I have yet earned the Mark, I will tell you truly—I have not. You are right then, I cannot know. But I can strengthen my nature, and have faith that I will withstand the pressures of my own passions, should such a tragedy come to pass."

Neral nodded solemnly. "I am proud to know you, Nishali. Your words are wise. I see your confusion, friends, so I will attempt to dispel it now. Millions upon millions of people have lived and died on Tahr. The total number is not known to me, nor is it knowable, for we do not even know when our world was born. We scarcely know anything at all about the lands and peoples living outside Greater Tahr. Only the Stone Elves possess such truths, and they have been silent for an age. The magical gifts of the elven people have blessed us with a great truth, the knowledge that the soul persists beyond death. This knowledge is truly a rare gift, and a grace from the First Father, this great and awesome wisdom, one that has not been made available universally to all people of all races. We also know, beyond question, that our choices in life lead to our choices in death. Additionally, we know that an ultimate audience with the First Father is not assured; it is an honor we must earn. We must finally acknowledge that there *is* wickedness and evil in the hearts of all, and that not all who pass through the Veil will find peace, Pheonaris. What lies Beyond?"

"It is unknowable, Goodfather."

"It is, child. Yet you wish to go?"

"I do, Goodfather."

"Why?"

A pause. "Because it is unknowable."

Neral smiled at this. "Well put, daughter of elves. And when you arrive Beyond, I am sure that you will be welcomed among those who await you. Yet for those who will neither remain beside us in eternal service to the land and our people, nor venture Beyond, what lies Next?"

Kender, Hand of Justice, spoke quickly. "We do not speak of it, Goodfather."

"No, Kender, we do not. Though today we must."

Mikallis could hold his tongue no longer. "Why, Goodfather? Why must we speak of this? What matter is the destiny of evil beings? Why do we discuss theology when we face a real threat that must be addressed?"

Neral frowned at the young Captain. "Please be patient, Captain. Am I given to pointless lectures?"

Mikallis lowered his head. "No, Goodfather."

Neral softened his expression. "Of course I am, Mikallis. I am old, and pointless lectures are my trade. Yet this one is not pointless. Hear me now, elven sons and daughters. I ask you to consider the eternities of evil spirits here today, because it is a matter of simple science that energies do not fade from this world. All things persist, transform, or become sustenance for another. Such is true with the spirits of evil, whose number is unknowable and unfathomable, and it is a concentration of those hateful energies that we now face. We must discuss what lies Next for these spirits of wickedness because, though you would wish to not think on them, they are thinking on you. The envy and hatred of ages has festered in their dark hearts for millennia. We all know how the cycle of evil progresses; Disorder breeds Evil, and the evil return to Disorder, where they spend their eternities in the depths of Fury, or as some call it, the Mawbottom. Yet we only think of the fiery pits of Fury in te abstract, for to truly reflect on their reality is too terrible an exercise. I tell you now that Fury is a very real place. As real as the air we breathe, as real as the citadel we have assembled in." Neral allowed the horror of it all to settle, pausing, a slight tremble in his hands as he folded them together, and continued. "The very marrow of Tahr awakens now, fueled by the horror of evils committed in ages past, and on through present times. Elves of Thornwood, we face the restless power of ancient Death, and it *is to be feared*."

**END OF PART ONE**

# PART TWO

# XVIII: THE MAW

hyla awoke just as the first beams of sunlight pierced the thick canopy of elms she slept beneath. She could have slept past noon, not merely because she was not naturally inclined to awaken early, but because she was thoroughly exhausted, having spent most of the night swatting away an insatiable armada of tiny biting insects. Her reddened, sunburnt flesh was covered in small welts, not only on her exposed skin but anywhere her clothing was snug. The assault had slowed a few hours past dusk, but did not stop completely, and as soon as she would find herself beginning to doze, another pinprick would startle her, leaving her scratching herself and swiping wildly at the dark, attempting vainly to murder the hungry little demons.

Sleeping late was not an option however, for she had heard the approach of some sort of animal just behind her. In her three days since leaving G'naath for the Morline, she had managed to evade the attention of predators, but she knew by the measured paces through the leaves behind her that her luck had run out. Shyla lay as still as she could, her head resting on her pack, hoping against hope that the animal would pass her by.

It did not, and suddenly Shyla's pack was yanked from beneath her head, tearing out wisps of auburn hair in the process. She yelped, scrambling to her knees to face the beast, and saw a hairy black creature backing away on its four legs, her pack in its fangs, growling and shaking loose her meager belongings. Shyla instantly recognized the creature from her grandmother's descriptions.

This was a wolf.

Quickly the frightened Shyla assessed her options as she knelt, coiled and ready to do...something. As the wild beast tore through her possessions, she remembered what Cindra had said, that wolves are pack animals, and that more would certainly be about. Quickly she glanced around, searching the forest for movement or eyes or teeth or other evidence that she was about to be set upon by a hungry mob of furry death, but saw nothing. The beast before her had torn her food free of its wrappings and was feasting greedily on a dried loaf of meat—but this wolf was considerably smaller than the ones Cindra had described to her. Terrified as she was of the animal, she was equally terrified of starving, and she could not let this wolf eat her only food.

"Hey! You! Bahhrrggghhh!" She yelled and waved her arms madly at the wolf, which jumped back, startled and whimpering, bowing its head between its forepaws. "Get outta here, wolf! I have magic, and I'll burn yeh to ash! Gaaahhh!" She feinted forward, and the wolf jerked back, unsure, then settled on its haunches, a pitiful whine escaping its throat. It looked across the few paces separating it from Shyla and placed its head on the ground, defeated.

*What is this?* thought Shyla. *These are the fierce wolves that I have been dreading? Bah!* Shyla stood then, heartened by the wolf's timidity, and stepped forward cautiously to gather her scattered belongings. The wolf sat there, panting, its tongue hanging out of its mouth, brown eyes following Shyla's movements. When she picked up the remainder of the loaf, rewrapping it carefully, the wolf perked up expectantly...then cocked its head in disappointment as she stuffed it back into her bag.

"This here be my food, wolf, and you can't have any! Now you get, go on now! Go!" She pointed to the forest, and the wolf looked to see what she was pointing at, confused. "I said get!" The wolf and slowly rose, its furry tail tucked protectively between its hind legs, and began to walk away. It turned back once, Shyla clapped her hands loudly, and the wolf bounded into the brush and was gone.

*Mawbottom, but that were close!* she thought. She quickly rolled her blanket, tied it to her pack, and made her way back to the trail she had left the night before. Shyla would wait for her breakfast until she had put some distance between herself and the wolf.

By midday, she discovered that she would likely die of hunger before that happened. The wolf had been following her the entire morning, carefully maintaining its distance, periodically reminding the little gnome that it had not forgotten her with another pathetic whimper.

Hunger and pity finally got the better of Shyla, and she relented. "Aw, for Fury's sake, wolf! C'mon, then." She cleared the leaves from a patch of trail, removed her pack, and laid out her blanket. The wolf approached cautiously. "Well, c'mon, ya stupid wolf, come eat." She tossed a piece of the meat loaf towards the animal, who warily sniffed the air as it approached. Its eyes looked first to Shyla, then to the meat; then, in a bound, the wolf snatched the meat up from the ground and retreated a few paces to begin its meal.

"Hmph. Big tough wolf," Shyla sneered, eating her own loaf and taking a drink from her waterskin. The dry meat was, aside from a mild hint of salt, mostly tasteless, but satisfying nonetheless, and she chewed happily as she considered the past few days. The parting with her family had been a sad affair, but a quick one, as she did not wish to satisfy the gossiping gnomes who stood at the gates gawking at her departure. She spent the entire first night walking, and most of the following day, as she had been well rested when she left–and, as Cindra Sandshingle had helped her discover, she was truly excited about this next phase in her life. She had left G'naath with instructions from her grandmother to go south and east, following a series of clearly marked trails to the Morline, where, Cindra assured her, she would meet with assistance. Her ultimate destination was the Grove of the Wood, equidistant between the city of Mor and the elven land of Thornwood, and her grandmother had promised her that if she were careful, and did not despair, and kept moving, she would arrive unscathed in but a few weeks' time. Beyond that, Cindra had said, she would face choices that the sorceress could not foretell, making her future unclear.

In the time that remained between her initial meeting with Cindra and her final departure from G'naath, Shyla had learned much from the old woman of the dangers of the world, her own nature, and her own abilities. She had learned better how to listen to the voices inside her, to hear fragments of the secret thoughts of others, and with concentration, even to ignite a small flame with only her will. Her threat to the wolf, however, had been an exaggeration; she could no more burn the wolf to ash than she could fly. In time however, Cindra had promised, she would learn to do such things, and more, if the elves chose to share such secrets with her. Shyla did not understand why the secrets belonged to the elves to bestow or withhold, nor from where her unique powers emanated, but there was little time for questions, so she tried to learn what she could without pestering the Lady with demands for further detail. It was excruciating. So many questions! The inquisitive gnome had gnawed a tear in her own cheek that day, stifling her queries. No matter. Cindra had promised her that all would be revealed, and Shyla trusted her grandmama.

Such a wondrous journey she now found herself undertaking, traveling through lands she had never even dreamed existed, spending her days walking through rich, bright, colorful life, no stone or soil overhead, only endless skies dyed in tints of blue and orange and pink and violet and countless other colors she lacked the language to name. It was all so exquisitely overwhelming, and even though Shyla had crept upward through her secret tunnel on many, many a night, she had only seen the world of Tahr from a very limited vantage point before this journey began, and never once in full daylight. She did not mind the stings and scratches. She did not bemoan her tired legs, nor her dirty clothing. Truly, if it were not for her mother and father, she would never, ever return to G'naath, and would live out her days wandering the world in search of new sights, sounds, and smells.

Tastes, however...the young gnome could certainly go for one of her mother's applecakes just then. Shyla knew she had but a few days' more food, and soon she would have to learn what in Tahr was edible and what was not. She would need to learn to hunt, Cindra had said, and catch fish, and forage for fruits and berries. This frightened Shyla. What if she at the wrong thing? What if she sought to hunt an animal, and instead found herself the one hunted? She carried only a short knife, hardly suited for battle with dangerous game. What if she could not catch any fish? She decided for the hundredth time to put the idea out of her head. Get to the Morline, Cindra had said, and you will find assistance there. With luck, she would find the great river before her food ran out. She refused to think further on the matter for now.

Shyla finished her meal, stepped off the path to relieve herself, and returned to find the wolf sitting on the trail, clearly waiting for her, its tail sweeping back and forth on the ground. *Odd*, she thought. She took a moment to examine the black, shiny-coated animal. Sitting on its haunches, it was not quite as tall as Shyla. Its fur seemed shorter than her grandmama had told her it would be, its ears...a wolf's ears were pointy, she had been told. This animal's ears were...well, floppy. She had expected, in her imagination, that a wolf would possess red, evil eyes, and fierce, sharp, jagged teeth. This wolf did not; even though its teeth were clearly sharp fangs designed to tear into flesh, they did not appear so fierce. Its brown eyes—no evil there, she decided. *Perhaps this animal is somehow deformed*, she considered. The idea explained why it might be without its family. That thought decided her.

"I'm an outcast, too, wolf," she said. The animal cocked its head, tongue hanging out again, then stood to approach her. It did so slowly, and Shyla reached out her hand, feeling an inexplicable urge to touch the animal. The wolf stopped just short of her reach, extended its head to sniff her fingers, and began to lick them. Shyla giggled with glee.

"Oh, wolf, yer silly! Why ya wanna be lickin' me?" she laughed. Her new friend seemed to enjoy her laughter, and began to prance around her, its keening whine now becoming a series of cheerful yelps. Shyla's sunburned cheeks reddened even further with laughter, and it was not long before the pair were rolling around on the trail, the wolf gently nipping at her, trying to encourage her to play some game Shyla did not understand. She discovered to her disgust during their wrestling that her opponent was a boy wolf, possessing the unmistakable attributes of a male. The young gnome squealed herself to fatigue as they grappled, and in time the two settled beside each other on the trail, breathing heavily, merely looking at one another in silence. After a time, Shyla spoke.

"Yeh be me first new friend, wolf. I s'pose yeh got a name, but bein' as I canna speak wolf, I guess that'll be yer name. Wolf. Do ya like that, Wolf?" Its tongue lolled out again, tail wagging. Shyla took that as a "yes".

Shyla rolled up her blanket and patted Wolf on the head, and the new friends continued along the trail toward the Morline. Shyla Greykin had never, ever been so happy.

~

On a westward trail somewhat parallel to the one Shyla walked, a small company of dwarves led by J'arn Silverstone rode south and west down the foothills of the Maw. Riding their sturdy yet diminutive horses, bred through generations to suit the dwarven people, the eight representatives of Belgorne made their way to the Morline, where they would secure (or design) passage to Highmorland, and then complete their march on foot to the Grove, where they would seek the knowledge and assistance of the elves. Some debate had ensued as they departed Belgorne, the forgemaster Garlan and the engineer Kelgarr coming to blows over whether they should ride straight for Thornwood or take to the Morline, where they would abandon their mounts and settle for making contact with the elves in the Grove. J'arn had already decided their path, but allowed the dwarves to fight it out, knowing that if they did not settle their differences before their journey began, the journey would be a long one indeed.

The strategy proved vain however, for had J'arn not separated the two, the fistfight would have become an axefight, and there would have been one less dwarf travelling with the company. J'arn had no illusions as to which of the two would have survived; Boot was a formidable fighter, with or without weapons.

The feud had begun nearly a decade ago, when Boot claimed he had warned the forgemaster that he was running the forges too hot, and would soon weaken the stone and steel struts supporting it. One support did weaken, and the forge shifted dangerously, killing one smith, injuring several others, and shutting down the forge for several cycles while the damage was repaired. Garlan maintained that Kelgarr gave no such warning, and implied that it was Kelgarr's incompetence in failing to see the danger that had caused the calamity.

The Prince of Belgorne did not personally witness any conversation between the two, so could not take a position publicly on the matter. Privately, he trusted Boot, and knew also that Garlan would rarely admit his own faults, even when the evidence was clear. In the absence of evidence, he would go to his grave before confessing an error. It was a frustrating trait of the dwarf, but his gruff, unyielding, never-apologize nature made him an excellent forgemaster, if a somewhat infuriating peer.

Boot pulled his horse up alongside J'arn, but remained silent. The two had not spoken in the two days since J'arn had broken up the fight, J'arn knowing better than to fuel the fire, and Boot still steaming. Since they had broken camp that morning however, Kelgarr's mood had seemed to improve.

"Smoke up ahead, J'arn," Boot stated. The air was thickening with the scent of burnt wood and foliage. It was not the first evidence they had encountered in the past two days of a smoldering Tahr, and they knew it would not be the last.

"Seen it, Boot. We'll be needing to find another trail, I'm thinkin'."

"Aye. If I remember, there's a junction not far ahead can take us due south. We'll reach the Morline sooner, but there won't be any docks."

"That's why you're here, Boot. That, and to keep Garlan honest," J'arn said.

Boot gave him a look. "About that, J'arn. The damned fool just had to stir the ashes. Ye know how I feel about the forgemaster, but I weren't tilting for a fight."

"I know, Boot. Garlan carries guilt for what happened that day, and 'tis easier to hate ye than to blame himself. In time, he'll make peace with ye. Could be this journey is just what it'll take."

"Could be it won't matter, J'arn. This is no pleasure trip we're on."

The prince sighed. *No, it most certainly is not,* he thought. The sound of singing reached their ears then, the twin brothers Narl and Fannor belting out the verses of a vulgar yet beloved drinking song about a dwarf with a fetish for stealing women's clothing. Soon the rest of the company joined the song, with even Garlan, J'arn, and Boot chiming in at the chorus.

> *Well, she never saw the lech'rous Jon, her eyes beneath her tresses,*
>
> *But when she woke the sneak had gone, along with all her dresses!*

The company laughed and sang and traded stories much of the rest of that day, their worries not quite put aside, but the sunshine and crisp autumn air doing much to remind the dwarves of Belgorne what they might soon be fighting for. The dwarves lived much of their lives within the halls of Belgorne, but unlike the gnomes, they lived part of their lives without as well. All the dwarven clans took turns with the responsibilities of hunting and patrolling the region surrounding the entrance to Belgorne.

They took the southern fork of the junction, and continued riding until dusk, when they reached the Morline. A small outpost and stable, manned by men, stood on the southern side of the river, just across a small bridge that spanned the still-narrow Morline. The great river did not widen beyond a dozen paces until it reached the Fang, a few day's ride west, where it was fed by several underground springs and a small series of rivulets that would nourish the waterway with melted snow in the spring. The rains the past few cycles had been plentiful, however, and where the dwarves crossed, the narrow river ran both deep and swift.

J'arn and Boot approached the outpost and were met by a trio of soldiers.

"Captain Marion at your service," the tall sentry addressed J'arn cheerfully. "What brings you to the Morline, gentlemen?"

"Hah! Did ya hear that, J'arn, he called ye a gentleman!"

J'arn shook his head and dismounted. "J'arn Silverstone, Captain," the dwarf extended is hand, grasping arms with the Captain. "Well met. We be headed down the Morline, on business of Belgorne. Tell me, can we stable our mounts with ye for a time?"

The Captain frowned. "Not with me, Prince Silverstone, the stable's not mine to rent. You'll have to speak with the stablemaster, Mister Jennings. Though there's room for twelve, and only our three mounts in residence, so I'm sure he'll be pleased for the business. But I think you might be missing an important element in your plan, sir. There's no dock here, and not a vessel to be had between here and the Fang, if even there."

Boot spoke up then, still mounted. "Aye, we assumed such, Captain. We'll be needing to assemble rafts, and quick. Any objection to us felling a few trees? Ye can have the firewood we leave behind, and we'll be happy to split it up for ye."

"No shortage of trees, sir, and they're not mine in any case. A question though—have ye brought any, ah, liquid refreshment with ye? Besides water, I mean?" The two soldiers at his sides noticeably perked up at this.

"Water!" This from Narl and Fannor, in unison, who had just approached. Narl continued, feigning indignation. "Whaddya take us fer, Cap'n? A gaggle o' monks?"

"Catch!" said Fannor, tossing a skin to the Captain, who opened the plug and took a whiff.

"*Fury*, sir, but that's not water. Tell you what, how would you feel about making camp tonight here, and in the morning, my men and I will help you fell those trees? Provided, of course, that you'd be willing to dine with us."

Boot laughed. "Ye mean drink with ye, and we'd be delighted, Cap." The dwarf dismounted smoothly. "Kelgarr, at yer service, though me friends call me Boot. If ye can hold yer liquor, tomorrow ye can as well."

"Challenge accepted, sir. Let us introduce you to Mister Jennings, and get your mounts settled."

~

Shyla and Wolf walked until night fell. When dawn came the next morning, the air was not as clear as it had been the past few days, the forest enveloped by a dense mist. She opened her eyes to see Wolf curled up beside her, snoring. The young gnomish girl had slept better that night, perhaps because she had better wrapped herself before she slept, perhaps because Wolf somehow kept the insects at bay, or more likely out of sheer exhaustion. She yawned deeply upon waking, and was assaulted by the stench of Wolf's damp fur and her own dried, pungent sweat. "Oof! Gonna hafta do somthin' bout that!" she said to herself.

The crudely drawn map she had brought with her, combined

with the instructions she had received from Cindra, led Shyla to believe that she would make the Morline this day. She had made excellent time since her departure from G'naath, facing flawless weather and easy trails, and her excitement at the day ahead was an instant tonic for her sleepiness. She did not delay in breaking camp. A bite of food for herself and

Wolf, and they were off, for today, she hoped, she might make acquaintance with the "assistance" Cindra had foretold would come.

The pair ran as much as they walked, the sunlight remaining obscured by the fog and by the crown of the forest until well past midday. The lift of the haze was gradual, and the trail they traveled widened as the forest on either side took on an enchanted quality, deeply emerald at moments, alternating between murky grey shadow and shining coppery light at others, with myriad touches of color tinging the leaves of the autumn trees.

Shyla had never imagined that such magnificent and diverse hues could be born of the same brown and black soil, yet here they were, all around her, above her, and beneath her. She nearly lost her footing several times while craning her neck upwards to admire the great variety of tree and plant and bird and animal life for which she had no names.

As twilight began to settle, Shyla was not concerned that she had not yet reached the river this day. She did not doubt that she was on the right path, for the sun had set to her right, and she could only be traveling south. No trails had cut across her own since the night before, and her sense of direction was almost faultlessly instinctive in any case, a skill developed and honed by a lifetime spent within a series of complex tunnels and caverns. Then Shyla glimpsed two small furry-tailed animals chasing each other around a tree just up ahead. Wolf took off in a sprint, doubtless to make a meal of them, yet he bounded past them and over a rise in the trail, becoming lost over the rim of the hill.

"Wolf! Wait up!" She laughed and dashed after him, but as she crested the hill, she froze.

The river.

Shyla had found the Morline, and Wolf had already begun splashing on its banks, as if he, too, somehow knew that this was his destination, and that it was time to celebrate a milestone in their journey. Shyla was suddenly uncertain, however, for on the far side of the river, across a narrow bridge, she saw smoke.

*Avoid the smoke, Shyla. Watch the skies for it, and if you see it, do not go near it. Turn and make haste the other way, as fast as you are able. A fire in the Maw will spread faster than you can run. It will jump streams and canyons. It will appear to be behind you, and yet suddenly leap ahead, surrounding you. And the fire may not even be your undoing, my dear.*

*The smoke will end your days upon Tahr just as easily.*

Shyla had seen plumes of smoke on the distant horizon repeatedly over the previous few days. Never had they been close enough for concern, however, and never until now had the smoke lain in her path. Mawbottom, she thought, so close to the river, what now? She stood on the rise, watching Wolf splash and swipe at the water, the sun now fully below the tree line, and only a bit of light remaining in the day. She could not, would not go back. Yet she dared not go forward. She must somehow retrieve Wolf, for the animal was surely too simple to know what the smoke meant.

"Wooolf! C'mon, Wolf!" She clapped her hands and hollered and danced around. Wolf glanced up at her once, then returned to his exploration of the bank. She continued to call, and he dipped in and out of view, and Shyla paced, suddenly realizing as darkness claimed the day that she was beginning to understand how her mother and father must be feeling right now. *I'll not abandon me only friend*, she decided, and made for the bridge.

The distance to the bridge was less than a hundred paces, and Shyla covered it quickly, though it felt like miles. The specter of smoke and fire and death reaching for her in the dark left her feeling as if a thousand needles had poked her flesh, the palpable, penetrating fear for herself and Wolf nearly paralyzing in its intensity. She did not stop to realize that she could not smell the smoke. She did not consider that if the fire were near, she would see the glow. In her frightened mind's eye, the very essence of fire was no longer a glowing, blazing, smoking thing, but a creeping invisible enemy that would snatch her life away without notice. *Get hold of yerself, girl! Are yeh that much a coward?*

Shyla quickly decided that she was, in fact, that much a coward, but she made the bridge nonetheless, and called out for Wolf. "Heeere, Wolf! C'mon, ya stupid beast, I got more food for yer scrawny hide! Wooool..."

A hand reached around Shyla, covering her mouth and stifling her cry. Instinctively, the young gnome bit deeply into the flesh of the strange hand, earning a scream and her immediate release. Before she could even fully turn around, Wolf suddenly arrived at her side, growling more fiercely than she had ever heard him growl. Shyla spun, pulled her knife free of her waist, coiled into a spring, and beheld her attacker.

Rather, her attackers. A band of dwarves stood before her, axes at the ready, the closest holding his hand protectively to his chest.

"Yeh best stay back! This here's a wolf, and he's fierce protective of me! We'll tear yeh to bits!" Shyla waved the knife before her frantically.

The light was just barely sufficient for Shyla to see the dwarves exchange confused looks. One marched up to her and slapped the knife from her hand smoothly. Shyla barely felt the gentle strike.

"Aye, little lady, and a mighty wolf he looks to be. Though yeh might want to tell him that."

"Huh?" she said, inadvertently.

The dwarf whose hand she had bitten spoke then. "Aye, yer protector seems to have sprung a leak."

Shyla glanced down to see Wolf in a cower, ears laid back, urinating on his own paws.

"Ah fer Fury's sake, Wolf. Yeh big pansy." Shyla deflated for only a moment, then straightened again, glancing fitfully among the dwarves and slowly backing away. "Well I s'pose ye'll be tryin' ta have yer way with me, then! But I'll warn yeh, I'll not let yeh near without leavin' a mark!"

The company of dwarves laughed riotously at this. Boot replied.

"Nah, little lady, ye need not be worryin' bout any such thing. Though after a bit o' moonjuice, Fannor here might write ye a sonnet."

"Aye, Boot! And it'll warm the cockles of your heart!" said Fannor with mocking passion.

"Boot ain't got no cockles, Fannor," this from Narl.

"My cockles are bigger than your cockles, ya damned fool," retorted Boot.

"Only if it's cold outside!" Narl replied. The dwarves fell into peals of laughter again. J'arn glanced back at them, and they quickly silenced themselves. He turned to address the young gnome, suppressing a grin.

"Little lady, I am J'arn Silverstone, Prince of Belgorne, and ye need not be afraid this night. Ye will come to no harm in our company. Ye nor your...wolf."

# XIX: MOR

ames Thallinson wedged his shovel triumphantly into the dense clay soil and beamed with pride. A waist-deep pit twenty paces square lay before him, the hole now prepared to be filled with gravel and mortar, the foundation for a new manor to be the home for some unnamed aristocrat or noble family. He and his four-man crew of laborers were expected to complete the chore within a cycle, yet the first spadeful of soil had been spooned from the ground less than six days before.

Despite having worked in Mor as a laborer for all of his adult life and adolescence, the gaunt man was not formidably strong. He was not formidably anything. James was not unpleasant, but also not particularly charming or physically attractive; nor was he ambitious, or possessed of even a basic education. He could not be described as simply "average", for even the most average of men typically possess some singular talent or defect. James had neither; his only outstanding quality perhaps being a pervasive simplicity that inhabited every aspect of his impoverished life. James had never led his own crew before, a fact owing to his prevalent and characteristic mediocrity, though the man never failed to find and maintain employment moving dirt or sand or clay from one place to another. James Thallinson had a reputation for sobriety, punctuality, and hard work, and the predominance of those qualities–combined with the lack of any noteworthy shortcoming in character—made him particularly well suited for the task of wielding a shovel. Eighteen years of digging into the soil of Tahr should, one would think, result in the creation of a sculpted man of great might and vigor; however, the rewards of such labors were meager, and James' diet was proportionally mean, resulting in an overly lean physique, an underdeveloped intellect, and an absence of the belief that anything would ever change.

Until eight days ago.

~

James had arrived at the worksite just before sunrise, early as was his habit, and found himself greeted by a pair of men wearing the distinctive cerulean robes of Kehrlia. James thought the wizards' presence curious, but not being a particularly curious man, he walked directly past them, intending to pay them no mind as he settled on a patch of grass to await his foreman. A voice behind him a moment later brought him to his feet.

"James Thallinson."

James faced the men nervously, a faint tickle of fear trying vainly to warn him, *Run!* Acknowledgment of his instincts came too late, however, as one of the men continued.

"Master Sartean D'Avers requires that you attend him at Kerhlia. Now."

Terror welled and roiled within James' heart and mind as the three walked the streets to the Keep of Kehrlia in the growing light of morning, and by the time they reached the steps, James Thallinson had vomited twice. He sobbed and blubbered his sinuses dry as his escorts remained silent, offering no explanation. James asked for none. He knew. He had misused his mouth. He had spoken the nickname. He had mocked the most powerful and feared man on the surface of Tahr, he had been heard, and if he was very, very lucky, he would die this day.

They arrived at the steps to the keep, but James could not ascend them. His legs would not obey his mind. He was frozen with dread, his feet obstinately refusing to do anything more than remain rooted in place. The silent wizards on either side of him grasped his elbows without a word, and he was effortlessly lifted from the path and carried up the steps, no longer trembling in fear, but now convulsing, the hammering of his heart threatening to split his veins and spill his lifeblood on the steps of Kerhlia before he even discovered the nature of his doom. James wished for death. He willed his very spirit to traverse the Veil as he was carried into the keep. He silently prayed and begged and bargained with any god or demon that would hear for his life to be taken from him. No response came.

His escorts released him onto the marble floor of in the center of the foyer of the Keep of Kehrlia, and somehow James Thallinson kept his feet, more from an accident of balance than as a result of muscular strength. His downcast eyes saw the hem of a black robe before him, and he squeezed them shut so tightly that the muscles in his face seized with pain.

"Remarkable, isn't it?" The voice of Sartean D'Avers echoed smoothly around the circular foyer, seeming to come from everywhere at once. A sound escaped the horrified throat of the man in response, some unintelligible expression of confusion and fear.

"Ah, forgive me, I see your eyes are closed, you must be preoccupied with imagination. Open them."

Somehow, James' eyes obeyed the command. Sartean continued.

"Is it not remarkable?"

"Ah-I-uhh," James emitted another equally incomprehensible utterance, followed by silence. Sartean let the silence carry for a moment.

"Come now, James Thallinson. You must admire the opulence. Look around you—a flawlessly calibrated radius of the most exquisite and priceless marble, as immaculately shaped as blown glass, its acoustic perfection causing my voice to reverberate from all directions simultaneously. Does the sound of my speech not seem to ring from deep within you, James? Is the effect not utterly *grand*?"

Despite his terror, James' eyes felt obliged to survey the foyer, his ears compelled to attend the quality of sound emanating from around him, comparing the wizard's description to what his senses experienced. He did not understand half of the words the sorcerer had spoken, but he did grasp their meaning. Aside from a flight of marble steps leading upwards and yawning widely behind the wizard, and two arched openings in the walls on either side of the stairs, the entranceway of the great tower was, to James' estimation, *perfectly* rounded, the azure and white marble appearing seamless, its meandering veins continuing uninterrupted along the walls, as if the entire vestibule were hollowed from within a single stone. The walls rose from the glossy floor at right angles, with a curvature evolving uniformly from a point intermediate between the floor and an inexplicably glowing ceiling that soared fifty feet above his head. James felt an overwhelming sense of vertigo as he imagined himself shrinking into nothingness. He felt entirely insubstantial as he stood in the center of it all, the enormity and grandeur overwhelming, and this only the first level of a tower he knew to extend to the skies.

"Do not allow yourself to be too overcome, James. I would imagine that the modest life you lead does not lend itself to spending much time in places such as this—though I will admit, no place quite such as Kehrlia exists. Tell me, James, about that modest life."

"Ah, I...sir?"

Sartean glided forward, barely perceptibly. "Now, James, if we are to have a conversation, you must contribute. I will forgive your awe, but I must insist you be more lucid. Here, perhaps this will help." The wizard allowed one hand to extend from beneath his robes, and gestured at the man.

"*Absharra.*"

James felt a bit of his fear diminish, and though not nearly at peace, he felt the paralysis of his mind part like mist before daylight, and looked up at the wizard's angular face for the first time.

"There. Now speak, James Thallinson. Tell me what a day in your life is like."

James cleared his throat and spoke. "Well, sir, I usually wake up before the sun and make myself somethin' to eat, if there's somethin' to eat, and try to get it eaten before anyone else wakes up. Then I go..."

"Anyone else, James? You mean you do not eat with your family?"

"Ah, no sir, I ain't got a wife, nor children..."

"No wife? Surely? A man such as you?" Sartean's tone was frank, and James could not tell whether the wizard was mocking him, though he suspected he must be.

"Ah, no sir, as it is, I ain't all that good with words, or women, or things like that, and I ain't got much money, well, none at all really, so I ain't found a wife. 'Sides, I live in the Common, so's I got no house for a wife to live in no ways." James looked at his feet.

"I see," Sartean said, his tone unchanged. "Go on, lead me through your day."

James continued. "Well sir, I eat, like I said, if there's food, then

I get dressed and head for whatever job I got to do. I'm a digger, and I dig for all sorts o' reasons, but mostly it's about the same, only thing different really is where I'm digging and what the ground's like. Sometimes it's just regular old dirt, and that ain't so hard, but sometimes it's clay, and sometimes–"

"I understand. So, for whom do you dig, James?"

"Huh?"

"Your employer, James. Who pays you to dig?"

"Ah, well, lately, last few seasons, I been diggin' for a crew that's assigned to the new construction details, but there ain't no pay, really. The city puts me up in the Commons, they feed us once a day on the job, and once in a while we'll get a little money for ale, but I ain't much of a drinker so I give it to my ma when I get it, and she brings me a little food when she can so's I can have a breakfast some days."

"Interesting. So, for how long have you been a digger, James?"

"All my life, sir. Since I was taller than a shovel, at least."

"That would be eighteen years, two seasons and a cycle, then, would it not? Since you became taller than a shovel, I mean."

James blanched. "Ah, I think so, sir, right about that long."

"Exactly that long, James." Sartean began to circle around James slowly, and spoke. "You began digging the week after your father died in a brawl over a woman he had bedded the night before, the young bride of a childhood rival and powerful merchant named Vincent Thomison, who cut his throat in a fit of jealousy, sawed off his head with the same knife, and deposited it on your doorstep for your mother to find. You were told that your father died in an accident while laying stone for the walls of Mor, and you did not learn the truth until the night of your twenty-third birthday, when you met Vincent Thomison at the same tavern in which he killed your father, where he would have killed you then as well, if not for the presence of a squad of city guards in the bar. He then told you that if he ever saw you again, you would meet the same fate as your father, and that was the last time you ever entered a pub, or had a drink of ale. You have led a completely penurious, anonymous and simple life for all of your thirty years, James Thallinson." Sartean paused his speech and his circuit, watching the color drain from the man's features. He leaned in threateningly from James' right side. "Until today."

James fell to his knees and began to bawl. "I know I was wrong, sir! I shouldn'ta said your name, or used that other name, or been shootin' off my mouth like I did., I was just havin' a hard day is all, and I lost my good sense–"

"Good sense has never been a thing you were overly possessed of, James. Stand up and be silent. I am not finished speaking."

James rose quickly, shoulders heaving, and suppressed his sobs to the degree he was able. Sartean continued.

"I know all there is to know about you, James, and I know that you fear me. I know the rumors that circulate around Mor about me, and I know why the people of Mor live in horror that the great and terrible Sardine Cadaver will invade their homes in the dark of night and steal them away to some dark dungeon, where they will be tormented and tortured to a slow death that they will pray to the First Father to hasten. Do you know why these rumors persist, James?"

James snuffled. "No sir."

"Master."

"Huh?"

"You will address me as Master, James."

The man nodded fervently. "Yes, si-yes, Master."

"So you do know, then?"

"Ah, I mean, I don't know for sure, Master. I don't know very much at all…"

"Yes, you do, James. You know that the rumors exist because they are *true*." Sartean paused for effect, allowing the reality of the grim admission to settle in the man's imagination. James' terror returned.

"Or rather, they have been true. You see, James, I had thought to bring you here to punish you. To allow your disappearance, and the eventual discovery of your broken body, to serve as a warning to those who would mock me. You must understand," Sartean began circling again. "I do not do such things out of vanity. I do them for the safety and security of Mor, so that its people will know that a society must, first and foremost, live in respect of law and Order, and by extension, respect of the people tasked with maintaining that Order. Do you understand, James?"

"I... I think so, Master."

"I do not think you do. Not fully. No matter, I will enlighten you. As Master of the Keep of Kehrlia, James, and leader of the Fraternity of Incantors, it is my duty to help protect Mor, even more so than the duty of the army, or the guard, for it is the power of sorcery that truly protects this kingdom from threat, not the pointy shards of metal that soldiers wield. If I, as the chief defender of this kingdom, do not command the fear and respect of the citizens of Mor, then how, I must ask, will I command that esteem from our enemies?"

James waited for a moment, to be sure that his response was required, then replied. "I... I think I do understand Master. You have to be strong for the kingdom, and that means sometimes you have to do things that are mean?"

"Yes, James, exactly that. You are a clever man, to understand so quickly. Tell me, how is it that you have not yet advanced to foreman?" Sartean asked, a sincere curiosity in his voice.

"Ah, well, sir...ah, Master, I guess maybe I just ain't been very lucky so far?" James responded cautiously.

Sartean stopped directly in front of James and placed his hand on the man's shoulder. James' blood froze. "No, James, you have not been very lucky. And that is why you are here. You see, James, in learning about you and your life, I have had a realization. Your story is not so uncommon. You live your life in a prison, a cycle of unfortunate circumstance and poverty, one that you cannot break free of, and in time, you no longer even feel the chains around your neck. Is this not so, James?"

James examined the floor. "Yes, Master," he replied truthfully.

Sartean moved his hand from the man's shoulder, and cradled his chin, gently, as a father would, and lifted the man's face to his own. "I know, James. I know. And your struggle has inspired me. Tell me, James, how does your body feel right now? Do not answer too quickly, take a moment, examine your own flesh, and tell me how it feels."

James did so. He considered the blisters on his hands and feet, the ache in his back, the exhaustion of his muscles that seemed to reach into his very organs. James had long ago stopped feeling the chain around his neck, he decided, and it had been some time since he had indulged himself in recognizing his own pain and weariness. "I am tired, Master. So tired. My body...every part of me hurts something awful. I don't even think about it no more, it's just the way it is. It's the way it's always been."

Sartean withdrew a small flask from his robes. "Drink, James. No, do not be afraid. Drink. Just a sip."

James unstopped the flask, drank a mouthful of the warm, bitter fluid, and handed it back to the wizard. As the flavor of the drink insinuated itself into his taste buds, his eyes slammed shut with disgust. The potion was thick and viscous, tasting like...like ash, and dandelions, and burnt hair. A succession of unpleasant tastes assaulted his palate, and the solution made its way down his throat, searing its way into his stomach–then, just when he felt he might vomit, a feeling of strength surged within him, a sense of youth, and potency, and boundless energy...

"Master!" James exclaimed, his terror and shame and weakness of a moment ago now less than a memory. He reached for the flask and the sorcerer pulled it away quickly.

Sartean smiled. "Easy, James, not too much. Tell me how you feel *now*."

James smiled at the wizard as he sought the words to describe the sensation. It was useless. "If you have a shovel, Master, I'll show ya."

Sartean nodded. "Do not show me, James. Show your foreman. And when he asks you how you managed to work so quickly, send him to me."

"I will, Master! May I ask a question, though?"

"Of course, James. Ask."

"Well, ah, sir, how long will this last? This feeling, I mean."

Sartean did not bother to conceal his hungry leer. "Only for today, James. Only for today. You will need to return in the morning."

# XX: THORNWOOD

his is ill-advised," Queen Evanti declared.

"More than that, completely unadvised, Lady," replied Neral, as he sat alongside the queen on the wooden bench beside the Lovers.

"Exactly my point. The Mistress was specific—this task is for Aria, though I do not understand it in the least."

"It is Aria's wish that Mikallis join her, Terrias, and if it is indeed her task, then it must be her decision to choose her companions."

The queen shot Neral a look. "She did not choose him. He inserted himself, and Aria did not object. They are not the same thing. And in any case, The Mistress did not divine that any companions were required."

"Nor did she divine that they were not, my dear. Would you send Aria on this quest unaided?"

"The Mistress is accompanying her, Neral. I do not fear for Aria in her company."

"Pheonaris is traveling with her to the Grove, Lady. Beyond that, her path is not known."

The queen was exasperated. "Fury, Neral, the boy will be a distraction!"

Neral smiled ruefully. "My dear, you think as a mother, not a queen."

Terrias Evanti looked far past Neral, as if focusing beyond the horizon. "I am both, Neral."

"You are. And you excel at both roles. But you are a queen first."

"Do not think to grease me, Captain Neral Evanti."

Neral laughed heartily. "I do not grease you, my esteemed Queen." He smiled mischievously, and Terrias warmed slightly. His expression sobered after a thought, and he continued. "I speak from the heart. You are a wonderful mother, and the equal of any ruler to whom our people have ever sworn fealty. Where those persons intersect, however, you are mired in confusion and uncertainty. I led elves once, and I was a father once. Your dilemma is not unknown to me."

The queen bowed her head. "Nu glahr ni, Neral."

"Your honor of me is kind, my lady. But I have heard those words a thousand times, and I do not require them from you to know your affection for me."

"It was spontaneous, Neral. You must know that."

"I do. And as we speak of affection, let us return to the topic of my niece."

At the elven council several days past, Neral had outlined the peril they faced, if ambiguously. When he had felt that he had conferred upon the elven leaders enough information to allow for an understanding of the scope of the looming threat, he deferred to the assembly to determine the best manner to wage a resistance against it. Voices were raised, horror was expressed, and more questions than answers bubbled to the surface. Neral answered what he could, but in truth, he had not held much back from the council—nothing, at least, that would make their path clearer. Their enemy was insubstantial, their tactics unclear; the only distinct fact was that the evil dead of Tahr were somehow causing violent changes on the surface of the world, and that they would accelerate the chaos to some cataclysmic end if they were not somehow opposed. The reaction of the elves was predictably hectic, until Aria noticed that Pheonaris was not only uninvolved in the discussion, but seemed to be...not present. When Aria stood, the elven leaders looked to her expectantly. They saw her looking to Pheonaris, and quieted. All knew that the Mistress was having a vision.

When Pheonaris surfaced again, after no fewer than fifteen turns of the glass, she opened her eyes and spoke.

"Aria and I must depart for the Grove at daybreak. There her path will become clear."

No amount of coaxing or questioning could cajole more details from the Mistress, and even Neral could not be certain whether there was more she withheld, or if she was devoid of further understanding of her vision. The Mistress maintained that the words she spoke upon her return to the present were the only guidance that would be given. Knowledge of from where that guidance came, and of the manner in which it had been conveyed, and an illumination of the dangers inherent in the young elf's path, would not be forthcoming.

A vote was taken, though it was barely a formality. It was agreed that Aria would go with Pheonaris, and the elves would await whatever wisdom resulted from her journey before they took further action. The queen gravely declared the matter finalized, and immediately upon her declaration, Captain Mikallis stood and made a declaration of his own: He would be accompanying Aria. All eyes were on the young elf, and the queen was dismayed to see him assert himself so inappropriately. She looked to Neral, whom she expected to chastise the young Captain. Instead the wizened old elf stated innocuously that he was sure his niece would welcome the Captain's protection. Aria's eyes widened at Mikallis, the queen's eyes narrowed at Neral, and the two men looked into one another, an understanding, or at least a covenant, passing wordlessly between them.

"You were quick to defend him, Neral," Terrias stated. She expected a reply, but none came.

"Do you intend to tell me why?"

Neral shifted uncomfortably. "I...yes, I was, Lady. Though I am not sure why, and I have thought about it often in the past few days."

"You spoke before considering your words, Neral? I find that unsettling for one in your position."

"I did not...ah, it is complicated, Lady. I cannot say that I understand it."

"Do your best to explain, Neral. I will be patient." The queen's word carried an air of command. Despite the gentle tone, Neral was compelled to respond.

"My Queen, perhaps I can explain it best this way. You heard Pheonaris' pronouncement. Vague, yet precise all the same. Little detail, but what was there was quite clear. Do you understand?"

The queen considered this. "I do, though not completely."

Neral nodded. "Nor do I, Lady. But I felt compelled to speak. I felt in the same way that it was somehow...necessary...that Mikallis accompany Aria."

"Do you mean that you sense some danger, Neral, some threat that he must protect Aria from?"

The elf shook his head. "No, not that, Lady. Not in the way you mean. I mean that...well, that his presence on this quest is somehow...ah, I hate to use this word, but I must. Ordained."

"Ordained, Neral? Did you have a vision as well? It did not seem so..."

"No, Lady, not a vision. But perhaps a premonition of sorts. I fear there is a danger, Terrias. To Aria, or perhaps involving Aria, one that I sense in a way I cannot describe. But I feel that the danger is not one that Mikallis can protect her from."

"Then why should he accompany her? I do not know why it upsets me so, Neral. I love Mikallis like a son. Just something...I feel that somehow his decision to go with her is *wrong*. Is it merely that I fear his motives? For the Father's sake, Neral, I know Aria is no child, and I know that when one cares for another they cannot bear the thought of them coming to harm. Surely that is Mik's motivation here, is it not? And if so, why am I so disturbed?"

"I think perhaps that you sense the same thing I sense, my Queen. I cannot know this for certain, but with your permission, I will stop censoring myself and speak freely."

Terrias Evanti did not want to hear what would come next, but knew she must.

"Speak freely, Neral. Your wisdom and insight are valuable. You are free to conjecture, without reproach."

"Thank you, Lady. Here is what I fear, the hazard I sense in my old bones. I fear that Mikallis is too possessive of your daughter, of my niece, of our Aria. More so than what he should be. I fear that he is a part of the threat she faces. I fear that she will spurn him, and he will react with great anger. I fear, Terrias, that Mikallis has the Fever for Aria, and that she does not share it."

"Oh, Neral, please tell me you do not know this. Please tell me that you did not send our Aria out into the world with this danger knowingly."

Neral was deflated. "I cannot say I did, Terrias, and I cannot say that I did not. You of all people know that the Fever is a rare and powerful thing. It does not merely affect those within whom it resides. Do not look at me that way, please, my dear Terrias. Even the king of Men, as you know, is not immune to the Flare. And among our people, it burns hotter. So hot that it can empower the one who carries it to persuade others to its cause. I believe, Lady, that when Mikallis declared his intention to accompany Aria, he persuaded me to support, and as he did, even as I caught a glimpse of what is to come, I could not remain silent. I was compelled, Lady."

Queen Terrias Evanti, for the second time in less than a cycle, recalled a young boy chasing conjured sparkflies, joyous and innocent. She recalled now how that boy grew to a man, how he came to love her, then to desire her, then to burn for her. She recalled how she had rejected him, not unkindly, but with finality, as she declared her love of another. The young man's Fever, a gift for some, a curse for others, became a smoldering, unreciprocated passion, steering him to a seething madness, relentlessly driving him to seek an outlet for his lust. His scorned love of an elven woman transformed itself into an insatiable lust for power, and as he ascended the throne of Mor over the early grave of his father, his passion consumed him. King Halsen of Mor was no longer the young whimsical boy; that part of him was long dead. He had become a haunted, ravenous man, consumed by jealousy, and in his hatred, he caused the death of Terrias' true love, her husband-to-be and the father of her dear Aria.

"Lady." Neral placed his hand on Terrias' knee. She recoiled. "Please forgive me."

Terrias stood, her demeanor suddenly decisive, her countenance stern. "There is nothing to forgive, Neral. I know the power of the Fever. What we do not know for certain is whether Mikallis is under its influence. Not yet. Come, Goodfather. Do not be downhearted. We will send a company to follow my daughter and ensure her safety. You will help me choose the elves. I will choose to continue to believe in the virtuous intentions of our young Captain Mikallis until he proves himself unworthy of that faith."

Neral stood. "And if he does, Terrias?"

Queen Evanti regarded Neral severely. "There will not be another Halsen to wound my family, Neral. Ni oash'e en." *I vow it.*

# XXI: HIGHMORLAND

Phantom stamped uneasily and Hope shied away from the great stallion, unsure of the cause of his discontent. Dawn was still not upon them, yet Barris was already awake, examining his unconscious patient, when the tremors began. The first sign of trouble was Phantom's agitation, followed shortly by a slight swaying of the pines within which they camped. The Twins were on the wax again, offering no illumination as they were now beyond the horizon, yet the dawn was sufficiently near to impart enough light for Barris to see the movement in the trees. No wind, Barris noted, and he felt an insidious queasiness that he could not place. The uncertainty lasted but a moment, however, as the sway of the trees became a violent, roiling wave, needles and leaves falling wildly as the very land beneath Barris began to quiver and churn. Hope whinnied in alarm, and struggled to tear her reins free of the tree she was tethered to. Even Phantom was losing his composure, rearing and kicking at an invisible enemy. Barris was leaning over his patient protectively as the violence of the tremor reached an apex. Then suddenly, as if nothing at all had happened, the forest was quiet and still, the wrath of Tahr spent, for the moment.

Barris had never experienced such an intense Tahrquake before, though he had heard stories of the great rending of the world that gave birth to the Morline and the Fang. Before this moment, he could scarcely have imagined the force required to open up the land in such a manner. Barris suspected that somewhere, great damage to the world had been done, and was disturbed in a way he had never been before.

Deciding, after a brief analysis and after collecting his own wits, that his patient was no worse for the experience, he went to Phantom and Hope to provide what comfort he could, though the two horses were already beginning to settle. Phantom had begun nuzzling against Hope, and was clearly having a calming effect on the mare. Barris spoke gently to the two horses for a moment, but did not get too close, for he could sense that Hope was still wary of him, and more than spooked from the tremors. He would allow her to quiet herself further before they broke camp.

Which left the question of what to do next. The young man–Lucan, Barris believed he called himself–was in poor condition, fevered and suffering some internal injury. They had spoken very briefly over the course of the previous several days. The boy had only been conscious often enough to give some vague explanation that he had fallen while riding, and to say that his horse, Hope, was his only friend. On discovering Lucan, Barris had determined very quickly that the boy would die without assistance, and the only solution he could envision was to bring the boy north with him, and leave him in the care of whomever was attending the Grove. The going had been excruciatingly slow. Barris had to tie the boy to Phantom, whose stride was far gentler, as he rode Hope and led the horses along the trail. He had done what he could to feed the boy and give him a crude paste of medicine the first day, but on the second, third and fourth days, he could only manage to get him to drink a bit of water, and Lucan's strength was fading fast. On this, the fifth day, Barris believed, the boy might die if they did not make the Grove. Perhaps even then. He had decided the night before that they would camp one final time, mostly for the sake of Hope, and then make haste north, not resting until they had reached the Grove. Barris estimated that they would arrive just before dawn the following day.

Now, however, he was unsure. The tremor had certainly felled trees and opened chasms in the trail ahead, and he would not know what obstacles would lie in their route until the encountered them. That would make travel at night perilous, and while Barris did not wish to allow this boy to die from thirst or infection, he was concerned that too hard a ride would kill him just the same. Phantom could make the Grove by sunset, and he suspected that Hope could ride nearly as hard for a sufficient distance. The boy, however...

There was no choice. The boy's body was failing, and Barris had done what he could in the way of his own healing abilities. If Hope could not keep up, then she could not, and he would share a saddle with the boy on Phantom; he felt confident that Hope would follow their trail. If the boy did not survive the ride, then he did not, and Barris would bury the boy with as much dignity as possible. He must try to make the Grove, however, so he washed the waste from the young man as best he could, dressed him again, wrapped him in a blanket, and secured him over Phantom's back with as much care as he was able. Barris had become practiced at the exercise, and the four were on the trail just as daylight began to pierce the canopy.

Barris had not ridden Hope at a gallop before this, and he was impressed with the ease at which she navigated the trail. The mare seemed to relish the workout, and Phantom followed a few lengths behind, his longer stride just swifter than a running walk. Barris slowed Hope repeatedly, allowing Phantom to come alongside so that he might check on Lucan. By noon he had only needed to stop a few times to retie the boy's binding to the saddle. After each pause, Hope joyfully returned to speed with little encouragement from the elf knight. By midafternoon, however, Barris began to worry that Lucan was nearing his end. The boy had not taken water all day. He had stopped sweating, his lips were cracked and desiccated, and the skin of his forehead was inhumanly hot. Barris increased the pace, knowing now that time was more important than caution and hoping that whoever was attending the Grove would have the talent to heal the boy, though he feared that Lucan was too far gone for any usual method of nursing to have any effect. The druids and druidesses of the Grove, however, could accomplish much more than usual healing, so he continued to ride, hope and possibility still not yet lost.

Just before twilight, the four reached a narrow brook that Barris knew to mark the territorial boundary between Highmorland and Thornwood. The springs of the Grove lay but a few thousand paces beyond the crossing. The water was shallow, typically cannon deep to Phantom at its deepest, and Barris and his mount typically would jump the stream in all but the worst weather. The vault was of course inadvisable this day, so Barris slowed Hope to a walk, dismounted, and began to lead her across the rivulet. Phantom followed closely behind, but as Hope's forelegs reached the far side, her rear legs sank in an unseen rift beneath the water that Barris had stepped over. Hope reared, and splashed, and began to panic as she sunk deeper, unable to kick herself free and instead sinking nearly to her stifles.

Phantom stamped and snorted behind her, distressed by the danger to his new friend, and Lucan began to slide off the stallion from the jerky lateral movements. Barris pulled on the reins as best he could, hoping to give the horse some additional leverage, but as he slipped in the mud it became clear that the effort was of no use. Barris looked around frantically for help, or something he could use...something...but he was alone, and there was nothing. Hope was stuck. He knew that there was no danger of the horse drowning in the shallow water, but she would certainly break a leg if she continued to panic, a sentence just as lethal. Meanwhile, Lucan was dangling precariously from the saddle, and Barris had to make a decision—save Hope, or save Lucan. Time slowed to a crawl as the terrible choice became clear.

Such a choice would be a simple one for most men, and even for most elves. While the life of an animal was to be considered precious, the life of a human was paramount. The decision, however, was not so easy for Barris. He did not merely love horses; he had an instant Bond with them, one that allowed him to feel their emotions as clearly as his own. The connection the Bond gave Barris with a horse was more profound than any rapport he had ever had with elf or man. Even though he knew what the world would expect of him here, perhaps what the First Father would expect of him here, his heart would not allow him to abandon Hope as she looked to him, screaming, terrified, with Barris her only chance at salvation. Yet a few paces away, a young man who had survived against all odds to reach the end of this trail was in grave peril, his head dangling between the hoofs of a massive and powerful stallion.

*Help me, Father*, he prayed, not ambiguously, but truly, humbly seeking divine guidance. In the space of a heartbeat, his panic cleared, and his mind focused.

*Inhale.*

Barris' eyes darted around the scene with otherworldly speed, his senses sharpened and his indecision washed away. His elven sight pierced the surface of the churning water, finding the boulder that Hope's hock was wedged against. Details surpassing those that ordinary vision could impart flooded his mind. He instantly discovered how he had missed the rift; he had trodden upon it, and Hope's hind hooves had slipped off the back side of the stone, her legs sinking into the mud. The cavity in the ravine was new, doubtlessly formed by the Tahrquake that morning. The rift was a result of the shifting of the great rock, only a small portion of which was visible above the muddy stream bed, but the fissure had filled with loose sediment, making it impossible to notice. As his understanding of how he had led Hope into danger dawned, Barris looked at Phantom and Lucan, his enhanced eyesight bringing the pair into close focus as if through a looking scope. Barris saw that the leather thong holding Lucan's leg to the saddle was tied tightly, the knot in no danger of separating. He allowed himself to sink deeper into the Bond with Phantom, and urged him to calm, all his will focused into steadying his friend, conveying to him the danger he posed to the one that Barris was obligated to care for. He sensed that Phantom understood, that the series of images he had sent had indeed reached the horse's consciousness, and as Phantom's heartbeat slowed, he knew that Lucan would be safe, for the space of a few breaths at least. Barris hoped that was all the time he would need.

*Exhale.*

Barris released Hope's reins and dove beneath her, his feet delicately finding balance on the underwater boulder, cramming himself into the space remaining between the rock and the horse's barrel, his shoulders braced against her ribs. He returned his elven focus fully to his own body, willing his life's energies into his legs and back, knowing that what he intended would come at a cost, but one he would bear to help this honorable beast.

*Inhale.*

Barris concentrated his entire being into a single great heave. He felt his eyes near bursting with pressure, his muscular legs swelling with blood and strain, tearing the seams of his leggings, the bones of his spine grinding against one another grotesquely. With agonizing slowness, Hope was lifted just enough from her muddy snare for her hooves to scratch out a slippery footing on the boulder. Her balance established, she bounded onto the land, kicking Barris a glancing but painful blow on the side of the head as she leapt.

*Exhale.*

Barris could not fall. He could not lose consciousness. Lucan was not out of danger. Blood poured from the gash on his scalp into his right eye, but he maintained his command of the power of his own life force, scrambled over to Phantom, and heaved the young man back onto the horse, balancing him and somehow summoning the presence of mind and dexterity to secure his binds once more. As he yanked the last knot tight, his vision clouded, and Barris knew that his moment of might and speed had come to an end, his power utterly spent.

"The Grove, Phantom. Get to the Grove, brave friend." Barris collapsed, his last thought a speculation as to whether Lucan was even still alive.

~

"Vicaris, a rider!" The student cleric turned abruptly from the group and rushed to the trail, sensing a horse and rider, though he could not touch the rider's consciousness.

The Vicaris had been lecturing the young aspiring members of the Order about the practical and ethical usage of the Sight, and heard Jerriah's cry of alarm before she herself sensed the approach. She stilled herself, closed her eyes briefly, and bowed her head. Her long silver hair flowed lightly in the breeze, the only indication that she was not a statue. The Vicaris listened with her bones, then opened her eyes again hurriedly, concern apparent on her aged features.

"Come, elves. Do not delay, to the trail." As one, the elven students turned to follow Jerriah with haste. The path curled somewhat beyond the tree line, so the mount and rider were not yet visible, but as Jerriah skidded to a halt and froze, there was no question that something approached, something that worried the young student a great deal.

"PHANTOM!" Jerriah turned back to his classmates and yelled, "It's Phantom! But...but no Barris!"

The great stallion walked up to Jerriah, and the student immediately began to untie the young blonde-haired man that was strapped to the saddle. Phantom stood motionless, ears flat against his head with anxiety. Jerriah's classmates approached, and together they laid the young man down on the trail. Once the boy was clear, Phantom immediately began to dance nervously. The Vicaris had just caught up to the scene; she laid her hand gently on the stallion's muzzle, and her concern instantly turned to shock. Without a word, the elderly elven woman vaulted atop the horse, and the pair broke south at a gallop.

Only a few seconds passed before the Vicaris and Phantom passed a lone riderless horse on the trail. The Vicaris sensed that this was Hope, friend to Phantom, and sent her will through the Bond to the mare, urging her with conveyed imagery to continue along the path to the spring that welled up to the northward in the center of the Grove. The Vicaris did not break pace, and raced down the trail just in time to see a bloody, staggering Barris climbing out of the brook. Barris saw Phantom, then the woman astride him, and stopped, awaiting her approach, his head sagging awkwardly, his arms hanging limply at his sides. The Vicaris helped the elven knight atop Phantom, and the trio turned back to the north.

"The boy," Barris croaked as Phantom drove the trail. "Does he live?"

"I sensed nothing, Barris. Quiet now, Knight, you are unwell."

Barris suppressed a cry and buried his head into the Vicaris' hair in sorrow as he clung to her. *So close*, he thought despondently. *So close.*

# XXII: THE PRAËR

ria wrapped herself tightly in her cloak, shuddering astride her bright white filly Sera. Her chill was unrelated to the crisp evening air. Aria, Captain Mikallis and her Mistress Pheonaris had made the Pinestroke, and what the young princess saw iced her to the core. The great wide swath of trees that marked the boundary between the Praër and the deep forests of Thornwood stood nearly lifeless, bereft of color, branches bare, needles wholly shed lying brown, dry and dead upon the ground. Aria had never seen anything so deeply unsettling.

Mikallis spoke first as the trio brought their mounts to a halt.

"Mistress, how can this be?"

Pheonaris did not immediately reply, struggling against her own sorrow. After a time, she spoke.

"Aria. What do you sense?"

Aria shook her head. "I...I cannot describe it, Mistress. Not death, not pain, but not unlike both. It is a horror. Perhaps that is the word. Horror."

Pheonaris nodded. "It is the same in my heart, Aria. Mikallis, do you sense it as well?"

The Captain thought for a moment. "I am not as well attuned to these things as you and Aria, Mistress. I feel...anger. Though it is from within, not without. Anger at whatever is causing this."

Pheonaris regarded the Captain. "It is precisely anger that is causing this, Captain. No, do not indulge in guilt. It is not your rage that is to blame; your anger is justified, and a proper reaction for a warrior. Yet there is as of yet no enemy at whom to direct that anger, Mikallis. I would caution you to disregard your rage, and learn what you may, so that when the time comes, you will be able to focus that anger at its proper target."

Mikallis nodded. "I understand, Mistress. I cannot but feel helpless, though. I do not know what is to be learned, nor what to listen for. I am impotent against this blight, and that inflames me."

Aria put her hand on the elf Captain's shoulder, and spoke gently. "We feel just as you do, Mikallis. Try to listen. You may hear something we do not."

Pheonaris smiled at the calming affect Aria had on Mikallis, and even on her own heart. *The young princess has a gift*, the Mistress considered. *Her very voice rides waves of harmony.* Pheonaris supposed, not for the first time, that the daughter of the elven Queen was properly named. The three sat atop their mounts silently for the space of a few turns as the light of day began to fade, and Aria was the first to break the silence.

"Mistress. I feel that we must not camp here. We must cross the Trine, and camp beyond the Praër."

Pheonaris nodded once, and wordlessly urged her sorrel colt, Spirit, forward. Aria and Sera followed, and Mikallis trailed the women. He and his own young stallion, a steel war steed named Triumph, assumed the rear guard. The riders passed beyond the gloom of the dying Pinestroke onto the rolling hills of the Praër, the name given to the vast clearing that dropped gradually yet unevenly over a distance of a mile toward the Trine Crossing. The Praër had been the site of many historical events for the elves of Thornwood; great battles and massive centennial festivals alike had been held here. The Trine was one of three natural boundaries that marked the lands of the elven people. To the east, the elven territory extended to the northern ranges of the Maw. To the west and north, no boundary existed, nor was any required, for the forests west were too dense and dangerous to be settled, and to the north, too few natural resources existed to make the conquest of the land worthwhile. The southernmost boundary was a long, narrow, winding brook just south of the Grove, a quarter cycle's ride south from the Praër, roughly where the legal border between Mor and Thornwood was drawn. The traditional southern boundary, however, was the Trine, for the elven people all lived north of it, where the land was tended pristinely and the life of the Wood was nurtured continuously, and the conscientious caretaking by the elven people contributed to create a land that tended and nurtured their people in return. The Rangers of Thornwood roamed the lands south of the Trine and north of the Grove, serving as a first line of defense against southern threats, and as a force of protection and order for the people of varying races and backgrounds that sought, for varying reasons, to live an isolated life in the wilds.

Aria had traveled the road between the Grove and the central communities of Thornwood repeatedly over the past twelve seasons. Her studies at the Grove and responsibilities of royalty frequently made the voyage necessary. In truth, those responsibilities had, in the past, been little more than ceremonial and traditional–attending weddings and funerals, and serving in various capacities during holidays and seasonal celebrations. That was as it would be until she earned her cloak in the Order this very season, and she assumed that even then, her duties would not change very much.

In her last trip north, only a cycle ago, she had seen that the Pinestroke was less healthy than usual. At first, it was believed that a mild disease had struck the trees, though no such disease had been found after extensive analysis. Less than thirty days before, when she had most recently passed this way, the condition of the trees was, to her knowledge, little more than a somewhat unpleasant ailment that would certainly be resolved soon. Yet now...a genuine blight, still of unknown origin, with no indications as to how far it might spread, or what it might ultimately portend.

Aria had never imagined that she, among all the elven people, would be a focal point in some vague and mysterious expedition to discover the nature of these forces that threatened the very world of Tahr. The slight blonde young woman did not fancy herself adventurous. Her life to this point had been remarkably carefree for the daughter of a Queen, and she had earned precisely zero experience in matters of great importance. *I am but a child*, she thought to herself, *a suckling babe compared to even the youngest leaders of our people.* Her observation was not an exaggeration. Her people could live for as long as a half millennium, and she carried less than a drop of knowledge when measured against to the vast wells of wisdom someone like Mistress Pheonaris possessed. Even a typical Ranger had lived a life more than five times the length of her own twenty-three years, and had surely witnessed events great and small that Aria had never even begun to imagine.

*I am placing too much importance on my place here*, she reminded herself, not for the first time. Over the past several days, Aria had wavered between two vastly differing notions. One was the idea that she was only a tiny piece of a greater puzzle, that she would most likely serve as no more than a carrier of a message to her people, a message she would somehow receive at the Grove. The message would be important, she believed, and she would be required to deliver it with precision and timeliness, but her role in this great evolving tale would end there. Her other notion frightened her, but seemed in her heart to be more likely. She, Aria Evanti, fledgling princess of Thornwood, would be instrumental in the struggle threatening her people–threatening all peoples–and she would not be up to the task. As soon as she would entertain that thought however, she felt...guilt. Shame. She felt that she must be arrogant beyond measure to think herself so important. *I am a child!* she exclaimed again silently. *If I were mature enough for this task, I would not even be thinking these thoughts!* Aria imagined that one who was truly essential to the safety of her people would not even begin to entertain such ideas. An elf of wisdom, Aria imagined, would ride to the Grove solemnly and await whatever knowledge or direction was to be given her, not waste her time in idle and fantastical speculation as to what her role would be.

Aria could not stop her mind from returning to the topic, however, no more than she could will herself to sleep while standing. The inexorable tide of daydreams and imagined scenes of abstract troubles would not relent, and she struggled continuously to not speak of them. *How foolish Pheonaris would consider me,* she thought. *Even Mikallis could not hide his derision.*

Mikallis. Now there was a topic she could think on that would distract her. The beautiful and brave elf was a dear friend to her, and more than once she had imagined what it would be like to have him hold her like a woman. She had been startled beyond speech when he declared, without asking permission, that he would accompany her on this journey. Such a thing was not done. Certainly not publicly, in a venue as grave as the last council. A part of her was flattered and flushed by the idea that the young Captain would risk such public humiliation on her behalf.

Another part of her, however, was appalled. It was not his place to speak so boldly. She cared deeply for Mikallis, and she did not lack a certain attraction to him, but she did not love him. Not in the way he would wish her to. And that was a thing she could not understand. She was physically attracted to the elf. His thick light brown hair, strong jaw, clear blue eyes, and muscular frame had turned the head of every unmarried elven woman under a century old, and some older. He was a serious sort, not quite brooding, but a bit dark, and when he spoke of anything, he spoke passionately. Aria had grown up alongside the young Captain—he was but a decade older than she, and he had been her most favorite elf for as long as she could remember. There was nothing they had not shared...well, next to nothing. The topic of romance had been a thing that they carefully avoided ever since Aria came of age, and despite the occasional awkward moment, the spark they felt for each other neither grew to a flame, nor caused them grief. Over the years they had settled into an easy and maturing friendship, one that only rarely threatened to become something more, and Aria loved the way things were. Mikallis made her feel safe, and beautiful, and cared for. He was more than pleasant to look at, even fantasize about. Yet she did not love him.

He loved her, though, she knew. If she had not known that before, she did now. No elf would speak as he did at the council otherwise. Aria could not say why she did not love her friend in return. She could scarcely define what love was, though she knew she had never been in it. The only thing she knew for certain was that after his declaration at the council, things between them would change. The day would come, perhaps soon, when Mikallis would make an even more bold declaration, and Aria would be forced to tell her dear friend, with no good cause, that his feelings were not shared.

She felt dishonorable. Wicked. How could she have allowed him to become so close to her over the years, when her instincts told her that he would someday want more than friendship? She knew the answer. She could not bear to lose his friendship, and the fantasy of him was a sweet thing she selfishly clung to, an inadequate substitute for real, passionate love. Aria fell into despair and shame as she thought more on the matter, and suddenly the idea of the world of Tahr coming to a violent end did not seem like the worst thing that could happen.

The three crossed the Trine without incident, and left the Praër of Thornwood behind them just as the Twins crested the horizon to the east. Pheonaris instructed them to make camp just off the trail, and they shared a meal of cheeses, breads, and berries, deciding that the disruption to the environment caused by a campfire was not necessary. They spoke of lighter things, sharing stories of travels past, and Pheonaris taught them a bit about the early history of the elven people, when the Airies, the Stone Elves, and their own people shared a community. When they had completed their meal, Mikallis bade the two elven women goodnight respectfully, with a slightly more exaggerated bow to Aria, and retired to his tent. The two women crawled into theirs.

Aria lay awake for most of the night, crying silently like a babe lost in the woods. Sleep came to the young woman in fits and starts, stippled with nightmares and dark emotions. She had just shaken herself free of another unpleasant dream when Pheonaris threw off her own blanket, pulled on her boots and reached for Aria. The Mistress' voice was commanding and terse.

"Tend the horses." Pheonaris threw the flap of the tent aside and raced to awaken the sleeping Captain. Aria did not delay in rushing behind the Mistress, immediately sending her consciousness to her Bond as she fastened her own boots, silently sending thoughts of peace and comfort to Sera. The princess did not know what threatened, but she knew that Pheonaris was not easily unnerved.

The three were protectively hovering near their mounts when the first jolt struck, a sharp convulsion coming from beneath them, as if a great fist had struck upwards from the center of the world. Aria's feet left the ground; she landed in a crouch just as the land bucked a second time, and a third. After but a few moments it felt as if the very ground was trying to beat them all to death. Mikallis strained to hold the reins of the horses, the ground beneath him bouncing him about mercilessly. Only Pheonaris was able to keep her feet; the Mistress' bent legs rode the tremors rhythmically. Aria could just make out her arms rising upward to the skies as the Mistress of the Druids of the Grove inhaled deeply and began to chant.

"Da, Nü perra ha na tahri. Da, Nü perra ha na tahri. Da, Nü perra ha na tahri." *Father, your power to the Land.*

A translucent golden glow, the color of morning sunlight, flashed from the hands of the Druid as she clapped them together above her, extending like a shimmering dome over the companions and their mounts. It rose to for several feet, then fell around them protectively– a barrier of sorts, Aria decided–and in an instant, the violent shaking no longer affected them. Silence and tranquility extended in a radius just large enough to envelop the elves and their horses. The quake had not yet relented, and as Aria and Mikallis got to their feet, and the horses glanced around them nervously, they could see through the protective veil a great rending, a tear in Tahr itself opening raggedly from just north of their camp, to and through the Trine a thousand paces away. While they could not hear it, the impression of a rushing wave of water was felt by all three. The pounding from the depths of Tahr stopped as suddenly as it began, but Pheonaris continued to hold the barrier, her concentration fierce. Her eyes met Aria's, and the young princess knew what was needed.

Bracing her hands on Pheonaris' shoulders, Aria sought deep within herself and located her own reservoir of life, calling upon it to strengthen her Mistress, though she did not yet see to what end. The Link was a thing practiced often in her training at the Grove; though it had never been required of her in more than an academic setting, Aria did not doubt that she could maintain the link until her life force was utterly spent.

Mikallis watched the women in awe as he used his Bond to comfort their horses. The golden dome around them thickened, and a great wave of yellow and brown water broke against it, sizzling and boiling as it sought entrance to their sanctuary, the odor of boiled mud the only intrusion into their protective bubble. The current was exceptionally fast and violent, carrying broken trees, stone, and even game animals with it. The detritus bounced off the dome harmlessly as Pheonaris and Aria held their enchantment, the water rushing over their position. The wave slowed, then stopped, and Mikallis believed the torrent would soon recede meekly...but then it reversed itself, coming back towards them from the south at nearly the same speed, bringing with it an endless murk of soil, brush, and drowning wildlife.

After a time that none of the three could measure, the surge of river and death slowed and fell back into the rent in the land, the lethality of the event passing, leaving Pheonaris and Aria dripping in sweat and trembling from their efforts. The Mistress and the princess both fell to their knees, and shin-deep muddy water rushed in to meet them. Mikallis released his concentration on the Bond– the horses were spooked but out of danger–and rushed to support Aria. She waved him off, knowing that Pheonaris needed him more.

Mikallis helped the Mistress to her feet, and as she stood unsteadily in the thickening mud, she commanded Mikallis, "Help me mount. Lead us from here. We must find a trail before the horses are mired."

Aria and Mikallis helped Pheonaris onto Spirit, then led their own horses on foot. The light of day had broken at some point during the flood, and though their bearings had been shaken loose, the way south was not difficult to find. The trail, however, proved much more elusive.

More than once, Aria and Mikallis got stuck to some degree, though the horses instinctively maintained a momentum that prevented them from sinking into the muck. On they plodded, through the wet, cold sludge of mud and debris, helpless to assist the countless small animals that struggled to free themselves. Pheonaris sat in her saddle upright, though Aria could tell she was not present. She appeared much as she had during the council, and the princess was certain she was in the throes of another vision. Aria's strength was fading fast when they finally ascended a small rise that had remained above the water line. The three crested the knoll, and twenty paces south, the trail mercifully appeared again. Aria and Mikallis hugged wordlessly in relief, and mounted their horses.

Pheonaris spoke weakly, her attention returned to the moment. "I am proud of you, Aria Evanti and Mikallis Elmshadow. Your composure protected us."

Mikallis dismissed the honor. "We would be drowned and lost forever without your power, Mistress. It was you who saved us."

Pheonaris smiled. "Well, if credit must be given for power, it is the First Father to whom we must give thanks." Aria and Mikallis nodded their agreement, and Pheonaris smiled humbly. "Though I will admit, the dome was not a terrible idea."

Aria laughed, the musical tone of her mirth somehow both inappropriate and timely. "No, not terrible, Mistress. And

Mikallis...how you kept those horses calm I will never know. Excellent work, Captain." Aria bowed graciously in the saddle.

Mikallis did not share the lighthearted mood of the women. "We survived. Many did not."

Aria shriveled, but Pheonaris' tone remained cheerful. "You speak with wisdom, Captain," agreed Pheonaris. "But let us not forget to be grateful to one another, and to celebrate that we yet live."

Mikallis nodded silently as they turned onto the trail, unfazed by the druid's attempt to find a bright side. They rode slowly, silently for a turn, then Pheonaris called the halt.

"Let us stop a moment." The three riders turned their mounts to face one another.

"Aria. Last evening, you said you had foreseen this."

Aria frowned, confused, and then recalled her unmistakable sense that they must cross the Trine and camp south of the Praër. "I...I would not say that I foresaw anything, Mistress. I suppose I merely felt uncomfortable within the Pinestroke."

"Was that all, Aria? Think, now."

Aria concentrated on recalling the feeling of the night before, a hint of...something...flowing just beneath the surface of her understanding. She could not give words to it, but she knew her feeling had been more than simple discomfort. Yes, she decided, there was something there. Something...ah, it was no use, her mind was a mess, and she could not focus.

"No, Mistress. It was not merely discomfort. But I cannot tell you what it was, only that it was not that. I am sorry I cannot be more helpful, I suppose I am not quite myself just yet. I will think more on it."

The Mistress nodded, and continued. "I spent a considerable amount of time in communion with the land this morning, as you must have noticed. I am sorry I was not more help in finding the trail, but my attention was required elsewhere." Mikallis and Aria listened. "I will not dissemble to you now. The quake of this morning is but a taste of what is to come. Understand me, just a *small* taste. This quake was felt from north of our homes to the Morline, to the deeps of Belgorne and west to the farmlands. Consider that. I am also reasonably certain that the Fang has awakened to some extent...and this was just a shadow of what is to come." Pheonaris paused to be certain that the gravity of her statement had settled in. The look of horror on Aria's face and the young Captain's frozen expression made clear that it had. "You have never expressed an ability to sense future events, Aria, have you? No, I did not think so. Yet the power of this event was sufficient to awaken that ability within you. To some degree, at least. It has also awakened something within me, and I tell you that we must make the Grove within three days. I cannot tell you why. I only know that at dawn, three days from now, you are due at the Grove, Aria."

Aria and Mikallis exchanged a look. The Captain spoke first.

"Mistress, I will do whatever is required of me without complaint. But this is not possible. It is six days at a hurried pace to the Grove. We have no food. We have no water. We will need to forage, and allow the horses to graze. Three days...Mistress, it cannot be done."

Pheonaris' usually gentle voice rang with an air of authority. "Do you mean to tell me Captain that there is none who can sustain such a pace? Because if so, I will tell you frankly that you are mistaken."

Mikallis reddened, but did not speak. Aria interjected.

"There is one, Mistress. Sir Barris. None other. Not without Phantom's endurance."

"It is not Phantom's endurance that makes such things possible,

Aria. You should know this."

Aria knew she was missing something, but she could only shake her head in response. "I lack your wisdom on the matter, Mistress. Forgive me."

"It is not a matter of wisdom, Aria. It is a matter of logic. Phantom is a great beast, perhaps the greatest living example of his kind today. Yet he is a horse. You must know this, do you not? Ah, I can see that you both are lost. Aria and Mikallis, hear me. It is through great personal sacrifice that Sir Barris impels Phantom to run as he does, without rest, without food, and when necessary, without water. It is the Bond, and the force of life that Sir Barris pours into that Bond that enables Phantom to endure as he does. Yet the knight does even more. Sir Barris does not merely offer what part of himself is required to accomplish this. He freely gives well beyond what is required, so that Phantom does not only succeed in such feats, but thrives upon them. That is why the pair are so renowned. That is why Phantom would run over the very lip of the Fang for his rider. Sir Barris has forfeited *years* of his life on this last circuit to Mor alone. Do not mistake me, Phantom is unique among horses. But Sir Barris is unique among elves, not in his power, but in his sacrifice."

As if on cue, Mikallis and Aria, in unison, honored the absent knight.

"Nü glahr ni, Sir Barris."

"Indeed," replied Pheonaris. "Though if you truly wish to honor Barris, you will not allow his sacrifices to be in vain. You will follow his example, and you will use your own Bonds to make this journey possible. There is no other way." She turned to Mikallis. "Captain, you are here voluntarily, and if you do not wish to risk—"

Mikallis placed his hand on his heart and straightened. "I will do as required, Mistress, with gladness in my heart, in service to my people."

"To all peoples, Captain. Thank you for your oath, I would expect nothing less. You are an Elmshadow." Pheonaris turned her attention to her novice. "Aria, I will not ask. You are the Princess of Thornwood, daughter of the queen, heir to the Seat of the Wood and ordained Druid of the Grove. Your path is determined by an authority greater than my own."

Aria felt herself strengthened by her Mistress' use of her titles. "You need not ask, Mistress. Though I must ask, how do I accomplish this? I am not so experienced with the Bond, not so much as you or Mikallis."

"You will learn, Princess. As will you, Captain. You must learn quickly. We will ride slowly until midday to allow our mounts to put the morning's horrors behind us, and I will answer what questions you have, but at noon, we will break south at speed, and we will ride until we make the Grove. We will do this because we must, and we will not fail."

Without another word, Pheonaris urged Spirit forward at a trot, and her younger companions followed. Aria kept her questions to herself for the time being, sensing that her silence was required for the moment. She could not, however, prevent her mind from turning over with anxieties.

*I* am *the Princess of Thornwood*, she thought. *I* am *an ordained Druid. And I will try, Father help me, but I will try.* Aria did not allow herself to further indulge her deepest fears, however. For in her deepest, weary heart, she believed sincerely that she could not accomplish what was asked, that she would die on this journey, and she would fail her Mistress; she would fail her people.

*I am but a child.*

# XXIII: THE MORLINE

ou talk pretty, Mister J'arn, but don't yeh come…hey, Wolf! What're yeh doin'? Get over here!"

Wolf decided quickly that Mister J'arn was just his sort of person. The dwarven prince made eye contact with the animal, and that was sufficient invitation for Wolf to bound towards him and begin a thorough investigation of the scents residing in the dwarf's most intimate areas. J'arn danced around to avoid the probing nose of the curious black beast, doing his best to remain stoic, but the laughter of his dwarves was too hearty to ignore. Within moments, the eight dwarves and one previously terrified gnome were laughing themselves into fits, as Wolf began barking and jumping at the prince, finally discovering a pocket that contained some morsel of uneaten food. Two of the three sentries of the Morline post joined the gathering, one announcing that dinner was about to be served. Wolf perked at the man's announcement, and despite a breeze coming from the north, somehow sensed that just beyond the crossing south, there was more promise than what was contained in J'arn's pockets. He took off at a run for the bridge.

"Come eat with us, little lady," offered Boot. "Ye can tell us all about why ye be out here in the woods of the Maw all by yerself."

*This is the help Lady Sandshingle promised*, Shyla was certain. She would not, however, put her guard down, not just yet.

"I'm little, Mister, and I'm a lady, but I ain't no little lady. That said, I could sure use a bit t'eat, if yeh'll have me."

J'arn interjected with a smile. "If your wolf has left any for the rest of us, ye be welcome to it. Come then."

~

The dwarves and men ate and drank with Shyla and Wolf, a filling meal of roasted fowl, boiled cabbage and sour loaves of bread. The thick, sweet scent of cooked fats mingled with pungent, steaming sprouts and burning wood, the aromas, to Shyla, redolent of home. J'arn insisted that Shyla eat her fill before being compelled to speak of her journey. The abundance of food brought the gnome her fill quickly, and as she sat and listened to the merry crew laughing and telling stories around the fire, she could not help but think about her family, and G'naath, and all she had left behind. A melancholy had nearly taken hold when Boot belched to shatter stone, and the dwarves offered their own gastric symphony in refrain.

Shyla was fairly certain one of the dwarves used a different instrument, and upon the realization, could not remain sullen. She giggled and stamped her feet in silly abandon, and the more she laughed, the less able she was to stop herself. The whole of the camp caught the contagion, including J'arn, and soon the usually solemn dwarf was laughing himself breathless beside her, cheeks darkening visibly despite his thick beard and the low firelight. Wolf, now full to popping and exhausted, glanced around dramatically at the dozen hysterical humans and wandered into the darkness, doubtlessly seeking a place of sanity where he could nap. The sight of the exasperated animal sent Shyla further into stitches, and she nearly laughed herself unconscious.

J'arn spoke when he finally caught his breath. "Lady, your

laughter is a melody. I have never heard such a thing." He smiled warmly at the gnome, and she smiled back.

"Shyla, Mister J'arn, yeh can call me Shyla. Shyla Greykin is me name." The dwarves and men quieted, sensing that this was the moment that they would hear the young gnome's tale.

Boot jumped in. "Well, ye know J'arn already, Shyla. I'm Kelgarr, though I s'pose the lot of ye can call me Boot now that we've shared a meal. This here's Narl and his brother Fannor." The brothers raised their mugs respectfully. "There be Jender, Starl, and Sergeant Turnn, but ye can just call him Rocks. And that sneaky lookin' fella over there be our illustrious forgemaster, Garlan. Ye be watchin' yerself around that one."

"Stuff it, Boot," Garlan retorted.

"Stuff it yerself, Garlan. Anyways Lady, ah, miss Shyla, that be our company. Now, the fine men here who have so kindly shared a meal with us, I know the Captain Marion, but his men..."

The Captain sensed his cue. "Aha! Thank you Boot! My dear bearded friend! I am your host, Captain Marion," the uniformed man stood and took a poorly balanced bow, "and these are my vennerade...my estimaded...ah, Fury, this is Mark and Ed."

The men laughed, and one spoke. "Privates Marcus Wellis and Edward Kalson, Lady, at your service."

"Hah! You said privates!" the Captain jeered.

"How's that moonjuice, Cap?" kidded Narl.

"Tip top, Nerl! Tip top!" The Captain sat back on his log–or rather, fell gently.

J'arn smiled and shook his head at the sloshed watch commander, and looked back to Shyla. "Well, ye know us now, Miss Shyla," he said, "or at least ye do a bit. Now I have to ask, what is a young gnomish girl and her...wolf...doing this far from G'naath? And, ah, forgive me for askin', but...how young *are* ye?"

Shyla felt all eyes on her, but did not blanch. Her trial felt like a lifetime ago, though she did not forget how vulnerable she had felt then. This did not begin to compare. "I'm twenty and three, Mister J'arn. And yer how old? Yeh look a bit young t'be leadin' an expedition, though I don't know much about dwarves, t'be fair."

J'arn did not quail, either. "I've got twenty-three years as well, Miss Shyla. And ye speak true, I be young for the job," J'arn raised his mug and motioned at his company, "but these here are the best dwarves in Belgorne, and with these fine companions, the job ain't more than a nature walk." The dwarves quietly raised their mugs to J'arn in kind, grateful for the honor.

Shyla continued. "Well, me tale's a long one, and I'll not be thinkin' yeh'll wanna hear all of it, but the short of it is, I been sent to find the Grove, and meet with the elves, and there I'm s'posed to be learnin' from their elders or some such. My grandmama sent me, and so that's where I'll be goin'." She paused to gauge the reaction of J'arn and his dwarves.

"The Grove," J'arn replied. "Miss Shyla, do ye know how far the Grove is?"

"Shyla be fine, Mister J'arn. Don't need no 'miss' in front."

"Then I'll not need a Mister. J'arn will do fine as well. But do ye know?"

Shyla considered how best to reply, and decided on the truth, or at least some of it. "Mist...ah, J'arn, I do not. Me grandmama Lady Sandshingle said I'd find help when I got meself to the Morline, and that was good enough fer me."

"Sandshingle!" exclaimed Boot. "Ye be Cindra Sandshingle's kin?"

Shyla cocked her head, stunned by Boot's recognition. "I am, sir."

"Well why didn't ye say so! J'arn, ye'll be knowing of the Lady Sandshingle, will ye not?"

J'arn shook his head. Boot continued. "Well, my little friend, ye'll have to forgive our prince. He's not yet heard every story there is to tell, but don't let that fool ye. He's a sharp one, and a Silverstone, and that's enough."

Boot told the tale, as he had heard it, of Cindra Sandshingle and her single-handed magical defeat of an entire tribe of goblins. The telling did not differ much from Shyla's version, and she said as much when Boot finished.

"The only part yeh got wrong was that when she went before the goblin king or prince or whatever he was, the wrinkled old fool didn't come after 'er with his staff. The coward tossed it up in the air and hid behind his chair, bawlin' like a drownin' goat, as they say. The Lady caught it, walked right outta the tunnel, not sayin' a darned thing to no one, and brought it back to th' Elders, sayin', 'yeh ain't got yerselfs a goblin problem no more'."

"Hah! She did not!" cried Boot.

"She did, and the way me Mama tells it, that *was* the last time we had a goblin problem, and that's a fact."

The dwarves raised their mugs and toasted the Lady riotously, and Shyla raised her own. Though her drink was already sweet enough, a delightful mixture of unfermented berry juices, it tasted all the sweeter knowing that it was in honor of her grandmama.

J'arn spoke when the voices died down. "Shyla Greykin, if ye are to see the elves, and are to be learning their ways, should I take that to mean that ye have magic of sorts?"

Shyla's expression remained serious, and she did not answer immediately. She was afraid now; afraid that her secret would alienate her from her new friends, afraid that they would shun her as her own people did. As she looked into J'arn's eyes however, she did not sense fear. Nor hatred. Only wonder, and perhaps...admiration? She suppressed the urge to dig deeper, to read into the thoughts and feelings of the dwarven prince, deciding that while it might be prudent to do so before speaking next, she would not violate this good dwarf so.

"I do, Prince J'arn. And I hope that won't make yeh hate me, nor yer company. But it is what it is, and I won't lie to yeh."

J'arn nodded, and the campsite grew silent. "One more question, Shyla. Why are ye alone?"

Shyla refused to let shame surface. She straightened and looked the prince directly in the eye, unblinking. "Lady Sandshingle weren't understood nor loved overmuch by me people, Prince J'arn. And I ain't exactly the favored daughter of G'naath meself. But I am favored by me Lady Sandshingle, and me papa and mama, and if that be good enough fer me, it'll have to be good enough for any."

Prince J'arn returned the gnomish woman's gaze, meeting her pink eyes. *So childlike*, he thought, but this was no child. The young gnome seemed to J'arn to be a complete contradiction. Small in stature, a head shorter than a dwarf, yet a spirit larger than life. Her demeanor had been somehow simultaneously wary and bold since their first meeting. Her pigtailed, bright auburn hair and freckled features lent her visage the personification of innocence, yet when she spoke, her words carried a dwarven sturdiness, and a surprising maturity. Surprising, because J'arn had traded with gnomes, and had listened attentively as his father treated with them. Before now, they had seemed to him like children, naive and temperamental, possessed of a certain narrowmindedness; not unpleasant, but less sophisticated and civil. Yet J'arn had to admit to himself that he had never known a gnome, not personally, and his sentiments were born of the natural suspicion of the foreign and unknown, rather than formed by any real experience.

No real enmity existed between the dwarven and gnomish peoples, aside from an occasional trade dispute or quarrel over hunting grounds, but a certain mistrust had survived even the centuries of uneasy peace between the races. Stories persisted of days when gnomes and orcs and trolls made common cause, often against the dwarven people. Those days were long gone, but when the last major treaty of peace had been drawn, a major tenet was that the leaders of the two races would severely punish any who broke the peace, whether with swords or provocative confrontations. The result was a forced tolerance, rather than a true alliance. In time, the old hatreds gave way to more pressing issues, then to common interests, and eventually to a tenuous forbearance toward one another, but no real friendship had taken hold. The dwarves of the present lived in a state of peaceful competition with the gnomes, their people segregated by many miles of stone and soil. The reclusive and geographically isolated gnomes relied on the dwarves as trading partners with the rest of the civilized world, and the dwarves relied on the gnomes for the gemstones and crafting materials they provided. They would bargain and haggle furiously, and tempers would sometimes flare, though any major disputes were quickly settled between royal envoys in the interests of peace, most often with both sides leaving the negotiations dissatisfied.

J'arn decided that perhaps that was the source of his opinions about gnomes; it was those heated negotiations he had witnessed that made up the majority of his contact with their people. It occurred to him then, as he listened to Shyla speak of herself and the love of her family with pride and self-assurance, that perhaps in his limited experience he had misjudged the gnomish people. Or, perhaps, this young gnome was unlike other gnomes. Perhaps both. J'arn became aware that his reaction was required, and that not Shyla nor dwarf nor man would speak until he had responded to the young woman before him. He also became self-consciously mindful of the fact that he had been staring at Shyla in silence for an uncomfortably long period of time, so he promptly returned to the matter at hand.

"Ye speak as a Lady of honor, Shyla Greykin. I and my company will honor ye as such." He turned to his company, considering his next words for a brief moment, then turned back to the strong and pretty gnomish woman.

"We seek the Grove ourselves, Shyla Greykin, and I know it to be true that we are the help Lady Sandshingle promised ye. It cannot be otherwise. Ye may accompany us to the Grove, if ye would, and we shall protect ye as one of our own."

A cheer rose from behind J'arn, his dwarves and even the men clearly fond of the young woman, and Shyla could not help but blush as the prince continued to look at her. *Well, I canna just stare back at the feller like a damnable fool*, she thought.

"I dunno what yer all cheerin' for, I didn't even say as I'd go with yeh drunken fools yet!" Her wide, toothy smile left no doubt, however, as the dwarves all fell into laughter. Boot leaned in to whisper at J'arn.

"Wipe yer beard, me prince." Boot clapped his friend on the back.

~

The night ended with most of J'arn's company falling into slumber where they sat as the stories ended and the moonjuice ran low. The men had prepared a tent for Shyla, and she awoke to the sound of Wolf barking and axes hacking wood. Daylight was already well established despite a thin overcast, and as she left her tent she saw the dwarves and men scurrying about under the volatile direction of Boot. The first of two rafts was already assembled, and a second was well on its way.

"Well, good afternoon, there, Lady Shyla!" greeted Captain Marion warmly, with a hint of playful sarcasm. "I didn't know gnomes slept so soundly–you missed the tahrquake! Or did you keep watch all night, protecting us from the dangers of the Maw?"

Shyla grimaced at the Captain. "Well it sure weren't yer drunken self wardin' off the orcs and trolls!" she said in return.

"Hah! You wound me, Lady. And after I prepared your tent with such care and reverence."

"Ah, don't yeh be wounded, Cap'n, I just tend to sleep a bit late is all. And what's a tar quake?"

"It's when the world shakes a bit. Sometimes they can be bad, other times..."

"Ah, yeh mean a stonecracker! I slept through that?" she asked, astounded.

"It wasn't much of one, Lady Shyla, no need to be alarmed. Must have been centered pretty far away."

Shyla was a bit worried for her family, but if she slept through it... "Well, what can I be doin' fer help? I'm a fair cook, if yer men be needin' lunch."

"It is not yet near noon, Lady, I jest. Feel free to wash and tend to yourself." Captain Marion bowed politely. "I'll need to excuse myself and return to helping Boot, or he'll have my head with that axe of his."

Boot bellowed on cue. "Ye be right about that, Cap! Shyla, get this animal o' yours out from underfoot! Dammit, Garlan, ye hacked that one too short!" Boot continued to holler and dictate orders, and even Prince J'arn seemed to scurry when he pointed.

Shyla called for Wolf, and walked down to the river, searching for a private place to wash her body and clothes. The freezing water invigorated her, and she had just enough beesoap remaining to lather Wolf a bit, since the animal desperately needed an improvement of odor. Shyla wrung out her wet clothing and dressed in her last clean pants and tunic, energized and enthusiastic for what the day would bring.

By midday the rafts had been completed, and Shyla marveled at the amount of work done in such a short period of time. The dwarves and men sat around the camp, shirtless and covered in sweat despite the cool air, and ate a quick meal of leftover fowl and cheeses that Shyla had helped prepare. The gnome could not help but notice the strong builds of the dwarves, all muscular and meaty, the most sculpted of which was J'arn. The prince caught her eye as she was assessing the finer points of his physique, and she turned away quickly to busy herself elsewhere.

"Ye can stop flexin' those spindly little arms of yours, my Prince, she ain't lookin' over here no more."

J'arn turned to Boot and regarded him severely. "Another word like that, Kelgarr, and ye'll be takin' night watch for the duration of the journey."

"Bah, Fury I will, J'arn, ye know damned well I'd fall right asleep. But I'll behave. She ain't unpleasant to look at though, is she?"

J'arn sighed. "She's pleasant enough, Boot. But yer wife wouldn't wanna hear ye say it, and ye be too old to make such an observation."

"Aye, ye speak true. Though tell me Prince, yer wife...what's her name again?"

"Ye said ye'd behave, Boot."

"Ahhh, that's right, ye ain't *got* a wife yet. Mistaken I was, I tend to forget at my age. Hmph."

Boot elbowed the prince as he stood, his meal finished, and J'arn threw out a foot to trip him as he walked away. Boot nimbly jumped it without missing a stride, and strutted away confidently.

"Maybe I'm not so rickety as ye think, J'arn! Ha!"

The dwarves completed their meal and began to pack their gear, and Shyla gathered her few supplies and reorganized her pack. Before an hour had passed, the eight dwarves had carried the two rafts to the bank of the Mor, moored them, and turned to say goodbye to their hosts.

Garlan addressed the men. "Captain, Marcus and Edward, ye have been a great help to us. Thank ye much." He shook the men's hands, and the dwarves all followed suit. Boot nudged J'arn and spoke quietly enough to not be overheard.

"Like he's the one to be thankin' 'em on our behalf. Presumptuous turd, ain't he?"

J'arn eyed Boot. "If he overstepped, Boot, it'd be my toes he stepped over, and I take no offense. Nor should ye."

Boot snorted but did not respond.

"Well, my bearded friends, it's been a pleasure," Captain Marion said. "And the same to you, Lady Shyla. I hope ya make the Grove in one piece, or no more than nine in any case."

"Nine would be ideal, Captain," said J'arn.

"Ten!" Shyla cried.

"Ten?" Boot asked.

"What about Wolf? C'mon wolf! Time t'go fer a ride!" Her companion hurried to her side and sat obediently.

"Ah, for Fury's sake, J'arn, I gotta ride on a raft for three days with that furbeast?"

Shyla glared at Boot threateningly.

"Well, as ye like, Boot," J'arn replied. "Ye can ride with me, Shyla, Wolf, and Rocks, or ye can ride with—"

"Aye, me prince. No need to get nasty. We'll be best o' friends, won't we, Wolf?"

Wolf cocked his head, unsure.

"Load up, dwarves of Belgorne!" J'arn exclaimed. "We sail!"

A process that should have been as easy as walking onto the rafts and dropping the lines became a disaster when Wolf realized he would be expected to sit submissively on the unstable, floating wooden log-thing. An hour later, all eight dwarves, one gnome, and one furbeast soaked to the core in river water, Wolf was finally too exhausted to further resist embarkation. The two rafts were unmoored and the ten travelers drifted slowly west.

"Captain?" Marcus asked.

"Yes, Wellis?"

"Does that girl really think that crazy pup is a wolf?"

"I think so, Wellis."

"Well why doesn't anyone tell her?" asked Edward.

"Why didn't you, Kalsen?"

"Are you kidding? That's one feisty little gnome. Didn't wanna make her mad," he replied.

"Well, there ya go." The captain smirked. "Me neither."

# XXIV: MOR

en seasons before the dwarves boarded their Morline rafts, as the last days of the unusually long and harsh winter gave way to the first hints of spring, Mila climbed the stairs of the Keep of Kehrlia, arriving at the door to Sartean's personal library hours before dawn. She knocked once, and received no reply. After several moments, she reached to knock again...

"Enter."

Mila smiled. *Always the posturing*, she thought, and entered the library.

"Why do you disturb me, Miss Felsin?" Sartean asked icily. He sat behind his desk reading, not troubling to glance up at the sorceress.

"Forgive my intrusion at the late hour, Master. I have news."

Sartean waited. Mila smiled amiably.

"Shall I await a messenger for this news, or have you brought it yourself? Perhaps it is a written message, hidden on your person?" Sartean looked the sorceress up and down. Her sheer gown clung to her flesh snugly. "If so, I do not know where you might have hidden it."

Mila laughed demurely. "Oh Master, you are so *lewd*." She continued to smile wryly as Sartean frowned at her irreverent comment. "But my news. I have abandoned my efforts to synthesize the phenarril plant as futile. It cannot be done." She paused, standing straight, chin out, back arched, her smile plastered on like a mannequin's.

Sartean raised an eyebrow, and stood slowly. "Yet you stand there grinning, so I can only assume that you have gone mad with the terror of how I will react."

"Oh, certainly not!" Mila said cheerfully. "On the contrary, I think you will be quite pleased."

"Enough, Mila." Sartean's tone darkened. "Tell me why you are here."

Mila sighed dramatically. "Oh, Master Sartean! Will you not allow me my fun? I have toiled for two years and have found your solution. May I not present it with a bit of flair? Indulge me just a bit more, will you please?" she said sweetly.

Sartean froze his expression, masking his emotions entirely. "A moment more then, Miss Felsin. Continue."

"With your permission, Master, I would prefer to show you. Would you accompany me to the labs?"

"Come here, Miss Felsin."

The sorceress walked around the desk obediently. Sartean grasped her hand, and they appeared instantaneously in the second floor laboratory, beside Mila's work area. The only light in the room came from a glowing blue orb of energy, slightly larger than a human head, hovering and wobbling a hand's breadth above her immaculately clean stone alchemy bench. She stepped before it and turned to Sartean.

"Your solution, Master," she motioned to the orb.

"What is it?"

"Not what, precisely Master, but closer to *where*. You will know that phenarril grows only beneath Fang's rim, and has never been found elsewhere."

Sartean rolled his eyes. "Yes, of course. I do not require a summary of the problem. I require a solution."

Mila lost her ability to pretend at cheerfulness, and decided just to get on with it. "Of course. Despite extensive search efforts, we have not located another source, and I have not been able to even get close to synthesizing an artificial version of the plant. Nor its extract. I have spent the last two years beating my head against this cursed table, and a cycle ago, I decided that I was asking the wrong question."

"Clearly. And what is the right question?"

"The *right* question, Master, is not *why* I cannot synthesize the plant. It is not *how* I might synthesize the plant, or its extract. The right question is, under what conditions will phenarril grow? In other words, *where*."

"And the answer?" Sartean was growing impatient.

"Anywhere I damned well please, Master, provided that I create the right conditions. So, I sent an apprentice to the rim to obtain air samples, and–"

"An apprentice? You did not obtain my permission."

"No, Master, I did not. Yet I sent him nonetheless, and he returned with several flasks of air from the rim, and a few minor burns, but nothing he won't survive." She eyed the wizard briefly to demonstrate that no, she did *not* fear him as much as he would like her to, and continued. "I have analyzed the air from the rim, Master, and while I cannot synthesize phenarril, I am certainly a sufficient master of the elements to combine the correct quantities of gases, particles, temperatures and light to create an environment equal to that which exists in the air that vents from the volcano. I have done so, and I have planted and grown a sprig of phenarril, right here in the lab, and I present it to you now."

With a flourish of her delicate fingers and a barely audible whisper, Mila evaporated the protective bubble of energy. In her hands, she held a healthy young violet phenarril, just mature enough to harvest a few drops of extract from. She placed it in the open right palm of her Master.

Sartean beheld the plant, and examined it. Its delicate yellow roots lacked any soil or even dampness, yet the stem was whole and the leaves a robust, vibrant purple, almost translucent, like a living amethyst, with thin white lines along edges of the broad round leaves.

"Will the extract's properties be consistent?"

Mila slid her hand between her breasts, into her gown, and removed a small clear vial with only a few droplets of fluid suspended within.

"You hold one of three identical plants that were conceived on the same day last cycle, Master. The first I have already milked, and analyzed its nectar. It is identical in composition and potency to the extract in our stores. This," she wiggled the vial, "is the extract from the second. I can test it now, if you like. I have prepared the reagents."

Sartean smiled savagely, and reached his left hand towards Mila's face. His middle finger traced a line from the center of her forehead and brushed aside a wisp of hair that had fallen into her eyes. His fingers drew a course down her cheek, resting beneath her smooth chin, and lifted it gently to his face. He leaned in intimately, close enough to feel the sorceress' sweet breath cease, and whispered.

"You have done well, Mila Felsin." The wizard's dark eyes held Mila's. She returned the stare, a hint of a tremble on her red lips her only expression.

Sartean withdrew. Mila exhaled.

"If you believe it consistent, then I will accept that as fact. The more important question remains. Can this be done at scale?"

Mila was looking forward to this question.

"I have already trained a team of four wizards to duplicate my efforts, Master. In a week, I could create a squarefield of this environment and begin planting."

Sartean laughed mirthlessly. "A team of four, and a squarefield?" he mocked.

"Well, yes, Master, for the quantities I assume you want."

"You assume much, Miss Felsin. Tell me, how much phenarril extract is required for a single day's dose of your flightfluid?"

"Approximately ten drops, Master."

"Yes. And how many drops will a mature phenarril plant yield?"

"Roughly twice that much, Master. Twenty drops, give or take."

"And how long is the life cycle, from planting to maturation?"

Mila began to redden. "Well, full maturity Master, most of a season, but that is only an estimate–"

"Yes. It is only that. But let us assume it is accurate. How many plants, Miss Felsin, do you believe can be grown in a squarefield?"

Mila was prepared for this as well. "The phenarril plant requires a bit of room to grow well, Master. No portion of it may grow under shadow. A conservative estimate is fifty thousand plants."

"Fifty thousand. Tell me, Miss Felsin, how many plants would be needed to sustain one person with a dose per day for one year?"

Mila did the math. "Three hundred thirty-six days in a year, one plant per two and one-half doses...that would be one hundred sixty-eight, Master."

"One hundred sixty-eight. Four growing seasons, bringing the annual yield of a squarefield to two hundred thousand plants, assuming your environmental experiment works at scale, which would roughly approximate four hundred thousand doses."

"Master, many would not survive continued usage for so long."

"How many people live in Mor, Miss Felsin?"

Mila froze. Sartean blinked slowly, awaiting her reply. "A quarter of a million, perhaps?"

"Over three hundred thousand. In the city alone." Sartean stepped forward.

"Yet as you say, Miss Felsin, tragically many will not survive continued use of the potion. And we must assume, adoption of its use will not be universal. So we do not need that many doses, do we?"

"Ah, no, Master. It would seem not." Mila was horrified.

"I will assume one hundred thousand doses per day will eventually be required. I would therefore require eighty-four squarefields of phenarril to be growing as soon as it can be arranged," Sartean shrugged, "though these things never go as well as planned. Call it one hundred. Tell me, how many wizards will that require to sustain?"

Mila was horrified. "Forty at least, Master."

"Train who you must. You will leave for the farmlands exactly ten days from today."

"Master! Me? I am not well suited—"

"You are perfectly suited, Mila. Or, rather, I believe you to be. Shall I instead assume your usefulness has run its course? You have trained four replacements whom I am sure would jump at the opportunity for such leadership."

Mila felt the noose tighten. "It will not be so simple as you extrapolate, Master. A phenarril plant will only yield a few dozen seeds per season, and I have only a few hundred with which to begin."

"I am aware of this, Miss Felsin. Assuming a reproduction factor of ten, it will take you five to six seasons to grow the four-point-two million phenarril plants needed to meet my objectives. You may lose half your seeds to incompetence, and you will still succeed. Will you not?"

"I will, Master. Though I must ask, are you naturally this skilled at mathematics?"

Sartean smiled. "This is not mathematics, child. This is arithmetic, and while I do not feel the need to answer your question, I will." Sartean leaned in again. "No, Mila. I loathe arithmetic. It is a base science imprisoned by rules. I have known about your discovery since the moment you did, and made these simple calculations a cycle ago."

Sartean stepped back, and handed her back the phenarril plant. "You are quite clever, Miss Felsin. A gifted sorceress. But the day that you will surpass or even surprise me is not coming." The Master of Kehrlia bowed his head subtly. "Thank you for your efforts, however. I enjoy your...*flair*."

Mila stood alone.

~

Ten seasons later, Master Sartean again received a knock that he had been expecting. A messenger had arrived with a brief handwritten note from the young sorceress.

*All delays have been resolved.*
*The caravan shall depart in five days.*
*-M.*

# XXV: THE GROVE

rellia, I have brought you some tea." Barris set the tray down on the small pine table beside the silver-haired Vicaris, and sat across from her. The woman leaned forward in her wicker chair and patted the knight on the knee. "You are kind, Barris, but it is a bit late in the afternoon for tea."

"Not for this tea, Vicaris. Your brew here in the Grove is amazing; I will drink my fill of it while I remain with you. I barely feel my aches from this morning." Barris moved to pour them each a cup of the steaming, sweetly aromatic beverage, and Vicaris stayed him.

Trellia smiled gently. "Do not dote on me, young knight. I have strength enough to pour tea. Here." She passed him a cup and saucer.

"Thank you. Your initiates do nothing but talk about your great leap astride Phantom, and how you sprinted down the trail like a battle-enraged warrior. You have made quite a stir, Trellia."

The Vicaris laughed. "I suppose I did leap, Barris, but Phantom sprinted. The young are always stunned to see me do anything besides lecture. They must think me little more than a dusty old nanny."

"Initiates think anyone older than fifty is dusty, Trellia. I am sure I strike them as ancient as well."

"Oh, you do, Barris. They marvel at the feats of endurance you and Phantom perform, though I think we both know that at your pace, you will be ancient soon enough. Lifting a horse, Barris? You spend your life energies like a soldier spends coin."

"Nonsense." The knight sat up straightly with mock indignation. "I will live forever."

"Perhaps, Barris. I worry about your young companion, however. He will be a bit worse for wear, I fear."

"He recovers well, I believe. Your healers are gifted and learned— all thanks to you, I would suppose."

"They are talented, but much credit must go to the spring." The Vicaris sipped her brew and smiled. "The same is true for the tea."

"Indeed," Barris agreed. "It is about Lucan that I wish to speak with you. It is expected that he will sleep for a bit still. Have you any notion for how long?"

"At least another day, although two or three seems more likely."

Barris sighed. "I am impatient to speak with him. There are many questions I have for the man."

"Let him rest, Barris. Whatever he has done, we will learn the truth. It is of little consequence in any case, given the current climate. There are much bigger perils to worry yourself about."

"Perhaps. Though I wish to know more about the young man. I saw his talent at the pub in Mor. Truly gifted with blades, and clever, if a bit roguish. His bond with his horse must have been strong as well, for her to alert us as she did that he was injured. Lucan piques my interest, and an abundance of curiosity has always plagued me, I fear."

"I thought nothing plagues you, knight. Are you not a paragon of virtue and discipline?" she teased.

Barris laughed then. "If only, Trellia."

"I must admit, I did sense worry from Hope about the safety of the young man."

"I'm sorry, say that again?" Something scratched at the surface of Barris' awareness.

"The mare. Hope. She was worried about Lucan," the Vicaris clarified.

"Have I told you the mare's name?"

"Oh. I am certain that the horse's name is Hope, however. Not the name given her by man, but the name Phantom expressed to me when he warned me that the three of you were in danger. When I sent her to the Grove, she responded to the name instinctively."

Barris' eyes narrowed in concentration. "Interesting. I did not learn Hope's name from her, nor from Phantom, but rather from Lucan. I suppose I had no reason to notice it before now, but Hope is certainly her soulname. I never made the connection, but now, as I consider it, I find it very odd that Lucan would know that. The horse was not elven trained, of that I am sure. How did he learn her soulname? I have never known a man to use the Bond, and such knowledge can only come from a very deep connection and understanding between species." Barris paused, seeing that the Vicaris appeared distracted. "Trellia?"

The Vicaris returned her attention to Barris. "A mystery indeed. You are right to be curious about the boy, Barris. There may be something extraordinary there."

A young male elf entered the humble shack sheepishly, and Trellia rose. "I heard it as well, Petahr."

"Very well, Vicaris. Is there anything..."

"No, Petahr, thank you." The initiate bowed and left.

"Have I missed something, Vicaris?"

"Well, not missed, Barris; you would not have heard it. There is a message from the queen for you, sent along the winds to me. Petahr must have been eavesdropping again. Nosy little cur, that one. Would you hear it now?"

"Of course." Barris tensed.

"She wishes you to await Pheonaris, Aria, and Captain Mikallis, who are riding at speed for the Grove as we speak. They will arrive in two days, at dawn, if all goes well. They will be exhausted and require your aid."

"My aid, Trellia?" Barris stood. "Is Aria in danger?"

"No, no. Sit, Barris. Do not be rattled. There are a few things that have transpired that we have not yet spoken of, I will bring you up to speed now. Come now, Barris. Sit. You are where you are supposed to be."

The Vicaris explained to Barris all that she knew. Since he had left Mor, she had received several messages from Thornwood via the system of magical communication the elves used between the Grove and the capital, a variety of the Speech that carried quickly, but not instantly, on the winds, utilizing the life of the land for conveyance. The elven leaders had convened, and Pheonaris had experienced a vision telling her that Aria would be needed to make haste to the Grove. The Vicaris also told him of Mikallis' impetuous declaration, and of the queen's belated decision to send a trailing company for protection. However, after Pheonaris, Mikallis, and Aria had withstood the surge of the Trine, Pheonaris' second vision had instructed the riders to increase their pace. The three would need to use the Bond as Barris did, in order to reach the Grove more quickly than they had originally thought necessary. The trailing company would never catch them, so the queen had recalled them.

"They will have difficulty, Vicaris. They and their mounts. The link between Phantom and me has developed over decades; it is not a thing that is quickly forged. I can help them recover when they arrive, but I should go to them and assist now."

"I would tend to agree, Sir Barris, but your Queen has ordered you to wait here. She must have good reason."

Barris thought for a moment, and forced himself to dismiss his disagreement. Terrias Evanti would most certainly have good reason, and he must trust her judgement. He had expected to leave this day, or no later than the next, to ride north, meet with the council, and return in haste to Mor. He admitted to himself that the order to wait brought with it a bit of relief, for as capable as he and Phantom were of making the journey, the cost was not insignificant. He also knew, however, that the order meant he would not be returning to Thornwood before his next audience with Halsen. The delay would make the timetable impossible, so he would not again see his queen for quite some time yet. It was as it would be.

"I dislike the news about Captain Mikallis, Trellia. The boy is too bold, and it makes me question his motives."

The Vicaris sat back and eyed Barris. "What is there to question? The boy is in love, and thus made into a fool. His motivation is clear."

"And dangerous. These are not times for dalliances, nor romances. Aria will have her fill of responsibilities, and any diversion of her attention is a hazard."

"You are right of course, Sir Barris. Though love is rarely convenient."

Barris considered this. He thought of his own ever-present feelings for his queen, and felt a tinge of shame as he swallowed his own words about dalliances and romances.

The two sat quietly for a moment as the light from the window began to grey. The storms of autumn would begin accelerating soon, and the shadow of winter was not far behind. The mildness they had enjoyed this season would before long give way to the tumultuous weather marking the end of another year. The realization caused Barris to feel the passage of time in his own life more keenly.

"Did the queen have any other message for me, Trellia?"

The Vicaris did not immediately reply.

"Would you wish that she had, Barris?" she asked mildly.

Barris eyes' widened, his embarrassment desperately seeking safe harbor, some dismissive thing he could say to dance away from the topic, but as he regarded his friend, the eminently wise Vicaris, he knew there was no escape.

Barris inhaled deeply and groaned. "Am I so obvious, Trellia?"

Trellia reached for Barris' hand. "Not to all, brave knight, but perhaps to your dearest friends."

He turned his hand over to hold hers. "*You* are my one dear friend, Trellia. And I am ashamed to discuss this with you."

"Nonsense, knight." She squeezed his hand and released it. "I swaddled you as an elfling, but over the many years, you have become more than a young knight to me, you have become my peer. We are elders of our people, despite our difference in age, and beloved friends besides. There should be no shame between us."

"Yet there is, Trellia. Though it is not an indication of any barrier between us. I have never spoken of this." Barris paused a moment. "If you see this so clearly, however, Terrias must as well."

The Vicaris smiled. "I would not be so sure, Barris. You are quite private and a bit mysterious, if I may say so. And in matters of the heart, even a queen can be dense."

"Terrias Evanti is far from dense, Trellia. You must know this."

"Oh, I do. But there is a reason I refused the Seat. My niece is wise, and strong, and I told my brother long ago that she would make a far better Queen than I would."

"I have never understood that, Trellia. You would have made an excellent queen."

"No, Barris, I would not have. I am too passionate, too blown about by my emotions. No, I belong here, in the Grove, with my spring and my students. I am a teacher, not a leader. I refused the title of Mistress for the same reasons. The very thought of being saddled with matters of state makes my heart cringe. Terrias however...she is not dispassionate, but she is much more capable of separating herself from her feelings. She suffered much loss while still very young, and her heart, like yours, is well guarded. It would not surprise me to know that she is completely clueless about your true feelings."

"I hope you are right, Trellia."

"Now why in Tahr would you hope that? If you two are to ever broach the topic, one of you must speak. It does not seem like you intend to."

Barris frowned. "It is not so simple, Vicaris. If she truly already knows how I feel, and she does not speak, then she must not share my feelings. If she does not know, then she must not be attuned at all to the notion, and therefore, does not share my feelings. How can I speak when I know that one of those realities must be true?"

Trellia fell into laughter. "Barris, you fool!" She continued to snicker, spilling her tea. "Ah, now look what you made me do." Barris, fuming, did not move to help her.

"You mock me, Trellia. I am glad you spilled your tea. I hope it was hot."

Trellia stuck her tongue out at the knight. "It was not," she retorted, still giggling as she waved her hand, the liquid evaporating into steam.

"Explain yourself, Trellia." Barris crossed his arms over his chest petulantly.

"Oh, Barris. Tell me, how do you know that my niece is not sitting on her oaken seat, right now, piddling herself with frustration, thinking the *exact same thoughts* about you?"

"*Piddling* herself, Trellia? Really?"

"Yes, Barris. Piddling. For all you know she's in a twist right now, mooning over you like a schoolchild."

Barris shook his head. "I see now what you mean. I do not think a queen would use the colorful descriptions you use."

"Oh, shut up, Barris. Now listen, and your shriveled, irreverent old friend will straighten you out. Do you not think Terrias Evanti is a woman? Of course you do, or why would you be so smitten with her? Ah–" she held up a hand as Barris tried to interrupt. "*Quiet.* Not another word from you. Now, if she *is* a woman, then she has desires just like anyone else. Do you know who for? Neither do I. But does it not make sense that it *may* be someone who is, perhaps, a bit shy about the matter? A bit shielded? Someone she respects, someone who is admired by her people, someone whose legendary strength and sacrifice are whispered about among children and the single women of Thornwood? Someone who is not around often enough to let the idea of love blossom?"

"You speak of someone who does not exist, Trellia, and if he does, he is certainly not me."

"See? That's why I call you a fool. Look, Barris, I don't know what Terrias Evanti thinks of you, aside from the fact that she has *always* spoken of you in tones of awe, as we all do. One thing is certain, however–you will never know if you never ask."

Barris shook his head again. "And if I do ask, Trellia? And she does not share my feelings? I am not worried about her laughing at me, Vicaris. I am not worried that she will be offended. I fear that the admission will cause her to feel uncomfortable with me, and I could not bear that. I would need to resign my position, and could no longer serve Thornwood as I do."

"Serve Thornwood as you do? You serve Thornwood by never spending more than a few days per *season* in Thornwood. You either train your knights and cavalry incessantly, or ride about the land of Tahr as an ambassador of Thornwood, on errands of importance to your people. Your service does not require close contact with Terrias. Although, perhaps, if you were successful in wooing the fair Queen, you might find yourself spending a bit more time among your own people. You have nothing to lose, Barris. Nothing more than your own fantasy of what *may* happen. If you cling to that fantasy in place of the real thing, perhaps you are not the brave knight we all think you to be."

There it was. The truth laid bare. The truth Barris refused to acknowledge, but knew was at the heart of his cowardice.

Barris gazed at his friend. "Trellia, I have fought battles with orcs and trolls and errant wizards. I have ridden to nearly every corner of greater Tahr. I have been slashed, hacked, hammered and harried for almost a hundred years. We have enjoyed peace for some time, but that peace may be ending. Something wakes in this world, and when its slumber finally ends, peace will be but a memory. This does not frighten me. Not in the least. But the thought of telling Terrias Evanti how I feel for her makes my mouth go dry and my spine turn to pudding."

Trellia stood and kissed Barris on the top of his head. "Well, now, don't you feel better?" she asked.

Barris stood and faced his friend. "Well, not particularly."

"A moment ago, you were just as terrified to discuss the topic with me. Now your heart is unburdened. Was it as awful as you feared?"

"No, Trellia. I should have talked with you years ago."

"You most certainly should have. And you now will recall that the fear of a thing is worse than the thing itself. Do you not train your knights in this concept?"

"I do."

"Then heed your own counsel, knight. Now go. I need a nap. You wear me out." The wisp of a lady hugged Barris, and the elf knight walked into the sweet air of the Grove, heartened.

# XXVI: THORNWOOD TRAIL

ria felt her life sliding from her grasp, her very youth draining from her as if Sera were drinking from the well of her soul. The sensation was not physically painful, nor debilitating, but extraordinarily difficult to regulate. The young princess had done as her Mistress had instructed, allowing the sheath of her spirit to leak like a sieve, feeding her own consciousness and her mount's thirst for strength. Aria struggled desperately to maintain a balance between the vitality she needed to remain awake and the power Sera needed to carry on. The challenge however was immeasurably more complex than that.

Pheonaris had done her best to prepare them in the few hours they had before they began their sprint. She explained how the Bond would allow them to open their reservoirs of elven strength, how when their mounts began to tire, the three must find the release within themselves to slowly let their energy trickle out to invigorate their horses. She had taught them that the sensation would be odd, but pleasant at first, and they must not give in to the urge to release too much too soon until they truly understood the nature of their Bond. That understanding would come on this journey, Pheonaris had said, and if it did not, they would fail.

The Mistress had not had time to explain how the demands on their own alertness would accelerate, and how their mounts would eventually begin to resist their urgings to continue to gallop. Mistress Pheonaris had said the words, but they did not begin to convey the true breadth of the demands on their spirits. It was not a simple matter of opening two channels and maintaining them. The first few hours were as taxing as any hard ride; the Bond was used only to help encourage their mounts, and sense the trail more acutely. Aria was already exhausted when they began, having helped maintain the protective barrier that her Mistress had erected against the rushing waters. She recovered quickly from the effort, though, as strenuous as it had been, and had begun to feel more confident that she would manage this ride without falling apart at the seams. This was an entirely different kind of strain however.

When she had assisted Pheonaris, the energies released were extreme and intense, almost violent, and she had lost all sense of time. The expenditure of her inner self seemed to be over as quickly as it had begun, and while she had been fatigued afterwards, the episode was contained within a brief expanse of time. However, they had now been riding since midday the day before, and night had fallen hours ago. This torture of her spirit would not end. The drain on her being repeatedly felt as if it were reaching a crescendo, but each time she felt that she or Sera would falter, she dug deeper, found more, and gave more.

Riding during the day was hard. Riding at night, however, was excruciatingly arduous. Energy was not enough. Alertness was not enough. She had to maintain a heightened sense of awareness to avoid losing her balance, since she was unable to anticipate the swerves and jumps Sera would make. Degrees of power factors more intense were required for Sera to maintain her footing, and keep a safe distance behind Pheonaris. Thirst. Hunger. Blisters. Absence of mind. Logs. Holes. Stones. Curves. Frustration. Impatience. Fear.

These were her enemies, and they attacked her relentlessly. They also attacked Sera, and the concentration and power required to combat them was unfathomable.

Yet Aria knew that she had it the easiest among them.

Pheonaris had made it clear that the journey would be twice as hard on Captain Mikallis. The maintenance of the Bond required a nurturing sense that came more easily to Druids, typically at least. The spirit of a warrior was sculpted differently. Hard edges, bursts of energy, fierce and violent releases of power–these were the tools of a warrior. Patience, longsuffering, gentleness, reassurance–a great soldier needed these skills as well, but they did not typically come naturally. Despite Mikallis' years of training, his ability to maintain his link with Triumph had faltered repeatedly, beginning at dawn that day. Whenever it had, it was up to Mistress Pheonaris to rescue the Bond, strengthening and supporting mount and rider with her own added energy and sustenance. Pheonaris had reassured Mikallis that in time, he would gain the ability to maintain such a pace without assistance, but it very possibly would take more than a three-day ride to develop the ability required.

Now, Aria felt that she was beginning to lose her link as well. She had felt Sera pass through many stages the past day and a half. First, simple thirst. Then hunger. Then a pervasive weariness. Frustration. Irritability. Anger. And now, a heartbreaking pleading, a failure to understand why so much was being asked of her, and a distancing from Aria's consciousness. An erosion of trust.

"Mistress!" she called out over the sound of hooves pounding dirt. "I am hurting her! She does not understand."

"She does not need understanding, Aria! She needs comfort, and love, and power. She must be made to know that she will not be forsaken, that your need for her is virtuous and vital!"

"I am trying, Mistress, but she feels so betrayed!"

"Then give more, Aria! I cannot help you, I must reserve what I can for Mikallis. Delve deeper, give more! More than she even asks! You must do this! Dawn approaches soon, and it will be easier, have faith!"

*How? How do you do this? How do Barris and Phantom do this?* Aria knew she must do something, now. She could not withstand the resistance against the Bond that Sera was expressing. She sensed her own resistance as well. A kind of bitterness, she felt, as she probed within herself. Resentment that she should need to feed this animal so much of herself, resentment that the sacrifice she was making was costing her seasons or even years of her own life. She did not know the eventual cost, and it frightened her.

*You are not merely giving strength to a horse,* Aria reminded herself. *You are sustaining a friend, and giving of yourself to your people. You must give more.* Aria knew that within this idea was the answer. She began to understand. The answer was not sacrifice—it was giving that was required. Giving freely of herself, for the good of her companion, for the good of her people. Her life was not important. Her duty was. *I am a Princess of Thornwood,* she reminded herself. *My life is for my people.*

Aria gave. She released her life willingly into the frightened filly. More. *Peace, Sera. Tell me what you need. I will not let you suffer. We will do this together. We are needed. All that we care for is at stake. Take what you need, dear friend. Take it all if you must. But ride with me!*

Aria finally understood the nature of the Bond. It was not sacrifice. It was not even a gift. *It is a sharing.* Aria freely allowed Sera to take what she needed. The balance she had tried so hard to maintain between her own needs and those of the filly was futile. It was not about balance. It was about complete and total surrender and unselfish release. *This is how Barris and Phantom achieve such feats. This is why their Bond is so legendary.* Aria realized that she could not put her own needs above Sera's, or even alongside them. She must put Sera first, and trust that her friend would leave enough for her. As she understood, so Sera's trust returned, and the pair no longer tore down the trail in terror and fatigue, but in harmony and faith in one another. The lifting of the emotional burden buoyed Aria, refreshing her.

What had been nearly two full days of agony was now a joy and a wonder, and as the night sky withdrew in deference to the light of the sun, Aria sent what part of herself she could to Mikallis. She found that she still had quite a lot remaining to give.

# XXVII: THE MORLINE

hat in bloody Fury...Garlan! Make for the southern shoreline! Rocks, on his tail!" J'arn shouted across the water to the forgemaster, and to his own navigator.

The rafts had reached a vast clearing that stretched for a mile on both sides of the wide river as the day had grown late, giving the dwarven company and guests their first good look at the Fang, the tree line no longer obscuring their vision. What J'arn saw chilled him to the bone. Flowing from the mouth of the volcano were several great streams of molten lava, the usually thin smoke trail emanating from the mountain now a massive billowing cloud.

"Mawbottom, J'arn, this ain't no overcast, it's smoke!" Boot stood to better view the sky surrounding them. "It's the whole damned world, J'arn, far as ye can see!"

"Easy, Boot. It may be both cloud and smoke. It is difficult to tell the difference in this light." J'arn was not convinced however. The sky did in fact look as if it were completely blanketed in smoke and ash. The winds had not blown this day, and J'arn reasoned that valley within which they floated could very well be trapping the smoke from the volcano. Perhaps when the winds picked up it would not look so horrifying. The rafts were drawn to a halt, and the company climbed onto the shore, legs rubbery from their extended ride on the river.

Wolf made as if he would go for a run to explore his surroundings, but decided against it, and lay down on the shore.

"Wolf's not feeling well, are yeh, Wolf?" Shyla tried to comfort the animal, sitting beside him, recognizing that the float had made her friend nauseous. "Yeh'll feel better in the morning, friend. We are camping here, ain't we, J'arn?"

J'arn nodded and made the announcement. "All right, let's get some tents up," J'arn ordered, sensing his dwarves' discomfort. "I don't like sleeping in the shadow of that damnable thing any better than you do, but I like the idea of floating into molten lava in the dark even worse."

"Do you think the flow extends that far, Prince J'arn?" asked Narl.

"I do not, Narl, but neither do I know for sure. Best to wait 'til dawn to find out."

Boot piped in to cheer the mood. "I'll get supper then, boys. 'Tis my turn, and ye be in for a treat tonight!"

Shyla jumped up. "I'll help yeh, Boot."

"Ah, Lady Shyla, I thank ye, but ye'll not need to worry yourself. I dunno how it is in G'naath, but cookin' ain't just womanwork among us folk. We all do our share."

"Well, in G'naath it is womanwork, Boot, mostly 'cause we're better at it. 'Sides, I got no other way to pull my weight. I ain't gonna be a burden to yer company, so ye can let me help or I'll spit in the pot."

"Hah! Ain't a little spit gonna ruin my stew, but I'll show ye me recipe. Ye can't be sharin' it with no elves though, now, hear me?"

"On me word as a Lady," Shyla bowed dramatically. "Can ye keep an eye on Wolf, J'arn? He ain't feelin' so good."

J'arn smiled. "I can, Shyla. Blast it Narl, ye can't carry that tent yerself! Wait there a turn, I'll help ye."

The company busied themselves preparing camp, and Boot demonstrated the finer points of preparing Rotriver Stew, a soldier's recipe he had learned from his father, passed down through the ages in his family. The hearty soup would not be ready until morning, since the fish heads needed to stew overnight, but tonight they would eat the meat of the enormous riverwhiskers they had fished from the Morline that day, fried and battered in the last of the lard and breadcrumbs they had brought with them. The plan, Boot shared with Shyla, had been for the dwarves to stop in Mor the following day to trade coin for more food, and when they did, he had an even better recipe he would share with her for slow roasted beef, provided they could find the right spices. Now, however, he was not so sure there would be time, as they had stopped earlier this evening than they had planned.

The tents were pitched and the dwarves found logs to set around the fire on the grassy beach. Boot and Shyla distributed supper, and the dwarves shared what remained of their mead and ale. From here to Mor, it would be water and dried foods, but this night they would enjoy one more substantial meal.

The meal was enjoyed and the fire died down, tenderly maintained by Boot just high enough to keep the stew simmering. The dwarves complained that the air was chilly, and wanted more logs on the fire. "It's all about the temperature, boys, ye gotta boil 'er up fast, then just keep 'er warm–"

"What good is tellin' us about the temperature of yer stew if ye won't share the ingredients, ye blasted stubborn old engineer?" This from Fannor. "Tell us what's in there, Shyla...least ye can do!"

"Least she can do, huh, Fannor?" Boot bellowed. "She cooked yer damned dinner, she did! Now drink yer mead and shut yer hole."

"Ahhhh, yer a hammer head, Boot."

"I'll hammer *yer* head, ye fool," Boot said, balling up a fist in mock anger.

"Hey, J'arn?" asked Rocks.

"Yeah, Rocks?"

"How much longer 'till winter gets here?"

Shyla interrupted. "Forty-one days."

The dwarves all looked at the gnome.

"Well, forty really, but yeh don't count the last one."

"How in Fury do ye know that, Shyla?" asked Rocks.

"Well, look up." The dwarves all looked up reflexively.

"Not tonight, I mean, can't see nothing tonight. But last night, the top Twin was kinda startin' to hide behind the other. Well, that only happens once a year, and it happens in the eleventh cycle. So, we're in the eleventh cycle now. Now, there was also this one big star kinda sittin' right there, under the bottom twin, all centered-like." Shyla tried to make the shapes with her tiny hands. "That means it be exactly thirteen days 'fore the end of the cycle, and when ya add up the thirteen days, minus today, plus the twenty-nine days in the next cycle, that'd be forty-one. The twelfth cycle is over on the shortest day of the year, and that be when winter starts. But like I said, ye don't count the last day, if yer counting ahead from today."

The dwarves all looked at Shyla incredulously.

"I thought she-gnomes never went outside, Shyla. How in Tahr do ye know all that?" asked Boot.

"Well, I maybe snuck out once in a while," Shyla blushed. "Or every night. Depends on how yeh count it."

The dwarves all laughed. J'arn asked, "Are ye sure yer' not goin' to study to be a Ranger, Shyla, and not a sorceress? 'Cause I don't think any of us know how to look at the night sky and know what day it is. That's what we have calendars for." The company of dwarves muttered their agreement.

"What's a Ranger?" Shyla asked curiously. "And what's a calendar?"

~

Shyla woke early, an uneasy feeling poking at her. The dwarves had set up a private tent for the gnome, and she could see a bit of light creeping through the narrow opening in the flap, but it was somehow...*wrong*. The morning was eerily quiet, and she did not believe anyone else was awake. Wolf slept soundly beside her. She rubbed her eyes, pulled on her boots, and stepped outside.

Shyla was not the first awake. The eight dwarves stood silently, gaping at the world around them. That entire world was grey.

Not merely the sky. The ground. The trees. The air. Even the river. Everything. An uncountable number of particles of light grey ash drifted slowly down from the skies, coating the Tahr with a thick blanket of soot. Shyla shuddered. As wondrous as the sight was, she knew it was bad. Very bad.

No one spoke. Boot walked over to the kettle to peer into his stew, and shook his head.

"Ruined."

For several turns nothing else was said, as the company wandered about in a daze. Jender finally broke the silence.

"Looks like the river's still flowin'. Got a bit of a sludge to it, but she's movin'."

J'arn nodded at the soldier, now also mottled in grey. He did not bother to inform Jender that it would take more than a few inches of ash to stop the Morline, sensing that the frightened dwarf had just needed to say *something*. "Aye, seems to be. Well, we'll be needin' to head out, boys. Leave the tents, we'll never get 'em clean. Pack yer gear, and let's float."

Shyla went back to her tent, and awakened Wolf. The animal stretched languorously, and made his way out of the tent. Shyla could not see his expression as she gathered her belongings, but she heard his plaintive whine. He stood waiting for her, ears laid back, as she exited the tent.

"Go on, Wolf." She patted him gently. "Go empty yourself, we're gonna be floatin' all day, looks like."

Wolf would not leave her side.

The dwarves quickly loaded up with gear—the larger items were already tied onto the rafts—and J'arn made the boarding call. Wolf was the first to the rafts, eager to be gone from the eerie clearing. He howled a long, unnerving note as Shyla and the dwarves secured their gear, urging the company to hasten away. The lines were dropped, and the rafts floated freely. While all knew on some level that the river had not slowed any since the night before, they all watched the shoreline pass before their eyes, and the sense of time decelerating was palpable.

Boot finally said it. "I hope Manera is safe," referring to his wife.

"She is, Boot," J'arn replied, his hand cupping his friend's shoulder. "Probably safer than we are."

Shyla did not find that idea particularly comforting, but understood how Boot might.

J'arn made a declaration. "We will not stop to visit the markets of Mor. We will sail until we reach the docks, then purchase fresh mounts and dried foods, and head north at the Highmorland Crossing. We will rest only as much as is absolutely necessary. We must make the Grove as quickly as possible. If there is help to be had, we must get to it."

None argued; all agreed.

They watched the Fang fade behind the tree line as the shoreline narrowed, its black and yellow clouds of sulfurous poison continuing to belch into the world, the angry red fissures now hidden behind the greyed forest canopy. The skies continued their unrelenting coating of Tahr, weaving a dense carpet that would soon silence and suffocate the land beneath it.

Shyla wept.

# XXVIII: MOR

artean stood passively before King Halsen in the great marbled throne room, hands folded before him and hidden within his rarely-worn set of maroon and brown robes. The tirade had been issuing from the frothing monarch for several turns, and no end seemed forthcoming. Four cowering heads of Treasury, Trade, Labor, and Agriculture stood beside the wizard in their frills and fineries, two on either side, flanked by a pair of stiff Defenders. An additional five pikemen stood behind the assembled supplicants, their presence making it clear that the rules of The Game were in full lethal effect. Eight more flanked the king, and the twenty-one men comprised the whole of the audience. Hundreds would regularly assemble in this hall, Sartean considered, and never had he had occasion to be present before the king in the throne room with so few in attendance. The resonance of that realization mingled with the echoes of the king's bellowing rant through the empty chamber, and the effect was unsettling, even for the formidable sorcerer.

Sartean knew that he must await the king's query before speaking, and thus busied himself admiring the marble columns and fine-woven tapestries that hung alongside the soaring stained-glass windows. On a typical morning, the light from the windows would be sufficient to brighten the hall. The architecture of the throne room and the curvature of the glass were designed to diffuse the sun's beams uniformly throughout. There were no beams this day; the glow of the sun was scarcely existent. The clouds and ash issuing from Fang choked the light, and only a filmy remnant of murky brightness penetrated the clouds sufficiently to reach the windows. Sconces therefore had been lit along the columns in of the hall, the scent of burning pitch lending an even more ominous feel to the gathering.

Sartean sensed that a question was bubbling to the surface, and returned his attention to the king.

"Tell us then, Master Alton," the king addressed the head of Labor, "WHY has nothing been done to repair the walls and address this damnable ash?"

The tall, bulky man was the only person present besides Sartean and the Defenders who was not shuddering in fear. He cleared his throat and replied. "Much has been done, Your Highness, but the problems exceed my allotted manpower. I have been doing all that is within my power and more to recruit more laborers, Sire, but without coin, I am helpless. My next and final option is to empty the prisons, and I have sent several requests to do just that, but as yet I believe Your Highness has not had occasion to approve them."

The king waved his hand dismissively. "You have my approval, Alton. But will it be enough?"

Master Alton deliberated briefly, then replied. "No, Sire. It will not be nearly enough."

"Coin, then." The king turned his gaze to Treasury. "Can you not make it available, Fennar?"

The head of Treasury shook his head. "Not without starving your soldiery, your Highness. Our greatest expense is our military. As I understand it, the morale among the men is already dangerously low, and the majority of the army has already turned to the submarkets for additional income." The master of Treasury swallowed. "Your Highness, our pay scale is woefully insufficient, and at the current rate, the coffers of Mor will be empty by the spring in any case."

King Halsen eyed the treasurer and held out his hand. Yan appeared from nowhere, placing a crystal goblet of wine in the monarch's fat fingers.

The king sipped slowly. "You are my treasurer, Master Fennar. If the treasury is empty, tell me, whose blood should spill?"

Fennar's knees unlocked, and the man barely remained upright. He replied unsteadily. "That is a decision only you can make, your Highness, and I will say only this in my defense. I am tasked with collecting taxes, counting coin, and distributing it as you dictate. There are no taxes to collect when there is no trade, and I cannot count and distribute what does not exist." The trembling man bowed his head and closed his eyes, bracing himself for what would come next.

King Halsen allowed the man's terror to take root for a moment, then spoke. "Don't soil yourself, Fennar. You may yet survive this day. Master Harris, however, your continued existence is not so assured." Halsen turned his gaze to the master of Trade. "Does Fennar speak the truth? Is there no trade?"

The slight man stuttered in response. "I, ah...well, Sire, the, the fact of the matter..."

"Collect yourself and speak clearly, Harris, or we shall replace you with someone who will."

Harris inhaled sharply and did his best to calm himself. He only just succeeded. "Of...of course, Sire. The problem is this." Harris took another brief moment to steady his voice. "The chief exports of Mor have traditionally been food and spices, Highness. We export cloth and crafts to the dwarves and elves as well, but those items are mostly bartered, with little tax revenue resulting. Our production comes primarily from the farmlands, and thus our influx of coin is most directly tied to the outputs of agriculture. In the past eight seasons, Sire, our volumes of food production...well, Sire, they have been barely enough to feed our own people. There is little left to export. We..."

"ENOUGH!" Halsen screamed shrilly. "Our walls crumble from tahrquakes. The blasted sun is blotted out, and ash blankets my kingdom. We need LABOR!" Halsen smashed his goblet to the floor, and even Yan did not move to retrieve it. The king stood, angrily leering at his kingdom's leadership. "Yet labor blames treasury, treasury blames trade, trade blames farming...we suppose that farming will blame the heat, or lack of rains, or rabbits, or some damned insect next!"

The head of agriculture spoke. "Your Highness, a great deal of the farmlands have been—"

Sartean silently congratulated himself on his choice of attire as fragments of skull mingled with brain matter and other gore splattered his garments. The halberd had sliced through the air smoothly at the silent urging of King Halsen, only a shifting of his eyes needed to prompt the Defender into action. The blade cleaved Master Harrington's head in two from behind, embedding itself deep within the man's chest cavity. The remainder of the man lay crumpled on the marble floor, and the Defender stepped on his back to yank his weapon free before returning to attention.

"It would appear we have a vacancy in agriculture." Halsen returned to his throne. "Sartean, will you be so kind?"

"Certainly, Sire." With a series of gestures and mutterings from the wizard, the blood and gore now spilling from the corpse boiled and evaporated, the gaping wound cauterizing itself to prevent further leakage. The scent of burnt flesh filled the air, Sartean nodded at the soldier who had done the deed, and the man dragged the carcass from the throne room. Within moments, a fine dry pile of ocher-colored dust was all that remained of the man's spilled life, and with a flourish, Sartean waved the dust into nothingness.

The king was amused. "You have become practiced at the task, Sar. Well done. Now, will you tell me precisely what we are to do about these issues?"

The Incantor nodded. "As you command, Sire. In our last meeting, I had conveyed that I believe I have a solution. I have begun field tests, and the results are promising. With a bit of luck, I believe we will have solved our overarching problems of labor and taxes by midwinter," Sartean turned his gaze to Fennar arrogantly, "well before the treasury runs empty. I will also quickly resolve the small matters of the wall damage and this infernal ash."

"How?" Fennar asked incredulously. Sartean raised an eyebrow at the man, then looked to the king. Fennar's eyes widened, and immediately raised his hands protectively over his head...too little, too late. The Defender's first blow was insufficient, owing to the man's feeble attempt at defense, but his second quick strike ended the screams.

King Halsen chuckled, and waggled a finger at the sorcerer. "You set him up for that, Sartean. We are appalled."

Sartean bowed his head slightly in deference, knowing better than to issue a response.

"Well, as much as I am inclined to take you at your word, Sar, I am going to need to see some evidence for myself that you've got this all under your thumb. What can you show me?"

"Much, Highness. May I suggest that you adjourn this assembly, so that we may speak freely...and privately?"

"Best that we do so, or at this rate I'll have the damned Defenders hacking at each other when we run out of councilors. Adjourned. Sar, attend me in my chambers in an hour."

Sartean stood silently as the other councilors quickly departed. "Something else, Sartean?"

"You may wish to call for a cloak, Sire, and assemble an element of Defenders," Sartean suggested.

"Dammit, Sar, can you not simply tell me what you wish to tell me in my chambers?"

"You asked to see evidence, Sire. That will require a short walk to the outer wall."

"The outer wall? Not so short a walk, wizard. Yan, send for my horse. I will meet you at the drawbridge, Sartean."

The wizard nodded and made his exit.

~

Walking through the passages of the palace towards the drawbridge, Sartean smiled at his remarkably good fortune. Harrington had been a moment away from informing the king that a sizeable percentage of the farmlands had been appropriated by Mila, and no amount of deflection on Sartean's part would have proven sufficient to stay the king's wrath. He had been tasked with finding a solution to the kingdom's woes only this cycle, and if Halsen discovered that the wizard's plans had been in the works for ten seasons, his suspicions would drive him to immediate and absolute violence. Sartean had not attended the council without protecting himself; no single strike of a halberd would have penetrated his defenses. He would likely have survived the encounter and escaped the palace, but not without initiating an all-out war between Kehrlia and the army. Sartean would accept such an outcome if it were necessary, but it was far from ideal.

The risk of that discovery was a now thing of the past. Harrington had kept Sartean's seizure of farmlands a strictly guarded secret, believing that his confidence would ingratiate him to the wizard, and assure his own wealth in the future. In truth, Sartean suspected, it was not his greed that had held the man in check for so long, it was his terror. The wizard had made clear and unambiguous the horrors that would visit the man if he spoke a word of their arrangement to anyone. His threats had lost their effectiveness, however, when the man had faced the king's wrath this day; better to survive the moment and worry about Sartean later, he must have reasoned. Perhaps he had believed that if he betrayed the wizard to the king, it would be Sartean's head split in two, and the man would leave the audience freed of both his secrets and the wizard's threats. *Perhaps your gambit would have succeeded, Harrington, if you had only awaited your turn to speak.* Sartean smiled at the thought. *No,* Sartean corrected himself. *You would have been begging for death by nightfall.*

Sartean had not needed to make similar promises of wealth to Master Alton. A steady supply of laborers was required to harvest the crops of phenarril that Mila Felsin had been growing, and that supply could not be secured without help from Alton, or at least without alerting him. His deal with the head of labor was much simpler. Alton's daughter Calli had been an apprentice at Kehrlia, and Sartean merely needed to assure her graduation—and survival—to obtain Alton's cooperation. He had barely needed to elucidate how dangerous an apprenticeship could be before the clever head of labor read between the lines. "Tell me what you require, wizard," he had said, "and you will have it so long as my daughter lives." Simple.

It had not been so simple to keep the disappearance of over a hundred laborers a secret, but Mila had done a commendable job in that respect. She had orchestrated a masterful system of recruiting that met her needs gradually, as the size of her harvest increased. She had assigned several wizards to the task, and only unattached, unmarried laborers were selected, men whose lack of connection to the world around them would prevent their departure from Mor from garnering undue attention. Her laborers served in a second vital capacity as well, allowing the sorceress to test her flightfluid potions continuously without raising suspicions.

She had settled upon her final recipe just over a year ago, and a significant supply of the drug was ready for distribution, but the climate in Mor was not quite ripe. Sartean bided his time, waiting for the king's failures at leadership to give way to desperation and paranoia, all the while positioning himself as a trusted and indispensable resource.

One obstacle had remained: Treasury. Master Fennar was not the most capable accountant, but he did possess a mastery of political and economic machination. The man was connected to all manner of industries and markets, and had amassed a lifetime of favors and alliances that would make him a formidable opponent when Sartean made his play for the throne. Sartean did not worry that the treasurer would side with Halsen against him in an eventual conflict; the man had his own designs, and would not brook any threat to the empire he had built for himself. *Yet with a word*, Sartean mused, *a single word, he brought about his own ruin.*

Sartean *had* intended to provoke the man with his unsubstantiated and arrogant declaration that he had found the solution to the kingdom's woes. He did not however expect that the fool would so easily take the bait. *Never underestimate man's propensity for stupidity*, he reminded himself. *Even the mightiest are but slaves to their own arrogance.*

~

Sartean walked beside the king, who sat in full regalia upon his armored steed. The pair had been making their way through the choking, ash-covered streets of Mor for the better part of an hour, and Halsen was losing patience.

"This had better be good, wizard." The king coughed himself breathless, and continued. "My cloak is ruined, and my lungs are filling with ash. So help me, I will strangle you myself if this is not worth the effort."

"My king, I would never inconvenience you so, were it not necessary. Here, may I?" Sartean reached towards the king tentatively, and Halsen nodded. He touched the king's boot, and within moments the ash clinging to the man had fallen away. "I wish I could do the same for your lungs, Sire." Sartean did not say that he could clear the man's chest of foreign particles with less than a thought. The wizard's ability to heal was unparalleled, but kept a closely guarded secret. Without that secrecy, the whole of Mor would be hammering at the stone doors to Kehrlia day and night, and the tower would be reduced to little more than an infirmary, a magnet for the sick and all manner of unclean human filth.

"Do not worry about my lungs, Sar. Worry about your...what is this?"

The squad rounded a corner near the northwestern reaches of the city, and before them lay an immaculately scrubbed avenue where a dozen men scurried about with brooms and brushes and pails. The ash continued to fall, but it never was allowed to accumulate. Teams of laborers moved down one side of the street and up the next, the result being a nearly spotless boulevard that was less soiled than before the ashfall.

"Impressive, Sartean. Though I doubt this can be duplicated in scale."

"It can, my king, but you have not yet seen the whole of what I have to show you. As we make the end of the street, I would direct your attention to the right."

They approached the corner, and to the right stood the northwest corner of the outer wall of Mor. Or rather, an improved section of it. An energetic and excited man quickly approached the procession and bowed to the king. Halsen motioned to his anxious guards to stand easy.

"Your Highness, it is an honor!" He then bowed to Sartean. "Master, I did a little more than ya asked, but we're 'bout done with the corner. We can keep going if ya like, I guess we just got a little carried away." The gaunt man stood proudly before the pair.

"I am pleased, James. How are you enjoying your new position?"

"Very much, Master!" The man grinned excitedly. "I like being a foreman! We got lot's o good men, and—"

"That will be all for now, James; please continue your work. I will see you in the morning."

"Yessir, Master! Your Highness." The man bowed again and ran off to continue to work.

"Forgive him, please, Highness. He is untutored in decorum."

"I don't care about his decorum, Sar. What in Fury have you got going here?"

Halsen shook his head in awe. From the corner where the northern and western walls met, and a hundred paces in either direction from the joint, the walls of Mor towered nearly twice as high as they had before. The color of the mortar clearly indicated that the stones had been freshly laid, and thirty men hurried about, mixing mortar, hauling gravel, and pulling stones up the walls with a well-organized series of pulleys and ropes.

"Is this why I lack laborers, wizard? I did not authorize a rebuild of the wall!" Halsen glared at Sartean.

"No, Sire, though I understand how it must seem. These men were assigned to repair a few cracks in the wall that appeared after the tahrquake two days ago. They have taken it upon themselves to be, ah, industrious, it would seem."

Halsen eyed the wizard. "I see maybe thirty men, Sartean. This task would have taken more than a hundred and fifty men to be completed in such a brief period of time."

Sartean nodded. "You are correct, Sire. I would calculate that a hundred and fifty is a very accurate estimate, if you include the labor needed to clean the nearby streets. My men, however, do the work of three."

The king scoffed. "One man does the work of one man, Sartean. Believe me, I have tested the concept extensively. What are you not telling me?"

"Your Highness, these men are under the influence of a powerful potion I have perfected since our last meeting. You will recall our last discussions."

"I do, and I had ordered you to find a way to magically enhance the efforts of my labor force. This..." He looked at the wall again, shaking his head. "This is the result?"

"It is, Sire. Now, I will caution, there are side effects–"

"To Fury with your side effects, Sar! You will resolve them, I have no doubt. Sar, this is amazing! But...how can we accelerate this? How much of this potion can you make?"

"More than you could imagine, Sire. I am a sorcerer, after all."

Halsen's lip curled in contempt, but he let the arrogance slide.

"What do you need, Sartean? Tell me what resources you require."

"I require no resources beyond those which I can already obtain, Sire. Kehrlia has worked tirelessly on this solution for your kingdom, and I have already begun preparations to distribute our potion as needed. Sire, if I am to address the matter of the ash and the vulnerabilities of the wall before these problems threaten Mor's stability and sovereignty, I will need to move quickly. We do not yet know what these quakes portend, but I can only assume they will continue. Yet that is not our primary worry, it is but one more complication we face. I only require your seal on a document that will enable me to work unfettered, and to direct the efforts of the citizenry to meet your objectives. Bureaucracy, Sire, is our greatest enemy, as evidenced by the failures of your most trusted advisors."

Halsen regarded the wizard for a long moment. "You shall have your document, wizard. However." The king turned his horse to face Sartean head-on.

"Yes, Sire?"

"I am not a fool, Sartean. I know what power you ask for."

Sartean nodded gravely. "I do not take you for a fool, Sire. And I know that what I ask is unprecedented."

"Indeed. Unprecedented and dangerous. Sartean, I will require frequent reports from you, and if at any point I determine that you are exceeding your mandate, or failing to meet it, I will withdraw my consent and punish you most severely. Do you understand what I am telling you?"

Sartean nodded again. "You are telling me, Sire, that if I do not wish to come to the same end as Harrington and Fennar, I will meet your objectives, no more, no less."

"No, Sartean D'avers. I am telling you that if you fail to please me, you will pray for a death as quick and painless as Harrington and

Fennar enjoyed. I recall that you are not a devout man, but I promise you, you will find religion before I have finished with you."

The king continued to glare at Sartean.

"I understand wholly, my king. I will not fail you." The wizard bowed deeply, and held his bow until the king spoke again.

"No, wizard, you will not. Continue your work, and I will prepare your document. Attend me at sunset." The king turned back to the palace, leaving Sartean to consider his threat.

The wizard did no such thing. After a moment to allow the king's squad to round the corner, he called to a nearby laborer.

"Yes, Master?"

"Find Master Vincent Thomison, and tell him his presence is required at Kehrlia immediately. You will find him at his manor. Tell no one, and do not fail to make clear that this is a summons, not a request."

"Yes, Master D'avers." The ash-covered man ran through the streets of Mor at a speed that impressed even Sartean.

# XXIX: THORNWOOD TRAIL

aptain Mikallis Elmshadow felt his consciousness slipping away again, his mind desperately trying to escape the turmoil and chaos that emanated from his heart.

He was failing Triumph. He was failing his people. He was failing himself.

He was failing Aria.

Night had fallen again, and the added degrees of concentration required were more than he could bear. For more than two days he had ridden without rest, the tortuous pace emptying him of all strength and confidence, leaving behind only a shell of the elf who had so boldly declared his loyalty to his beloved princess a few short days ago. He had withstood the stares. He had withstood the murmurs. He had even borne Aria's distancing, for he knew that his worth would be soon proven, and his honor and loyalty would win her heart. Yet he had been the first to falter, a wound to his pride that had festered and bled, its stench so thick within Mikallis that he could scarcely breathe. Each time the young captain called to Pheonaris for assistance a new wound opened, deeper and angrier than the last, his very soul now a lacerated mess of shame and dishonor.

*I am nothing. I cannot even keep pace with the woman I have sworn myself to protect. I have shamed myself before all of*

*Thornwood, and my love will never be returned.*

The rhythmic pounding of the saddle against his bruised and battered thighs was the only sensation his body was aware of. His eyes had long ago stopped being able to focus. He knew he held Triumph's reins, though his link to the Bond was but a thread, only strong enough to know that it was Pheonaris and Aria preventing his mount's heart from surrendering to the peaceful embrace of death, and the promise of rest it whispered.

Mikallis only knew shame and self-loathing. Nothing else mattered. Nothing else was even real. Nothing existed beyond the knowledge that his Aria would by now have lost all respect and admiration for him.

*My Aria*, he thought. *She is not my Aria. She has never been my Aria.*

The admission burned like hot coals in his stomach, scorching his guts, boiling his very blood. The feelings he had for Aria were beyond love. Beyond desire. Beyond passion. They were all. Mikallis would scorch the very world to protect her, to earn her love, to feel her kiss.

To possess her.

The noblest part of Mikallis knew that his obsession was wrong. That it was not elven, not even human. That it was centered in lust and hunger, not selfless, real love. Yet he could not extinguish it. He did not *want* to extinguish it. He only wished to sate it, to bathe it in Aria's own love and passion. Nothing else would soothe him. Nothing else would satisfy.

As the miles wore on, Mikallis' heart skipped between competing ideas of grief and determination. He would somehow complete this ride, he would persist, he would earn her respect again, her love was not lost. Then...it *was* lost. It was *never* his to lose. It could never be.

She did not appreciate his devotion to her. He could never make her *see.*

*No, I will. I must only survive this moment. Dammit, Triumph, run!*

He had forgotten how to communicate with his mount. Five years they had ridden together, and before this ride, he had known every inch of the stallion's spirit. He could inspire him with a thought. He had loved the horse, as he imagined that a father would love a child. Now Triumph was failing him, in this of all moments. As the Captain's desperation reached a climax, his link with Triumph began to fade, and he needed to constantly remind himself that this was his companion, his friend. Yet his friend resisted him.

The cut that his shame rent within him when he first called to Pheonaris for help that first dawn was painful. The gash he suffered when Aria, unprompted, send a part of her will to support him...this was the injury that broke Mikallis' spirit. She had only moments before called to Pheonaris herself. A part of him was saddened to hear her pain, to hear of Sera's pain. He had eventually admitted to himself, however, the larger part of him *hoped* that she would falter, that they would be forced to stop and rest, that his own weakness would be mitigated by the idea that only the powerful Mistress could maintain their pace. As soon as he had admitted that to himself, he found himself longing for Aria to withdraw her spiritual support—not because he did not need it, not because it did not comfort him, but because the withdrawal might mean that she had begun to fail, and he would not seem so inadequate in comparison.

This did not happen. If anything, he felt Aria's support *increase* over time. He saw her spine straighten, saw Sera's stride lengthen, and his jealousy and despair grew overwhelming as he watched his Aria ride with pride, strength and poise.

*She is not your Aria.*

The war within Mikallis raged on, and his heart weakened. The riders rounded a turn, and Triumph nearly rode straight into the wood. Mikallis barely pulled the reins in time to turn the charging horse. They rode on, Mikallis no longer even aware that he was not alone, the slight tendril of consciousness remaining to him only sufficient to keep him on the saddle. Aria sensed the danger.

"He is weakening, Mistress!"

"I know, Aria! You cannot help him, he will not make the Grove!" Pheonaris called back.

"We must not leave him! I cannot!"

"You must, Aria! You must ride on, we must ride on!"

"Can you not stay with him, Mistress? I can continue—Sera and I can go on!"

"No! I must accompany you! You must trust me, Princess of Thornwood! Let go!"

Aria's heart broke. She knew her friend must feel so ashamed, so alone. Her dear, prideful Mikallis. She sensed the distance between them increasing as Triumph slowed.

"He will join us later, Aria! Let go! Now!"

Aria let go. She knew she must do as her Mistress directed, but it tore at her to abandon her friend, to abandon Triumph. *Such pain they must feel,* she knew. The sound of hooves behind her faded, and the reduced exertion of her spirit was both a relief and a source of sorrow. She closed the distance between her and Pheonaris, and settled back into her pace.

Behind her, a haunted cry split the night air.

"*Ariaaaaa!*"

~

Aria and Pheonaris continued through the night, and the trail widened enough for Aria to bring Sera alongside Spirit. Pheonaris looked over her left shoulder to see Aria and Sera approach, and made room on the trail for the pair.

They raced beside one another in silence, Aria comforted by the closeness to her Mistress. No words needed to be spoken for each of the two women to know what the other was thinking. Aria was terribly saddened at the thought of Mikallis' sorrow, and Pheonaris would know this. The sweet brave elf would be crushed by what he saw as his own failure, but Aria knew that his shame was misguided. She did not fault him. She did not see his inability to keep pace as a weakness. She only just had learned the complexity of the Bond, and she knew that it was not a thing that could be explained, only discovered. That discovery would come between horse and rider in its own time, she understood. It was not a matter of character or strength. Aria sincerely felt that it was little more than luck that she had stumbled upon an understanding of the Bond, and she could no more fault Mikallis than she could congratulate herself.

Yet Mikallis would not see it that way, she knew.

Aria suspected, however, that her Mistress would see another angle. She would see Mikallis' presence on their journey as a distraction, no more. Aria was as safe as anyone could be in Pheonaris' presence...further protection was not needed. Mikallis would not know this; the Captain saw life through military eyes, and would not know her Mistress as Aria did. The woman was not merely capable of great power. She was wise and intelligent. Pheonaris possessed a sensitivity to her surroundings that only a century of training and experience could impart. Aria had seen evidence of this countless times during her tenure as an initiate. Mikallis would not know this, and his concern for Aria would not allow him to leave her fate in another's hands, not when the world faced such looming dangers. Pheonaris would understand this, but that understanding would not cloud her judgement. No, Aria decided, her Mistress would not be glad to see Mikallis struggle as he did, but neither would she lament his absence. In times such as these, pragmatism was required.

Pheonaris eventually broke the silence, her voice only slightly raised to carry over the sound of beating hooves.

"Dawn approaches, Aria. How do you fare?"

"We are well, Mistress. Sera is uncannily strong. How do *you* fare? You must be exhausted."

"You know I am not, Aria. You have learned how the Bond works. Spirit's comfort refreshes me. She is well, so I am well."

"What is the cost of this, Mistress?"

"Life, Aria. The cost is life. You must by now know this as well."

Aria did not ask the more specific question that was foremost on her mind, for she knew that Pheonaris understood what she had asked, and had chosen not to answer.

"The trail narrows ahead, Aria. You may take the lead if you wish. Do not look back to me, concentrate on the trail ahead. We are but a few hours from the Grove. Lead me home."

"Yes, Mistress," Aria replied, and gave Sera her head. The filly kicked at the trail enthusiastically, pleased to surpass Spirit. Aria could almost sense the pride coming from her friend.

The women raced on as the morning light advanced. There would be no sun this day, Aria observed. An overcast had thickened from the east during the night.

# XXX: THE MORLINE

hyla sat beside Wolf on the log raft, stroking his fur and brushing the ash from the animal's eyes as it continued to fall unabated. The Fang was well out of sight by then, and no longer northwards of them but due east behind them, as the Morline meandered northwestwards through the gently sloping basin between the Maw and the lands of men. Despite the distance between the company and the fuming mountain, the fall of ash had barely relented, and the mood of the travelers remained sullen and hushed.

Shyla's curious voice ruptured the stillness. "J'arn, is it hard to ride a horse?" the gnome asked the prince. "I seen the ones at the stable, and it looks hard."

J'arn nodded to Shyla. "Aye, Shyla, I have been considering that. 'Tis not a simple thing, particularly for one so small as you. I do not mean any insult, mind you, but it is a matter of strength. A rider uses their legs as much as their hands, and ye be at a disadvantage."

"Ye saying me legs are short, J'arn?" Shyla teased.

"Yer legs are just lovely, Shyla. But they ain't exactly pikes now, are they?"

"I s'pose not. Yers ain't neither, though."

J'arn laughed. The gnome had a way of brightening any situation, he noticed. "In any case, Lady Shyla, it will be necessary that ye share a saddle with one of us."

"Ain't all that easy for a dwarf neither, me Prince," Rocks added, poling the raft steadily. "Can't speak for the rest, but I ain't used to a full-sized mount."

"Ye will manage, Rocks. We'll not be able to ride as hard as with our dwarven steeds, but we'll make much better time than on foot."

Rocks nodded, and the matter was laid to rest for the moment until Shyla spoke again.

"What about Wolf?" she asked.

"What about him?" J'arn asked.

"Well, he can't ride no horse. He just s'posed to run alongside? He ain't much fer doin' as yeh tell 'im."

J'arn did his best to find a delicate way to reply, but none came to him.

"Shyla, Wolf might be best off stayin' behind at the docks–"

"Well, *that* ain't happenin', J'arn," Shyla interrupted. "I ain't leavin' Wolf behind fer nuthin'."

"Ye may have no choice, Shyla..."

"Nope."

"Well, ye can't–"

"Nope." Shyla scowled at J'arn, daring him to argue the point. J'arn was about to do just that when Boot interjected.

"Yer little spat may be for naught anyways. We got us another set o' problems."

The three looked to the engineer, who had spent the better part of the day poring over a series of maps. "C'mere and look at this, J'arn."

J'arn and Shyla shifted over to see the map Boot had laid out on the deck.

"We got us a heck of a run northwest after we hit the docks. Look here." Boot pointed to a shaded area on the map. "There be Gas Gorge, smack dab in the middle of the trail headin' to the Grove. We'd pass her by if we sailed on straight to Mor, but we can't get around her comin' from the docks."

J'arn sighed. Shyla asked, "What's Gas Gorge?"

"It's a crack, Shyla. A crack in the ground. The gorge be deep and treacherous, and some kinda bad air tends to accumulate in there– poison, some say. It ain't too bad when the winds are blowin', but they ain't been, and I ain't sure we oughta take that road. In fact I'm pretty sure we'd better not."

"We can't float all the way to the Northern Road, Boot," J'arn said. "If we do, we'll need to head south into Mor for mounts, and we'll add a day at least to the journey, likely more. We need to cut northwest, and the only place where we can do that *and* buy mounts be the docks."

Shyla listened as she concentrated on understanding the map laid before her. She could not make out the words very well, since the handwriting was foreign to her, but she could see where the Fang was marked, and was able to roughly establish where they must now be, based on the marking for the docks. Shyla understood direction well, and it did not take long for her to understand what the map portrayed.

"What's this squiggly line right here," she asked, "running west and north-like where the Morline breaks south?"

J'arn replied. "That's the Boiler, Shyla. It's a fork off the Mor that runs northwest to the springs."

"Well, ain't we headed to the springs? Ain't that where the Grove is?"

Boot answered. "Aye, Shyla. That's what I was about to mention to me prince, here." Boot looked to J'arn, eyebrows raised expectantly.

J'arn returned the stare. "Ye be crazy, Boot. No way can we take the Boiler, not on these rickety things."

"What's so bad 'bout the Boiler?" Shyla asked.

"Whaddya mean, rickety?" Boot replied, incensed. "These rafts can take a beating, J'arn, ye can bet a bag o' emeralds on that."

"What's wrong with the Boiler?" Shyla asked again.

"Ye can't be serious, Boot. I ain't tellin' ye about yer business, but can't no raft make the Boiler."

"*What in Mawbottom is wrong with the boiler, damn yeh?*" Shyla shouted.

Wolf's ears flattened against his head. The riders on Garlan's raft looked back at the hollering gnome.

"Apologies, Lady Shyla," Boot responded. "The Boiler's a rapid, she's fast and rocky and narrow, and..." Boot saw her confusion.

"It's a really fast river, Shyla. Really fast. It breaks off from the Morline—and yeah, it heads right where we be goin', but it's dangerous. Too dangerous for a raft."

"J'arn, I disagree with ye. These rafts can take 'er."

"Ever run the Boiler, Boot?"

"Can't say as I have. Have ye?"

J'arn knew he had erred before Boot even replied. "Well, no I haven't, Boot—"

"Then ye can't know we can't make it. Look J'arn, if we *can* take the Boiler, we'll get most of the way afore nightfall, if the stories about the speed ring true. We'll have a day's march the rest of the way. Look here...it ain't *even* a day's march from where the Boiler drops us off. And there be somethin' else. I ain't sure we're gonna find us any mounts at the docks, besides. Ye see what we're floatin' in? The damned skies are fallin', and for all we know, it be worse in Mor proper. Would ye be wantin' to sell yer own mount in these times?"

J'arn signed, again. Shyla, Rocks, and Boot all stared at the prince.

Rocks spoke up.

"Prince J'arn, if we can make 'er in under two days, 'stead of seven or eight, I say we give it a go."

"Seven or eight *if* we get mounts," Boot corrected.

"Two days *if* we survive the damned thing, and *if* we march the rest of the way without making camp," retorted J'arn.

"I ain't tired a bit, J'arn. How 'bout ye, Shyla? Need yerself a nap just yet?"

Shyla shook her head, smiling.

"Rocks?"

"Well, me arms are a bit tired, but I 'spose if ye can spell me a bit...sure, I'll be holdin' up, I'm thinkin'."

J'arn hung his head in thought as the three turned to him for a decision.

"Boot, I just ain't sure. The Boiler is *bloody* fast. It comes down to yer rafts. I'm no engineer, ye know that. But I know we're gonna take a poundin'. I need ye to put yer pride aside and tell me. Can these rafts make it?"

Boot considered before responding. He had of course never ridden the Boiler. None of them had. He could not know how treacherous the rapids would be. What he did know was that all Fury was breaking loose on Tahr, and the only help his people could hope for would come from the magic and wisdom of the elves. He looked to his prince. The young leader wanted an answer, not speculation. J'arn was hesitant, understandably so, and he needed reassurance.

"Well, J'arn, the rafts are sound. I designed 'em sturdy. We got as many crosslogs in the water as deck logs on top, and a hundred ties on each raft, tight as can be. We could lose half our knots and still hold together. I took a close look at Garlan's raft afore we floated this morning, makin' sure the damned fool hadn't banged his up too badly. She was rock solid, solid as when we first tied em' together. I say we tie everything down a bit more snug-like, just to be sure."

J'arn needed more.

"Aye, me prince, these rafts can make it."

The prince nodded. "I didn't bring ye along for yer looks, Kelgarr. Garlan!" he called. "Drag back a bit, we'll be takin' the lead!"

Narl dug his pole into the murky bottom of the Mor, allowing J'arn's crew to come alongside.

"Dwarves, we got us a bit of a problem, but we think we have a solution," J'arn addressed Garlan's crew.

"Ha!" Fannor barked. "Pay yer papa, boys!"

Jender and Starl groaned, and each tossed Fannor a coin.

"What's this?" asked J'arn.

"Well, we're takin' the Boiler, ain't we?" asked Fannor, smiling from ear to ear beneath his carrot-colored beard.

J'arn's eyes narrowed. "Aye, we're taking the Boiler. Could ye hear us talkin' from upriver? Didn't think we were so loud."

"Nah, we're just smart, is all," said Narl. "Fact is, Garlan here saw it comin' first."

"Did ye now, Garlan?"

"It's a damned fool idea, prince J'arn. I know why ye wanna do it, but these rafts can't take it."

Boot jumped up. "Ye call me prince a fool again, Garlan, and ye'll be whisker bait, I swear it."

"I didn't call J'arn a fool, Kelgarr, nor would I ever. It's you I call a fool, and I know it be yer damnable pride that makes ye think these floating trees can ride the Boiler."

"Pull us closer, Rocks. We're about to be short one forgemaster."

*"Shut yer traps before I shut 'em for ye! Enough!"* bellowed J'arn, the rare sound of his raised voice freezing the company stiff. "Garlan, it be my decision, not Boot's. Ye be out of yer element here. Boot, ye swallow that tongue o' yours *now*." J'arn paused a moment to make certain the dwarves had settled.

"Prince J'arn," Starl broke the tension. J'arn looked to the man.

"If we take the Boiler, are we gonna get out o' this cursed ash a little faster?"

"Might be, Starl."

"Well ye got my vote then, if ye needed it."

The rest of the dwarves all murmured agreement, all except Garlan.

"I didn't need yer vote Starl, but I'll take it. Boys, ain't no time for democracy now, we're gonna have to get to work. Now, the river's widening. See that inlet comin' up? That means we're not far from the fork. I've made this trip a dozen times with my father, and he's shown me where the Boiler starts more than once. It won't look like much when we hit the split, just a little lazy lookin' channel off to the right, but don't let that fool ye. My father says she narrows quick, and she's fed from a dozen inlets between here and the springs. She'll get fast, and faster, don't ye doubt. We'll be ridin' the Boiler before noon, I be thinkin' half an hour at most. I want every last pot, kettle, pack and sack tied down tighter than a corset, and retied again. Shyla, ye might want to tie yer Wolf down. Don't gimme that look...better he whine than fall off in the rapids. If he hits the water, we can't stop, won't be no way to stop. Boot, what else?"

Boot spoke up. "I cut an oar for each o' ye, they ain't much but they'll have to do. Fannor, pass me those four on top o' the pile. Shyla, grab 'em, don't let 'em fall in now. We're gonna need to tie in some handholds. Jender, cut me nine lengths o' rope, long as yer arm..."

"Ain't much rope left, Boot," Starl said.

"How much?"

"Not enough to do all the tyin' ye be askin' for, and make handholds besides."

Boot thought for a moment. Shyla looked around at the dwarves, and chimed in.

"We all got bootlaces, Boot. Will that work?"

"Aye, Shyla, good idea. Ye won't wanna be wearin' those if ye get knocked off anyhow. Use yer bootlaces then, yer gonna need to thread 'em between the logs now, and get some gloves on after, or ye'll blister up as ye paddle..."

Ideas became orders, and the dwarves worked diligently. Shyla managed to secure Wolf as best she could with J'arn's help, so that the struggling animal was tied and flattened to the center of the raft. He had snapped threateningly at the pair more than once, but at last relented, sensing that he had little choice but to comply. He whined continuously, but even Shyla was not swayed.

"It's for yer own good, ye furry pain in the pants. Yer a Wolf not a fish, and if yeh fall yer a goner." She worked to soothe the disconcerted animal as best she could.

After a time the rafts were made as ready as they could be to withstand the ride, and J'arn called back to Garlan, "Stay on my tail now, the fork's comin' up!"

Seven oars and two poles worked the water, and the sturdy crafts cruised right up the center of the fork, leaving the Morline to wander to the southwest as they entered the Boiler heading northwest. At first, there was no perceptible difference in speed. The Morline had widened considerably and slowed a bit before the fork. The Boiler began to narrow slightly, however, grassy shores becoming steep embankments, and their speed increased. As they navigated the stream, the falling flakes of ash seemed to come at them at an angle, the illusion created by their accelerating pace.

"Well, we're makin' good time now, ain't we?" Boot said excitedly.

"Aye Boot, seems like!" J'arn replied. "Center now boys, keep to the center. Watch how I'm paddlin'."

J'arn knelt and hunched at the front of the raft, steering left and right with his oar as they passed the first inlet. The flow of water from the north pushed the raft to the left, and the paddling dwarves compensated smoothly, their pace steadily increasing.

"Fury, J'arn, we're movin' now!" Shyla declared, grinning. The ash began to blow around them, rather than coming to a rest and sticking to their clothing and the deck. "This has gotta be faster than a horse!"

"About that fast, Shyla, but we'll be gettin' even faster here in a bit, I'll bet. How's the raft holding up, Boot?"

"Ain't no different than the Morline, J'arn. 'Less we hit somethin', don't matter how fast we go."

"Pass me one o' those oars, Boot, this pole's useless at this speed." Boot rose and walked back to relieve Rocks. "I'll take the rear, Rocks. Rest yerself a minute. Shyla, let me an' J'arn steer, rest yer arms a bit."

The dwarves on both rafts took shifts resting and manning the oars, and despite the increasing speed, or perhaps because of it, the steering became easier for a time, their oars used more as rudders than as paddles. They passed several inlets, made several meandering turns, and the company navigated the stream carefully, always maintaining a path along the center. The land of Tahr flew by, and a flock of hundreds of small birds paced the crews for a time, eventually veering off and giving up the chase.

"The ash!" Shyla exclaimed late that afternoon. "The ash ain't fallin' no more!" The dwarves had barely registered the change, their concentration fixed on piloting their rafts. A cheer arose as they all realized the gnome was right, and Narl and Fannor broke into a song about a fictional fleet of dwarven pirates.

"Quiet, dwarves!" J'arn interrupted the song. "Looks like the channel is starting to narrow up here. Everyone on an oar now, and watch me!"

The channel did narrow dramatically. The rafts were roughly four paces square, and the Boiler had maintained a width of roughly forty paces for the past hour. No longer. The width of the stream suddenly halved, and their speed subsequently doubled. What had been a smooth, fast, flat journey quickly became a breakneck ride, the wind pulling tears from J'arn's eyes as they accelerated.

J'arn kept his gaze upriver, and suddenly, he could see why the Boiler was so named.

# XXXI: THE GROVE

ria and her snow-bright filly Sera flew the remainder of the Thornwood Trail like feathers in a gale. The princess was not quite relieved of her sorrow over Mikallis, but neither was she shattered. Aria had consciously decided that she would not allow herself to mourn the decision to leave him; all was as it must be, and so she would enjoy this ride with Sera, and allow herself to become hopeful that the Grove would bring rest and understanding of her role in the struggles to come. Mikallis would join them, and in time the episode would be forgotten.

She did not want to forget *this* moment, however. The air was crisp and cool, the leaves of the wood scattered and piled on the trail but still retaining many of the bright vivid colors of autumn. They had passed a herd of deer, several rabbits and all manner of woodland life as they rode. All parted before the storming pair in deference, as if they somehow knew that even their future relied on the successful journey of the princess and her Mistress.

Pheonaris had not called to her in an hour, and Aria was grateful for it. She enjoyed taking the lead, flying through the wood as if she and Sera were the only sentient beings in all the world. Her body was sore, but her spirit was soaring, and despite the gloomy skies and chilly air the day was perfect. Her long ponytailed hair bounced behind her, blue cloak flowing freely as she moved in rhythm with her horse and flung the miles behind her dismissively.

The trail opened suddenly onto a grassy hillock, and the riders slowed at long, long last, cresting the hill and looking down upon the secluded valley of the Grove. Pheonaris pulled alongside her, and they slowed their huffing mounts to a trot, then a stop.

"Tell me, is it not wonderful, Aria?" The beautiful, wise Pheonaris spoke reverently, smiling.

"The ride, or the Grove?" Aria asked.

"Both, certainly, but I speak of the Grove. I cannot but leave my heart here when I go, and I so do love to return to it." Pheonaris inhaled deeply. "What do you smell?"

Aria also inhaled. The air of the Grove *was* different from that of the trail. Perfumed aromas of flowers and pungent wild plants mingled with steamy, humid scents that emanated from the underground hot springs that nourished the herbal flora of the enchanted land. "Life, Mistress. All the life of the world. It is the best air in all of Tahr. I miss it dearly as well when I go."

"It is home," Pheonaris expressed simply. "Let us go to it."

The women started down the rise and Aria spoke.

"Thank you for allowing me to take the lead on the last stretch, Mistress."

Pheonaris halted her mount. "Aria. Wait a moment, please."

Aria turned Sera. "Yes, Mistress?"

"The lead is yours to take whenever you wish. Do you understand?"

"I...thank you, Mistress, I think so."

"I see perhaps that you do not. Aria, hear me now. You are the Princess of Thornwood. You are no longer my initiate. You bear the full authority of your station. You are my superior."

Aria frowned. "Mistress, the day that I feel myself your superior will never come. I am still but a novice–"

"It is not a matter of how you feel, Princess. It is what is. I certainly hope that you will always allow me to advise you, and teach you as is my responsibility. But it is only that which I offer, advice. You must choose to heed it or not, as your obligations require."

Aria shook her head emphatically. "Mistress, I could never ignore your advice. You are wise in so many things."

Pheonaris smiled. "You honor me, Princess, but the day will come where my advice runs contrary to another's, and you must allow your own wisdom and conscience to guide you. When the queen is not present, you *are* Thornwood. May I make a suggestion?"

"Ah...of course, Mistress." Aria was exceedingly uncomfortable.

"When we are alone, if you allow it, I shall call you Aria, as I would speak to a student, as a friend. And you may call me Pheonaris, for I consider you my friend." Aria nodded vigorously, her agreement passionately clear. "But when we are among our people, particularly when we are discussing matters of state, I will call you Princess, or another of your formal titles. You must feel free to order me as your mother the queen would. Perhaps the formality will help you remember."

Aria bowed her head. "Pheonaris, I do not like this. I do not wish for things to change."

"I know, child. I know. Yet change things do, and they always will. It is as it must be."

Aria looked upon her teacher, her Mistress, her friend. The Mistress of the Order of the Grove sat silently, returning Aria's gaze. It became clear to Aria that she must give her friend her first order.

"Your counsel is wise. Let us continue then, Mistress. Though I would ask..."

"Yes, Princess?"

"If I am in danger of making a complete and total fool of myself, you will stop me?"

Pheonaris laughed joyfully. "I will try, Princess Aria of Thornwood. I will most certainly try. Now let us see what trouble Trellia has caused in my absence. After you, Lady." The Mistress bowed demurely in the saddle, and Aria walked Sera down to the valley.

~

"Vicaris, the Mistress arrives! With Aria!" Fani announced excitedly. The senior druid ran up the flagstone path to greet her long-missed friends.

"Fani! Ah, it is so good to see you!" Aria exclaimed, rushing ahead to meet her. Pheonaris had said something as Aria had called to Fani, but she did not hear it over her own voice. The princess quickly dismounted Sera for the first time in days.

"Noooo!" Pheonaris yelled, too late.

As soon as Aria left the saddle and her feet hit the soil of Tahr, her knees buckled and her head began to swim. She fell to all fours, shivering and struggling for breath. Sera threw her head, visibly upset and frightened.

"Aria, what's wrong? Vicaris! Come now!"

Pheonaris approached, chanting softly under her breath, and gingerly dismounted Spirit, steadying herself and maintaining physical contact with her colt at all times.

"Princess, listen to me. You must reconnect with your Bond. Stand now, touch Sera, it will help."

Aria could not stand. She could not even try. She felt as if she had died, her soul unreachable, her body a ragged bag of lifeless skin and sinew. Her Mistress was speaking, but as if from beyond the Veil, words blurring and swirling in the air, incomprehensible and distant. The Princess collapsed the rest of the way to the ground as Barris ran up.

"Mistress! You did not tell her!" Barris scolded as he laid his hands on Sera, who by then was losing her own sense of balance.

"I tried, Sir Barris. She shot ahead and I did not stop her in time."

"Fani, I must stay with Sera. Get the Vicaris."

"I am here, Barris," Trellia moved to kneel beside Aria and placed her hand on her sallow forehead.

"She is cold as snow. What happened?"

"She dropped her link too suddenly," Barris replied as several druids and initiates approached, two carrying a cloth stretcher.

"We heard your call, Mistress. What must we do?" asked Petahr, concern becoming panic as he saw his Princess shuddering on the ground.

Barris barked instructions. "You must carry her to the cabin, quickly now. Fani, run ahead and set up a cot beside Lucan, and throw more logs on the fire. Everyone else, gather blankets. She will need to be kept as warm as possible. Her spirit is in shock. You will know how to treat this, but you must first warm her. *Go!*"

Aria was loaded onto the stretcher and whisked to the cabin quickly, the druids and initiates racing about in an organized but harried fashion, carrying out Barris' orders. Pheonaris and Barris slowly walked Sera and Spirit to the stables that sat on the near shore of the Spring.

"She will recover," the Mistress affirmed, primarily to herself.

"She will, Mistress. Do not fear for her. Better she learn the lesson now, while she is in safe hands."

"I should have told her sooner. It is my error."

"And not the last you will ever make, Mistress. Be at peace, Aria will be fine," Barris promised. "But where is Mikallis?"

The Mistress gave Barris a loaded look. "We must speak about Mikallis, Barris. I fear that we may have a situation there."

Barris nodded. "I fear the same thing, Mistress. I assume he could not keep the pace?"

"No, though I am sure he will not be far behind, a day at most. His pace is not the problem."

"Perhaps his pace is exactly the problem, Mistress."

Pheonaris understood the entendre, but shook her head. "It may run deeper even than that, Barris."

~

Trellia and Barris sipped tea with Pheonaris in her private home, huddled around her small dining table. The humbly appointed cabin bore a musty, humid odor, but not an unpleasant one. The cabin had remained closed for the better part of a cycle as Pheonaris had traveled to the capital. The setting could best be described as orderly yet chaotic—hundreds of small trinkets and books and keepsake items adorning the many shelves around the cabin, colorful handmade chimes hanging silently in the windless air, and stacks of parchment balancing on nearly every flat surface in the sparsely furnished log home. The initial impression was that of a hoard of inconsequential items, but a closer look revealed that everything one saw had either a use or a history, and was in its proper place. The small house was divided into four equally sized rooms: a small area for entertaining, a kitchen, a bedchamber, and a library. Barris and Trellia sat quietly, awaiting Pheonaris' cue to speak, but the woman seemed distant, and they both sensed that something ate at the Mistress.

"Share your thoughts, Mistress," Trellia invited.

Pheonaris pulled her gaze from the window. "I scarcely know where to start, Trellia. I suppose we must first discuss the fact that these are not ordinary clouds rolling in."

"Fang," Barris declared frankly.

"I believe so, Barris. I am a bit too fatigued to confirm as much, but after I have slept, I will know for sure."

Trellia shook her head. "No need, Mistress. It is the mountain. Either Fang caused the quake, or the quake woke Fang. I sensed this yesterday, and confirmed it myself. Ash is falling throughout Greater Tahr. We are only just outside the mountain's reach, and only until the westerly winds again blow."

Pheonaris appeared crushed. "So much will die," she said. "This has happened before, in the first age of Tahr, and the devastation was atrocious. If Neral's forecasts are accurate, and I have no reason to believe they are not, even the Grove will soon become a blighted land of death." Pheonaris explained all that she had learned in the elven council. Barris and Trellia listened in dismay as the Mistress described the feared causes of the affliction affecting the world, and the omens of war, evil and horror that were coming to bear.

"The outlook is nothing short of total and complete destruction," Pheonaris concluded, her tone more miserable than Barris had ever heard it, all the charm of her spirit spent.

"Let us hope it does not come to that, Mistress," Barris said after a moment, lacking a better response.

"Hope is not a strategy, Barris. We cannot let the land die, or its people will soon follow."

"I assume you have a strategy then, Mistress?" Trellia asked, Pheonaris' gloom proving somewhat contagious. "Other than blind hope, I would gather? If so that is good, for I am not blind, but neither am I especially hopeful just now."

"A strategy...no. But a belief that one will soon emerge, yes."

"Not much better than blind hope, I fear, Mistress."

"Perhaps it is a bit more, Trellia. As you have no doubt learned by now, I have been given to know that Aria is somehow to be instrumental in our opposition to these forces that threaten. Although..." Pheonaris paused, and her shoulders seemed to heave slightly as she suppressed a sob. "I had expected that we would have learned that strategy, or at least some of it, upon arriving here at the Grove. It was clear in my vision that we were required to arrive this morning, at dawn, yet the day passes and I have not yet discovered anything at all. I am afraid that perhaps we were a bit too late, or perhaps my failure in preparing the Princess for the end of our ride has caused her to miss some sign–"

Trellia interrupted the Mistress, embarrassed and saddened to see her superior so distraught. "No, Pheonaris. I do not believe divination works like that. A future is but one of many paths, it is not scheduled so strictly. You are tired, and filled with self-doubt. You must not despair."

"I agree with the Vicaris, Mistress. Perhaps Aria is right where she is meant to be, and the way forward will soon become clear." Barris reached for the Mistress' hand, and spoke gently. "I know what you feel right now, Mistress. The breaking of the link of the Bond takes a toll, not only on your strength, but on your heart. You cannot serve yourself or your people until you have rested." Barris squeezed her hand, and stood.

"Come, Trellia. Let us go see how our patients fare."

Pheonaris scowled. "Barris, do not dismiss me as so helpless."

"I do no such thing, Mistress. I dismiss your doubts, however. After you rest, you will do so as well."

The Mistress wiped her eyes, nodded in compliance, and rose feebly. "You will wake me, if Aria wakes?"

"*When* Aria wakes, Mistress," Trellia corrected, hearing the despair and guilt in her Mistress' voice.

# XXXII: THE BOILER

ne hand on yer oars, one on yer straps! Looks like we're in for a ride! Shyla, watch for–"

The front of the lead raft struck something solid, and J'arn's words were cut off as the craft skipped atop an unseen obstacle. He barely managed to avoid falling headfirst into the water as Shyla grabbed his belt and pulled him back. She had set down her oar to catch the unbalanced dwarf, and it bounced off the deck into the water as Garlan's raft violently collided with their own from behind. There was no time to resettle themselves or assess the damage, as the pair of rafts jumped another rock. Wolf yelped in fright.

Boot had managed to remain balanced as they struck the first boulder, and as Garlan's craft smashed them from behind. The second, however, threw the dwarf from the log deck, and the hollering engineer flew into the water.

"*Boooot!*" Rocks screamed.

Boot gasped and clawed at the surface of the water as he rolled within the rapids between the two bulking crafts, tons of soaked wood threatening to smash him at the surface, rocks and logs battering him from below. The dwarf could barely swim in calm waters; in the raging flow of the Boiler, he was at the mercy of the currents. He lost all sense of up and down, desperately inhaling whenever he sensed his head bob above the water, exhaling violently whenever his battered body struck a stone. At one point, he tumbled completely end over end, and his legs stuck out of the water, the corner of one raft smashing and grinding the bones of his ankle against the other. The pain was severe, but as nothing when compared to the tortured burning of his lungs.

Above the surface, Wolf barked and snapped, terrified. The dwarves had all lost their oars, and were clinging for life to their handholds. The rafts bounced and smashed and crashed wildly among the rocks as the river became shallower and more treacherous, but somehow, they held together, only three logs having come loose. J'arn was yelling unintelligible orders while he gripped his own strap, knowing they were not heard, nor could they be heeded if they were. The loose logs now rolled murderously between the two rafts, adding to the threat faced by the drowning engineer.

Shyla looked over to the other raft just in time to see Garlan bark an order to Starl and dive into the water headfirst.

Boot was no longer fighting. He rebounded between rock and raft, concentrating only on where his next breath might come from. His body bled and tore, but the dwarf paid it no mind. Only air. *Please, one more breath.* He willed himself to float to the surface as he fought against the scorching urge to inhale. Pain became panic, and he forced his hands over his nose and mouth to fight the need to breathe. Finally, a log struck him in the ribs, and he could withstand no more. Boot inhaled deeply, river water flooding his lungs, and he managed two quickly completed breaths before his eyes glazed over, and his limbs went limp.

Darkness.

~

The battering seemed to go on for an eternity. Then suddenly, as soon as it had begun, it stopped. The Boiler passed over a shallow natural dam, and on the other side, the waters pooled and the two rafts spilled into a basin, slowing quickly. The stream widened quickly into a small, quiet pond lined with lush green trees that had not yet suffered the ashfalls of the east, the grey and emerald scene impossibly serene and placid. J'arn and Shyla looked at one another solemnly, then to Rocks, and to Garlan's raft.

One terror had passed, the other only dawning, as Narl and Fannor were the only two dwarves visible.

The pair of brothers paced the edge of their raft, calling desperately to their four missing comrades. J'arn, Shyla and Rocks joined the call, and Rocks saw Garlan first, a hundred paces to the east, pulling a limp dwarven body onto the shore.

"Paddle! Get to the shore!" J'arn knelt and paddled with his hands, desperately trying to alter the raft's direction, but the river behind them still thrust them forward despite the relative calm of the pond. Gradually, excruciatingly sluggishly, the raft altered course towards the shoreline. J'arn looked back to Narl and Fannor, and saw that they were not paddling, but standing in stillness, staring silently off towards the mouth of the Boiler. J'arn followed the line of their gazes.

Floating face down, two dwarven bodies bobbed and swirled in the current.

J'arn screamed to Narl and Fannor to rescue the floating dwarves, his mournful cry shattering the stillness of the scene. He and Rocks paddled furiously towards the shoreline, and Shyla slapped at the water desperately. Her tiny hands had little effect on the raft's direction, but she did what she could.

~

On the shoreline, Garlan slammed his hands upward repeatedly into Boot's gut. Pints of water were expelled, but the dwarf did not breathe.

"Damn you, Boot, I'll kill you for this."

Garlan pinched the engineer's nose shut, and breathed into the pallid dwarf. Three, four, five times he filled Boot's lungs...finally rewarded with a mouthful of vomit and river water. Garlan jumped back as Boot gasped, coughed, and clawed at his own throat. The forgemaster rolled the dwarf onto his stomach, and let the engineer finish emptying himself of water and bile as J'arn, Shyla, Rocks and Wolf made the shoreline. Shyla immediately united Wolf, Rocks moored the raft, and J'arn ran to Garlan and Boot.

Narl and Fannor had lifted their friends aboard, and were not far behind.

~

"I didn't even see 'em fall, me Prince," Narl said weakly through tears and snot.

"Nor I, Narl," Fannor sobbed as J'arn, Rocks and Garlan helped the brothers gently carry their drowned friends ashore. Shyla sat beside Boot, who now sat upright, watching the four carry out the solemn duty. Wolf had limped off into the woods.

"They were still on the backside of the raft when I went in after Boot. Nothin' ye coulda done, ye can't help what ye don't see," added Garlan. The dead dwarves were laid side by side, and Shyla could not help but notice their bare feet. Somehow, their unshod feet made them appear more lifeless, as if their lack of boots was the result of some final indignity faced, one that all would eventually suffer. Shyla shivered, and Narl knelt down to close their milky white eyes.

"I shoulda been watchin', Starl." Fannor knelt beside his brother.

"Ah, Fury, I'm so sorry, me prince. I'm so sorry." Narl and Fannor embraced one another, weeping pitifully.

J'arn spoke quietly and slowly. "It was not your fault. The responsibility was mine. I shall hear none claim otherwise, nor lay blame on another. The Boiler was the path I chose." The prince eyed Garlan, then.

Garlan frowned. "I suppose ye fear I'll blame Boot, prince."

J'arn did not respond, but looked to the engineer, who was being helped to sit upright by Shyla.

"Well, ye need not. He spoke his mind, and he were right. His rafts held. And even if they didn't, this ain't his fault. It ain't yours neither, J'arn." The prince moved to speak, but Garlan did not allow it. "Don't say it, Prince J'arn. The world's gone to Fury. We're doin' a job. Best we can. Might be we all die. Ain't a one of us 'fraid to. I've lost dwarves. Brave dwarves. Hard workin' dwarves. Made choices I regret. But they were the choices I thought best. Ye can't know what's comin', and ye can't change what's come. I ain't worried about Starl and Jender. They be half drunk in Stonarris already, ye can bet a bag. These..." he motioned to the bodies. "These ain't Starl and Jender. Not no more. We gotta bury 'em, bury our guilt with 'em, and get on with it."

No one spoke for several turns.

J'arn broke the hush. "We must bury our friends, and continue on to the Grove. Rocks, will you untie our boots and bring them? Kelgarr, can you travel?"

Boot took a tentative step. He nearly fell, Shyla catching him.

"No, me prince. Ye can leave me a bit of food, and I'll catch up. Won't be more than a day behind."

Garlan shook his head and spoke forcefully. "We're already leaving two, no more. Narl, Fannor, with me. We'll make a stretcher, and we'll march. Not a word, Boot."

Boot nodded.

"Shyla. Will ye help us bury our friends?" J'arn asked.

Shyla nodded. "Aye."

Wolf padded up to Boot, and sat at his feet, sullen. Boot sat beside him, pulled him close, and began to cry silently as the grey light of day faded to black.

~

Starl and Jender were laid to rest, their own waraxes used to chop markings into the nearby trees, so that their graves could be found later. The company vowed as one that their bodies would be retrieved, and returned to their families. J'arn slung Starl's axe over his back, and would carry it until they returned to Belgorne. Boot insisted on carrying the other, but it was impractical as he would be carried himself. Rocks carried it in his stead for the time being.

J'arn took point, and Shyla and Wolf stayed on his heels, followed by Garlan, Rocks, Narl, and Fannor, who carried Boot's stretcher. As much gear as they could transport was tied atop Boot, and the eight companions trudged northwest, roughly following an outlet that would serve as a directional guide, at least throughout the night. There was no trail, and the march through the dark forest was made with difficulty, but the eight managed.

The wood was eerily silent. No wind, no howls of wolves or other nocturnal creatures. It seemed to J'arn that the entire world held its breath in anticipation of the coming clouds of smoke and ash, for there was no doubt that when the easterlies again blew, the ash would reach to the Grove and beyond.

Paces became miles, miles became hours, and the light of dawn began to glow. J'arn called a rest, and the company shared what remained of their dried meats and nuts. No banter was exchanged; all sensed that idle chatter would be an insult to their fallen comrades. With a word from J'arn they resumed their journey, and they marched several more hours before another rest was called.

"We'll make the Grove before nightfall," J'arn declared. "Relieve yourselves, and let us complete this march." The dwarves and Shyla all sought a moment of privacy.

"C'mon, Boot. I'll take ye to empty yerself," Garlan offered.

"Aye, Garlan. Thank ye." The forgemaster helped the engineer limp a few paces into the forest. He propped Boot up against a tree and made to leave.

"Garlan."

Garlan turned. "Aye, Boot."

"The trouble between us. I... I was wrong."

Garlan shook his head and ran his fingers through his salt and pepper hair. "No, Kelgarr, ye weren't wrong. I lied from shame. Blamed my failures on ye. Ye weren't wrong."

"I know yer shame now, Garlan. Know it well."

"But ye won't lie about it, will ye?"

Boot considered. "I might if I could, Garlan. I just might."

Garlan stared at his feet, then walked back to Boot.

"We got a job to do, Boot. Ain't no room for anger between us."

"Ye saved me life, Garlan. That ain't the reason I be sayin' all this, but it ain't fer nothin', neither."

Boot held out his arm. Garlan grasped it. The feud between the forgemaster and the engineer died forgotten in an unnamed wood in the forests of Tahr.

"Now get, forgemaster, before I foul me pants."

"Thought ye already had." Garlan deadpanned.

~

The eight marched on. The going became easier as the trees became taller and more sparsely rooted. The canopy of broad leaves and thick branches nearly blotted out all light, save for an unbroken, dusky, greenish glow filtering down from overhead. Shyla was in awe, but Wolf was spooked, and walked beside her with flattened ears and a tucked tail. A mist had thickened as they walked, and the formerly challenging march became a monotonous plod, easier on the legs, but harder on the heart. They walked for hours; then, just when the remaining light began to fade and the company began to fear that they had lost their sense of direction, the mists thinned, and the eight broke free of the forest's grasp.

The battered and weary company emerged from the wood onto an embankment. A hundred paces from the ridge lay a steaming spring, the inviting glow of candles within cabins, a small stable, and a spattering of busy elves.

They had reached the Grove.

Shyla grinned and took J'arn's hand. "Thank yeh, Prince J'arn. Yeh be good as yer word."

Wolf sprinted down the embankment, sensing food.

# XXXIII: THE GROVE

ucan felt the dream slipping away. For days, he had dreamt of wars and terrors, battles and beasts, sliding from one scene of horror to the next. There had been moments that he knew he was not *here*, that he was elsewhere, somewhere, asleep and unable to wake. Those moments fled, and returned, and fled again, the nightmares ebbing in and out like a tide. He now stood upon a rise, overlooking a grand scene of combat, and beside him, stood the elf. The woman he had fought alongside. The woman he sensed he knew, yet knew he did not. The woman he had come to expect at every scene, the ever-present, silent elf. Now she faded, his dream faded, and he knew that he was returning to the place he was from. He was not sure he wanted to. He sensed that he was important here, that he was needed. Unlike in his true life, his real life...

Lucan opened his eyes, and the firelight flickered on a pitched log ceiling. He blinked, and inhaled, and was surprised that there was no pain. Slowly, he turned his head to the side to survey his surroundings.

Beside him lay the elf.

At the same moment, Aria stirred from her own dream, the princess returning to consciousness and leaving the man that had stood beside her to stand alone, the man that she knew, yet did not.

Aria opened her eyes, blinked, and inhaled. She heard a stirring beside her, and turned her head. Looking back at her was the man. The two looked at one another silently for a moment. They spoke in unison.

"Hello."

**END OF PART TWO**

If you have enjoyed reading *Omens of Fury* and would like your copy signed, please email me at **sean@seanhinn.com**, and I will be delighted to make arrangements with you.

Also, please connect with me on Facebook and Twitter; it would be my pleasure to speak with you personally about *Omens of Fury*, its characters, and The Days of Ash and Fury series.

**facebook.com/TahrSeanHinn**
**twitter.com/SeanHinn**
**seanhinn.com**

*For a sneak preview of Volume Two, continue reading past the acknowledgements...*

# ACKNOWLEDGEMENTS

*Omens of Fury* is my first book, and from the moment I wrote the first scene with Barris standing before Halsen, I have been obsessed with the story at the expense of all else. I first wish to thank my family, Emily, Joey, Sean, and Bella, for not only tolerating that fixation, but encouraging it. Without exception, my repeated calls from my office of, "Who wants the next chapter?" were met with enthusiasm. You guys are the best, and without your inspiration, *Omens* would never have been finished.

I also wish to acknowledge Amers – you know who you are – for always being the very first to like my posts about Omens of Fury on Facebook (back when it was still titled *Tahr*), and unfailingly having something kind to say. The same gratitude goes to my best bud Scott, who read every word of the story within hours of it first being written, providing feedback throughout the composition of the book.

Mostly, I thank Emily, the smartest person I have ever met, for always knowing when to gently criticize a style decision–and for endless hours of stimulating debate about commas. This book is as much your work as mine, and I love you more than I could ever express.

I *very* much wish to thank MAPLE ESTUDIO for the gorgeous cover re-design, and I am also deeply indebted to the talented Dr. Debra Doyle for her excellent work in preparing and polishing this second edition of the book. Thank you, Debra... your brilliant application of editing magic has made this story shine.

Finally, I thank you, my first readers, for embarking on this adventure with me—in particular, my very first fan, Todd S. from Junction City, Ohio. Like you, I cannot wait to see how it ends.

# VOLUME TWO

## I: MOR

Sartean D'Avers sat silently in his library; he would make Vincent Thomison wait. The merchant had been called from his manor to attend Sartean at the Keep and had arrived fully an hour prior, covered in ash and incensed at the summoning. Sartean knew this. Master Thomison would have certainly learned of the violent demise of Barrington and Fennar earlier that day. Violent, unexpected mortality had a way of causing one to evaluate their place in the pecking order, and so the Master of Kehrlia seized the opportunity to unbalance Thomison with the subtle display of power.

The masters of Trade and Treasury had failed at The Game, and their failures had proven fatal; in the throneroom of Mor, The Game was all. While the wizard did not personally strike the fatal blows, Thomison would nonetheless suspect that it was Sartean who had orchestrated their deaths.

*And he would be correct, in a sense at least,* Sartean considered. Though, he would not begin to fathom the complexity of Sartean's course. Not yet. First, Sartean surmised, his guest - Master Vincent Thomison, de facto ruler of both the legitimate and underground markets of Mor - would be hard pressed to see beyond his own indignation at being kept lingering at the wizard's pleasure in the grand vestibule of Kehrlia, where no seating was to be found. *He will be pacing now,* Sartean imagined. *Deciding whether he should seek out an apprentice to remind me that he has arrived. Perhaps he is considering leaving. He will be-*

A booming knock at the door to the library interrupted the thought.

*Interesting,* thought Sartean.

"Enter."

An apprentice stumbled through the heavy door, shoved roughly from behind. "Master, I tried to tell him—"

"He tried to tell me that I must wait at the bottom of your damned stairs, wizard. I grew tired of waiting."

Sartean raised his eyebrows, looking up from a book on his desk. "That will be all, Criss. You may leave." The apprentice bowed and hurriedly departed the library. "Master Thomison, how good of you to come. Please sit." Sartean motioned to the indigo velvet chairs that sat before his imposing black marble desk.

Thomison removed his crimson cloak and unceremoniously tossed it onto the chair on the right, ash billowing from the garment in a cloud. He sat in the chair to the left.

"You play games with me, wizard. I am not one to be kept waiting. Only one in Mor has the power to summon me."

Sartean nodded. "Yes, only one. As for your wait, I was unaware that you had arrived."

"You lie."

Sartean made no effort to hide a smirk. "Do I?"

"Your apprentice told me that you had been notified of my arrival an hour ago."

"Ah. Well, perhaps he did; I have been engrossed in my work. Surely you dismiss much of what your own subordinates report."

"I dismiss much, wizard, though I overlook nothing. Why am I here?"

Sartean regarded the man. The merchant was a contradiction. Fine garments, the finest, his silken white shirt immaculately clean, leggings of the most luxuriously black material, nearly iridescent. His clothing had been tailored perfectly to fit his lean muscular frame, his boots dirty with ash, but clearly of premium quality. Yet, the man beneath the fine clothing had the look of one who worked much of his nearly fifty years out of doors. Deeply tanned skin, rough hands, eyes pinched by the sun, salt and pepper hair trimmed neatly but not overly short, no jewelry visible aside from a single platinum band on his right hand...Vincent Thomison appeared to Sartean as a lifelong soldier, suddenly come into wealth.

"I asked you a question, wizard."

Sartean's tone carried a hint of shadow. "Master Thomison. Perhaps we have gotten off poorly. Let us begin with an understanding, then." A pause, for effect. "As you only allow one to summon you, I only allow one to address me as 'wizard.' I shall address you as Master Thomison, or Vincent as you prefer. Am I being clear?"

Thomison's lips pressed together, though he continued to hold Sartean's gaze, pausing a moment before replying. "Very well, Sartean, we have established our nobilities. First names will do. Now, I have much business to attend to today, and I would very much like for you to get to the point. Perhaps you might have noticed; Mor has gone to Fury these past days."

"Not quite Fury, not yet, but I agree. It is a dangerous time we live in."

"For some, perhaps. I see nothing but opportunity."

"As do I. You have no doubt heard of today's audience in the throne room."

"How did you pull it off?"

Sartean demurred. "I am sure I do not know what you mean."

Vincent's face curled. "Sartean, we are men of power. You have invited me here for a reason. Clearly you have business to discuss. Let us dispense with deception and wordplay, agreed?" A pause, then a slight nod from Sartean in response. "Good. Now, Barrington and Fennar died today as much by your hand as by the halberds of the Defenders." The merchant did not phrase his statement as a question.

Sartean allowed a slight grin. "Ah, you are certainly too perceptive. Although, if we are to speak freely, I feel it only fair to warn you of the consequences of violating my trust."

"And I feel it only fair to warn *you* that I would not have visited you today without precaution. If, today or anytime in the foreseeable future, something unpleasant should befall me, there is a standing bounty of ten hundred thousand scales on whomever is found responsible for my death, to be administered by my estate, and my instructions are to suspect you, chiefly. If I die, Sartean, the killer will find themselves the target of an army of assassins from within Mor, and many from without. My personal safety mechanism is layered and secure, I assure you."

"Yes, yes, of course," Sartean responded, waving his hand dismissively. "It would seem that we are both well protected. Yet I still require your assurances. What we discuss now *is* dangerous, despite our precautions. How do I know I can trust you?"

Thomison laughed. "Well, obviously, you cannot. No more than I can trust you. My assurances, like yours, are empty words. We are not moral men. We are not bound to promise. However, I will say this: so long as our objectives align, you will not find a more loyal ally. I will add that I enjoy confidences: they beget power. I do not break them without due consideration. Your reputation implies the same."

Sartean studied the merchant. *Yes, he will do nicely.*

"Very well. Let us then continue from where our conversation today began. You had mentioned that only one here in Mor has the power to summon you."

"Only one in Greater Tahr, Sartean. In *all* of Tahr."

"Yes. And only one may call me 'wizard.' That number seems a bit high to me."

Thomison sighed. "I know what you mean. Yet Halsen is the devil we know. My business interests have flourished under his rule, and I need only bow and scrape on occasion. I have no desire to upset the order of things."

"Business. Yes, that is the point, is it not? We measure success differently, you and I, but it comes down to business, in one sense or another. Tell me, how has business been for you lately? Most recently, I mean?"

Thomison frowned. "You'll know of course that gold doesn't flow like it once did in Mor. Though I glean my share."

"It hardly flows at all, Vincent. There is a reason Fennar and Barrington are no longer with us, and their insolences before the king were merely a punctuation to their failures."

"Failures orchestrated by you, no doubt. Yet you still have not told me how you accomplished it. Nor why."

"The 'why' should be easy enough to discern. The two held more power than they were entitled to, by my measure."

"There is more, Sartean. Much more that you are not saying."

Sartean smiled. "Of course there is. You will also know that the work of repairing the walls after the quake has begun."

"Oh, definitely. Quite a job, that. And the rumor is that the laborers assigned to the task are working eighteen hours per day, at an inhuman pace. Your doing? I suspected as much; only magic could make men work like that."

"More specifically, a magical potion. I call it—"

"Speedsap then?" Thomison shook his head. "Impossible, not stable enough. They would be dying in droves."

"A derivative of Speedsap. I call it Flightfluid. Much more stable, albeit quite addictive." Sartean's smile deepened.

Thomison did not immediately reply. The men regarded each other silently for a moment. "Who's distributing it? Who's manufacturing it? I would have heard about this by now if it were happening in scale. A test, then?"

"No, come now, Vincent. Would I be so foolish as to make such a move without an endgame already arranged?"

"I would not assume that, no."

"The manufacturing process is well under way. I do, however, require a more efficient mechanism for distribution." Sartean let the idea settle.

"I'm listening," replied Thomison.

Sartean stood and began to pace behind his desk as he spoke, the scarlet hems of his midnight robe grazing the floor. "How would you like to assist me in achieving my own objectives, Vincent, while simultaneously solving the two biggest problems you yourself face?"

"Still listening," said the merchant.

"We will need to work quickly. I have already secured the support of the throne in beginning immediate distribution of Flightfluid. The kingdom of Mor is in dire need of solutions, Vincent. The ash of Fang falls. The walls crumble as Tahr quakes. The treasury is nearly empty, and we have no trade; Halsen has thoroughly succeeded in alienating every race and kingdom in Greater Tahr."

"And you do not care a fig about any of it, Sartean. Don't try to sell me on the idea that you do."

"Oh, but you are mistaken there. I care a great deal. Who would want to inherit a broken kingdom?"

"As I suspected. You eye that gaudy seat in the throneroom."

"Not exactly. I like my tower. Though, certainly I would make a far better king than Halsen. Sartean mused, "Hmm. Perhaps I could install the throne here, in my library, yes? I don't see why not..."

"Why in Fury would I deliver the throne to you, Sartean? I already made it clear: I like Halsen in charge. He is pliable and predictable."

Sartean stopped his pacing, and turned to face Thomison. "And a complete and total failure. You pretend these days, you and I both know it. Ah, no need to be offended, Vincent. I offer no insult. The truth is what it is. Like you, I am not without sources of information. Your own coffers are emptying, not filling. There is simply no more gold to go around. While you have considerable reserves, they are not bottomless. You want Halsen replaced as badly as I do; pretending otherwise implies that you have ambitions of your own."

"If you believe I seek the crown, you could not be more mistaken. I have absolutely no desire to wear that uncomfortable piece of metal, nor attend to the duties its wearing requires. I enjoy my comforts as they are."

"As they once were." Sartean waited.

Thomison shifted uncomfortably. "Very well, Sartean, I admit that things have been difficult of late. But you have no idea how much wealth I possess. I could outlast a hundred Halsens."

"Oh, I am sure you could. But you do not strike me as a man who is content with *survival*, no matter how comfortable that survival may be. And you are also astute enough to know that it is not Halsen of whom you must be wary, but rather the people of Mor. When the army's salaries stop, and they will by spring, it will no longer be gold that serves as the currency of Mor; it will be blood, and the blood of the wealthy will be spent first."

"And you can assure otherwise?"

"I can. And I can assure that you are at the very center of it all, providing the people with a potion that reduces hunger, increases productivity, and, of course, is available at a reasonable margin of profit."

"You have enough of this potion, Sartean? And you will continue to?"

"I do, and I will."

Thomison shook his head. "I'll assume you do, although I have my doubts. But the fact remains, we're still just shuffling cards. We're not increasing the flow of gold into Mor, but rather redistributing it to ourselves. The well will run dry, and we'll be right back where we started."

"Now Vincent, don't be so shortsighted. The men of Mor are not the only people of Tahr that would benefit from such a marvelous concoction."

Thomison raised his head at this. "Your ambitions run deeper then."

"Wider, Vincent."

Thomison thought for a moment. Who? The dwarves? Unlikely. Elves? Never. G'naath...perhaps...*ahhhhh.* Thomison realized. *He thinks to expand to the south...perhaps even the west?*

"Assume I see your logic on all points. What of Halsen, then? You seek the kingdom, yet he has an army. I do not relish the idea of civil war in Tahr, even if I am enriched by it. The result is far too unpredictable. And I don't see you dirtying your own hands in this. You're no assassin."

"We are in agreement on those points, Vincent. Although, didn't you say something earlier about having access to, how did you put it, 'an *army* of assassins?'"

Made in the USA
Middletown, DE
20 March 2019